THE INSUBORDINATE

THE INSUBORDINATE

SIMON LENNON

Pine Hill Books

The Insubordinate

Fiction (Political, Satire)

Published by Pine Hill Books

ISBN 978-1-925446-28-9 (electronic)

ISBN 978-1-925446-29-6 (paperback)

78,000 words

Cover image: Molong, 2011

To my middle-born daughter

PREFACE

The harshest isolation in the world today is that which the ideological West imposes, or threatens to impose, upon our own. If this novel is as much satire as drama, it's because political correctness is no less ridiculous than it is cruel.

The protagonist is a woman because the story arose from the reticence of the principal female character in my novel *A Young Man's Tale* to speak about race. Her self-censorship was mine.

Initially, I set the novel in a fictitious New South Wales town with a local council chamber, named Denley Vale. After discovering beautiful Molong in the course of my work, I realised I'd found a real setting for the story. I trust the gracious people of Molong appreciate the compliment I intend.

THE REMARK

A newcomer could take up home in the town of Molong and live there the rest of a long and happy life, without hearing anyone talk of the summer Jessica Rawlins came home from university. If the newcomer mentioned her name, townspeople would say it was only a story: that such awful things couldn't happen in so pretty a place. They'd point to the boards of gold-decal names in the Cabonne Council chamber and say there'd never been a mayor named Hector Xiedergrain. There wasn't even a Pickled Pepper Café anymore.

The people who'd lived in Molong, central western New South Wales, during the early years of the twenty-first century were much the same people, through their many generations, who'd always lived there. The National Trust had classified Bank Street for being cultural heritage in the early Austen-European style, although few people outside the Molong Historical Society and not everyone in the society knew what Austen-European meant.

At the lower end of Bank Street were the shops, where irregularly spaced columns and painted wooden pillars held aloft corrugated-iron awnings, sheltering the footpaths from sun more than rain. Comfortable chairs much like a lounge room at home accommodated women waiting at the Bliss Beauty

Salon, below photographs of model women in alluring styles. Hairsprays aromatised the cool conditioned air.

By several mirrors along a wall stood black-vinyl swivel chairs, in which women there for their hair sat with smocks draped over their clothes and around their necks; adjustable frames set different sized customers to each hairdresser's height. Some customers faced their reflections. Others read magazines, only looking up when the hairdressers asked them if they liked what they'd done. Most conversed, while cut snippets of hair fell to the floor.

Sitting in the chair in which she sat every Tuesday morning (the salon being closed on Mondays), was the once more beautiful Mrs Xiedergrain. She was tall, befitting the wife of the mayor, with high hair sculpted in style for another public week of her husband's civic duties. Instilled in her skin were the perfumes, potions, and lotions she'd wash away a little each day. "Charlie Quinn and I have the same understanding I've had with all the proprietors of the *Molong Express*," she said, gazing through her image in the mirror. "I'll believe everything I read in his newspaper, provided he doesn't print anything about me."

Patiently grooming her was Lynne Delaney, the owner of the salon. Lynne stood with her skin creamed to be young, her dark hair held in place.

It suited them all to forget Lynne had worked there since finishing her education at the Molong Central School, too many years earlier. If any of her customers knew she was forty-four years of age, or even if her husband of more than twenty years or their two children knew, then none of them mentioned it; how her latest young assistant came to know was purely by chance, but she too never mentioned it. Lynne had trained the procession of similarly groomed young women passing through the salon assisting her, dressed in their clean white blouses and skirts. Together, they convinced customers they were as beautiful as the women in the photographs hanging from the walls.

At the end of the morning, Mrs Xiedergrain studied her new, same hair in bright reflection. "Thank you, Lynne," she told the woman in white.

"We'll see you again, Tuesday, Mrs Xiedergrain."

The mayoress, as the wife of a mayor was known, smiled. "You get me through the week."

Lynne opened the door for her customer to leave, as a tall and purposeful man almost twenty-five years of age appeared on the footpath before them. Derek Saxby stood dressed in a business shirt and trousers for the people he met. His collar was open; country New South Welshmen only wore ties for special occasions. He held his brown bush hat in his hands; the late summer sun was still bright enough for people to wear their hats whenever they walked too long outside.

"Good morning, Derek," Mrs Xiedergrain smiled broadly, stepping forward and placing her hand on his. "You're much too handsome to come into a salon."

"I'm here to see Jessica."

"Who?"

"Jessica Rawlins. Over there."

Mrs Xiedergrain turned around. Standing at the rear of the salon, under a bright light from the ceiling and wearing her white blouse and skirt, Lynne's latest young assistant was holding a long broom. Her watch, a small gold oval on a thin band a gift from her late mother, reflected the light from her wrist. Her blonde hair was bound in a bun, and her blue eyes watched the people watching her. Most obvious among her delicate facial features were her softly defined cheekbones. Shorter than any person watching her, although she was five and a half feet tall, Jessica was twenty-two years of age.

Mrs Xiedergrain turned back to Derek, pulled her hand away from his, and drew a long breath. "My husband's efforts with the Chinese to restart the mine should be good for your real estate agency, Mister Saxby."

"It should be good for all the businesses in Molong, Mrs Xiedergrain."

"Quite," she said. "Good day, Mrs Delaney."

"Good day, Mrs Xiedergrain."

The mayoress left the salon and the door closed behind her. Jessica, carrying her broom, moved towards Derek.

"Jess," said Derek, "Can we have lunch today? I want to ask you something."

"I'm seeing Susan and Briony, if you want to join us."

Derek stepped back. "I'll leave you to talk about me without me," he smiled. "I'll see you tonight." He departed. Jessica resumed sweeping the floor.

Some customers noticed Lynne's assistants' young faces, checking to see if they recognised them from their last appointments or from the schoolgirls once in school dresses. They talked about people they knew and people they didn't, gently asking questions of the women working on them without much interest in their replies.

"And what have you been up to lately?" a customer asked Jessica, as Jessica washed the old woman's feet.

"I saw an old movie in Manildra on Saturday night, Mrs Tancred, with my boyfriend."

"I like romances myself," she said, not really speaking to Jessica. "Saturday night, I shared a very pleasant little meal with my husband at the Wing Hang restaurant."

The beauticians normally listened just enough to progress the conversations customers wanted to have, but Jessica was new. "I don't particularly like Chinese food, Mrs Tancred."

"Ooh, dear," said Mrs Tancred, pulling back her foot a short way. Jessica reached out to continue washing it.

Lynne interjected. "I think Jessica likes Chinese food very much," she said, "but not while she's watching a movie in the Amusu Theatre."

Mrs Tancred didn't speak anymore after that. When she'd left, and only they were in the salon, Lynne spoke to Jessica about it. "You're very good with them," said Lynne, "but please, whatever they like and dislike, you like and dislike." Her voice was polite but firm, almost maternal. "If they tell me about a restaurant they've visited, then I say I've not eaten there for some time so they can tell me about it, even if it's been my favourite for years or I hate it. It makes them feel best about themselves, and that's what they're paying us to feel."

Lynne spoke like a tutor to her pupil. Jessica dutifully accepted her instruction.

"They assume I agree with them about everything," Lynne continued, "but they can't make that assumption if I express an opinion about anything. I put them at ease, save them from thinking anything too difficult, and let them talk about whatever they choose. They don't talk about anything with which we might disagree, and neither do I. If they can't talk of matters agreeable, they won't talk, and they want to talk. It's a game they pay us to play. That's what we do, and why they come back."

By the time Jessica arrived at the footpath chairs and small tables of the Pickled Pepper Café for lunch, Briony Keyte was already there; Briony was always the first of the three friends to get away from work. Wearing a long seamless frock and with large round sunglasses over her eyes, Briony didn't need to enter a contest to know how beautiful she was. Working as a sales assistant in a ladies-wear shop along Bank Street, her customers liked her to model the fashionable clothes and millinery they contemplated buying.

Soon joining them was Susan Hodgeson, with her button nose and large brown eyes. Wearing another patterned blouse open well below her neck, Susan worked in the post office, selling stamps and other items at the counter and accepting letters and parcels for postage. When her work allowed it, and it often did, she pondered the pottery she forged from her mother's clay, wheel, and kiln and offered for sale from a shelf. Her first ever show opened that Saturday night, promoted with colourful little cards in piles at the post office, Bliss Beauty Salon, and Briony's place of work.

The three young women each sat with their handbags slipped under their chairs. Shielding Jessica and Susan's eyes from the sun were sunglasses much smaller than Briony's, while the awning above let Jessica rest her sunny-day hat on the spare chair at their table. Jessica's white blouse and skirt was conspicuously a uniform aside her friends' clothes, but she had evenings and weekends to wear something colourful. There was too little breeze through the dry air.

Briony sat studying the menu, the same each time they sat

there aside from one recent deletion. "There's no asparagus sauce," laughed Briony.

"Shush," said Jessica. Approaching them was the waiter, in his blue-striped apron over immaterial clothes.

"You must love being Volunteer of the Month," the waiter said to Briony, although she continued studying the menu without seeming to notice him. People had often said as much to her since the mayor announced her award. "Ms Keyte?"

"I'm sorry," she said quickly, looking up at him. "I forgot to be polite."

"Briony!" snapped Susan.

"I'll have a goat's cheese salad and diet cola," Briony told him. He scribbled her order on the pad of paper in his hand.

"The same," said Susan. The waiter added ticks beside the first order.

"I'll have the penne marinara, please," said Jessica, "and a glass of apple juice." Briony glanced down towards Jessica's waist below the rim of the table, while the waiter scribbled down her order and took the menu away.

"We're still trying to decide whether you changed, Jess, or we changed," said Susan, more pointed in her comment than disappointed.

"Young people always change," Jessica hedged in reply.

"Some do," said Briony, before laughing. "Molong never changes. Even if it did, we wouldn't notice the change."

"Except for the asparagus sauce," said Susan, before turning back to Jessica. "I don't know what university taught that you couldn't learn here." The waiter set an empty glass before each of the women. "It didn't teach you to be a hairdresser."

"I'm earning money for my journey to London," insisted Jessica, her coming of age incomplete.

"Derek won't like that," said Briony. "He's done well in the years you were away."

"He wants to ask me something, tonight."

"What if he's trying to work up the courage to ask you to marry him?" grinned Susan. "What will you say, Jess?"

"Why 'no', of course," interjected Briony, "at first. You want him to be jealous." The waiter set three bottles of cold drink before the three women.

Jessica opened her small bottle of apple juice and poured some into her glass, unaffected by what affected her friends. "I'll use my biology degree somehow."

They began sipping their beverages. Jessica's apple juice was the sweetest taste she'd experienced since breakfast; she drank it a little too quickly.

"If the mayor can get the mine operating again," said Susan, "you could work there."

"Mines don't need biologists," Briony fobbed her off.

"The Chinese might bring other businesses," Susan retorted. "They say there'll be three hundred of them coming if the mine goes ahead."

"Will they stay?" asked Jessica.

"I hope so," laughed Briony. "If they all bring their families, there'll be more of them than us!"

Jessica smiled. "Not that we can mention it."

"Yes, we can," beamed Briony, as the waiter laid her plate of salad before her. "It'll be wonderful."

The waiter set a similar plate before Susan. "We'll celebrate," said Susan, gazing over her meal. "This'll be Chinatown."

"The mayor will want a big civic reception," smiled Briony, glancing at Susan, "but he won't invite *some* people."

Susan raised her eyebrows in tiny protest on Jessica's behalf. Jessica hadn't cared.

The waiter set a plate of penne marinara before Jessica. "Thank you," she said, collecting the pasta on her fork before looking back at her friends already eating their salads. "Why will it be wonderful?"

"What do you mean, Jess?" asked Susan, chewing a portion of lettuce.

"It's diversity," explained Briony, nodding her head at the waiter hovering over them.

Jessica never spoke with food in her mouth; she kept her mouth closed while she ate. The pasta was a little too spicy for her liking, but she finished chewing her mouthful and swallowed it. "I don't want to be a minority."

"A minority?" asked Susan.

"A racial minority," explained Jessica, "not in my hometown, not in my country."

Briony and Susan looked around them, causing Jessica to look around too. People at other tables quietly ate their food.

"We know you've been away," Briony told Jessica, "but you can't talk like that."

"It's a terrible thing to say," Susan added quickly.

"Chinese people wouldn't want to be a minority in China," Jessica elaborated. "Asian countries don't allow all this immigration."

Briony leant towards her, speaking softly enough not to be heard at other tables but loudly enough for the waiter to hear. "You're being divisive."

"How could you?" snapped Susan, gritting her teeth. "We thought you were our friend."

"Why shouldn't I be your friend?"

Briony looked up at the waiter. "Can we get another table?" she asked him.

The waiter looked around. Seats at two tables were empty, but he hadn't yet cleared away the used plates and cups from one or set the clean crockery and cutlery on the other. He stared down at Jessica. "You will have to leave."

"Why?"

"Please," he said. "Our customers don't want your type of person here."

"What type of person?"

The waiter looked at Briony and Susan. "I'd like another table," snapped Briony. She picked up her handbag from the ground and stood up, leaving her meal and partly drunk glass of cola.

"I'll go with you," said Susan, doing the same.

"Why?" asked Jessica.

Briony looked at the waiter. "We didn't know her," she tried to assure him.

"You're my friends," complained Jessica.

"We are not!" Susan told her, glancing quickly at the people looking at them from other tables.

"I'll make up this table for you," said the waiter, leading Briony and Susan to an empty table. Jessica watched the waiter pull out the chairs for Briony and Susan to sit down. Without acknowledging Jessica staring at him, he took their meals to their new table. "I'll replace your drinks," he told them, slipping away.

"I won't mention it again," Jessica from her table told Briony and Susan. "We can talk about your award, your pottery."

"Have you finished reading that book?" Susan asked Briony.

Briony resumed eating her meal. Susan did the same. They conspicuously concentrated their sights upon their food.

Jessica noticed a middle-aged man staring at her. She looked at him and shrugged her shoulders. He looked quickly at his meal.

The waiter brought clean napkins and fresh glasses of cola to Briony and Susan. Alone, Jessica collected some pasta and sauce from her plate onto her fork.

"I think you should leave," the waiter told Jessica, standing tall over her table.

"I'm eating my lunch." She lifted the fork to her lips and took the pasta and sauce into her mouth.

The waiter leant forward and picked up a spoon piled with sugar from the sugar bowl. He tipped the sugar onto Jessica's meal.

Jessica looked at the plate of food she could no longer eat and up at the waiter. Calmly, she lifted her glass and poured the last of her apple juice into the sugar bowl.

"How dare you!" he told her.

Jessica picked up her handbag lying on the ground under her seat and hung it from her shoulder. She returned her hat to her head and stood up from her chair.

"Not yet!" said the waiter, hurrying back inside.

She realised Briony and Susan were watching her, when their faces quickly turned back to their meals. "I'm sorry," said Jessica.

The waiter rushed back to Jessica. "Your account," he told her, handing her a small slip of paper.

"You're joking," said Jessica, "aren't you?"

"Must I call the police?"

"I'll pay for the apple juice. I enjoyed that."

"We don't want your type thinking you can get away with anything," said the waiter.

"What is my type?"

"You will pay for the meal."

Jessica opened her handbag hanging from her shoulder, removed her purse, and offered the waiter the four dollars her drink had cost.

The waiter didn't accept her money. "The account is for sixteen dollars."

"You ruined my food," Jessica told him. "The pasta was too spicy anyway."

"Please, Jessica," interrupted Briony. "Haven't you said enough?"

"It's only twelve dollars," added Susan.

"Madam," said the waiter. "I can have you arrested."

"After what happened with the asparagus sauce," seethed Jessica, giving him sixteen dollars, "it's a wonder anyone comes here."

"If you come here again, asparagus sauce will be all that we serve you."

When Jessica returned to the salon, Lynne Delaney was sitting alone, casually examining her fingernails. "How was your lunch?" asked Lynne.

"Really weird," replied Jessica, pulling her hat from her head and tidying her hair. "I said something to upset Sue and Briony." Jessica checked her face in the mirror, preparing to slip into a washroom to tidy herself. "The next thing I know, they're at another table and the waiter's telling me to leave."

"You must all be having a bad day."

"A bad hair day, you mean."

Lynne laughed. "They can all come in here and we'll dolly them up."

"We can charge the dumb waiter an extra twelve dollars."

2

THE POLICE

Briony and Susan remained at their table in the Pickled Pepper Café, without eating or drinking anything more. Through Briony's voiceless mind reverberated a word neither one of them uttered. In the predicament in which Jessica had placed her, the safest action was inaction. Briony dared not risk getting involved, but she had to say something before anyone imputed Jessica's words to her. Were it not for the waiter, she could've pretended not to have heard.

The people around them might also have heard. "I don't know what came over her," said Briony, loud enough for those people to hear.

"She's so rude," said Susan, glancing around. "I could kill her for saying such a thing. It was so embarrassing."

"She's never said anything like that before, ever. I never liked her." Briony leant towards Susan and dipped her voice. "This could ruin me."

"I've got my pottery show to think about."

"There are other salons," said Briony. "We've got other friends."

"People know we disagree with her."

"Do they?" asked Briony, looking around at the customers eating their food. "You know what happened to Fergus Millane.

What if somebody thinks we didn't contradict her enough? You heard the waiter threaten to call the police. We should have offered to call."

"Saying what she said isn't illegal, is it?"

"If the waiter reports her and we don't, then people might wonder why we didn't. They'll say we let her say what she said."

"She changed at university."

"We'll find Sergeant Vaughan."

The two women rose from their chairs without finishing their salads or cola. They left money for the cost of their meals and generous gratuities for the waiter in the centre of the table, before hurrying away.

People with enquiries of Sergeant Vaughan usually stopped him when he walked through the town, but Briony wouldn't wait. With Susan struggling to keep up, she led them to the far end of Edward Street and the stone-walled police station.

Briony pushed open the police station door, ringing a small brass bell overhead. Sergeant Vaughan at his desk, reading the weather reports on his computer screen, looked up. The sergeant kept his thinning grey hair short and neat, with a comb barely visible through his shirt pocket. Thirty years accepting small cakes from shopkeepers and elderly women who brought them to the police station had made his belly large, but he laughed boisterously and insisted that everything was muscle behind his pale blue cotton shirts and crisply ironed dark blue trousers.

Constable Tarrant, recently graduated from the Police Academy in Goulburn and still thin in his uniform, turned away from a memorandum from the Commissioner to all New South Wales police. Seeing the young woman enter, he sat upright in his chair. Susan smiled, and dipped her head.

"Good day, Sergeant," said Briony, stepping towards the counter. Susan followed close behind.

"Good afternoon, ladies," said the sergeant, standing up from his desk. The constable rose, too. "This is a lovely surprise." The sergeant and constable stood before them. "Two good citizens," smiled the sergeant, pulling a small metal charity tin on the counter towards them.

Briony glanced down at the tin and notice affixed to it. "Eugene Gallagher," she read, "that poor man." The human immunodeficiency virus in Eugene had manifest into Acquired Immune Deficiency Syndrome, whereby the young man could die. Briony took a five-dollar note from her purse and pressed it into the tin.

Susan opened her purse. The smallest note she carried was ten dollars. She hesitated, before slipping it into the tin.

Briony reopened her purse. She popped in another five dollars.

"What can I do for you?" asked the sergeant.

"We need to report a crime," said Briony.

The sergeant's smile slipped from his face. The constable stepped a little bit forward.

"At least we think it's a crime. If it's not, then it should be."

"Ten dollars each is a perfectly fine donation."

"It's Jessica Rawlins."

The sergeant was the only person to remember everyone's name in Molong, as everyone in Molong knew his. "She's a friend of yours."

"Not now," snapped Susan.

"She said something offensive," explained Briony.

"Jessica?" said the sergeant. "I knew her parents."

"Deeply offensive," added Susan.

"She seems so sweet," said the sergeant.

"That's what we used to think," resumed Briony.

"What did she say?"

Briony turned her head away. "I don't think I can repeat it."

The sergeant looked to Susan. "I wouldn't have believed it," she added.

"She said it," said Briony, "right before our eyes and ears, only a few minutes ago."

"We thought you should know," said Susan.

"Yes, of course," said the sergeant, shaking his head. "What precisely did she say?"

"She said Asians aren't like us," said Briony. "They don't want us around."

"Goodness me," said the sergeant, collecting his thoughts. "I didn't think we had anyone like that in Molong, not since Fergus Millane."

"Is what she said illegal?" asked Susan.

The sergeant turned to the constable. "Racial vilification is illegal," responded the constable.

Briony turned to Susan. She smiled.

"The law is ours to enforce if not to make," the sergeant told them, "defending and protecting the community. Where is Jessica now?"

"At work," said Susan.

"The Bliss Beauty Salon," added Briony.

"I know."

The ensuing silence was awkward, until Briony spoke up. "I'm thinking of learning to speak Chinese."

"We should be going now," said Susan.

Briony looked at Susan. "We've done enough never to mention her again."

"I might need to speak with you further," said the sergeant.

Looking back at him, Briony hesitated. "Yes," she replied. "You can say we reported her."

"At any time," added Susan.

"Thank you," smiled the sergeant. "Thank you both of you for bringing this to my attention."

Briony tilted her head slightly as she smiled at him. "Goodbye, Sergeant."

"Goodbye," said Susan, looking at the constable. He smiled, but rarely spoke with the sergeant around.

"Goodbye, ladies," said the sergeant.

The bell rang above them as Briony and Susan opened the station door. The door closed after them.

The sergeant again turned to the constable. "I'm sure it's a misunderstanding," said the sergeant, "but having reported it, those two young ladies expect us to do something." The problem of Jessica was his.

"We could charge her with breaching the peace," enthused the constable, his eyes wide and alert, "causing a public affray?"

The sergeant raised his hands gently ushering down the constable's exuberance. "I'll speak with her," he told him, "and quietly try to resolve it." The New South Wales police service didn't oblige officers to prosecute wrongdoers if they could maintain the peace without prosecution. A police record would blemish the town as much as Miss Rawlins; he hadn't become a police officer to prosecute anyone. "She mightn't have broken any law."

The sergeant picked up his mobile telephone from his desk and walked around the counter. From the stand near the door he took his blue police cap, the crest of the New South Wales state police force sparkling from its centre. Their black leather police jackets hung from thick wooden coat hangers, but the day was warm enough for him to leave his jacket behind.

"This might require my pistol," said the sergeant.

The constable stepped forward; the sergeant had famously never drawn his gun in action. Police had no cause to carry guns in most country towns, where the most likely offences were traffic infringements. At the end of each day, police firearms were locked away at the stations.

"I'm teasing you, Tarrant," smiled the sergeant. The bell rang above him as he left the station.

Walking along Bank Street, another man's voice broke his thoughts. "Good afternoon, Sergeant."

"Hello, Sam," he smiled at the man at the door of his shop, without interrupting his stride. The sergeant only removed his police cap from his head when he greeted people older than he was and when he entered homes, offices, and shops.

Entering the Bliss Beauty Salon, the sergeant removed his cap. Among scores of intricate beauty accessories, various trays maintained neat arrays of combs, scissors, and brushes. Others organised curling wands and rollers. Dozens of aerosol cans adorned with bright and black logos stood on shelves and tables, as did bottles of dyes. Dressers cut, coloured, and styled customers' hair better than they needed to be.

Lynne Delaney was at her desk and book of appointments. "Good afternoon, Sergeant."

"Good afternoon, Lynne," he replied, more officiously than he normally spoke with her. Instead of mulling around the chairs in the waiting area looking at the magazines, waiting to be offered a cup of tea or water biscuit, as he normally did, he looked past Lynne towards Jessica sweeping the floor. Jessica stopped sweeping.

"Can I offer you some tea, Sergeant?" asked Lynne.

"Jessica," said the sergeant, "what did you say to upset Briony Keyte and Susan Hodgeson?"

"Not you, too," sighed Jessica, nearly dropping the broom. "All I said was that Chinese people wouldn't want to be minorities in China and I don't want to be a minority in my country. I don't see why we need all this immigration."

The sergeant shook his head. "Why say such a thing, Jessica?"

"Why forever not?"

He stepped closer to Jessica and spoke so that only she heard him. "It was racist."

Jessica dipped her head. "Conversations with friends aren't so private anymore," she muttered.

In the quiet, Lynne spoke up. "Jessica mentioned only this morning how much she likes Chinese food."

"You should apologise to Susan and Briony," the sergeant told Jessica.

"Why did they tell you?"

"You're lucky they did," said the sergeant. "How do you respond to people saying something offensive?"

"I can't think of anything that offends me, however vehemently I disagree with it."

"What if you did?"

"I'd try to understand them."

The sergeant looked to Lynne. "I want to see if we can get Jessica out of this without any more trouble."

"Why does anyone care what I say?" asked Jessica.

"Please Jessica," the sergeant told her. "I'm trying to help you, but I can't if you're going to make it difficult. You must be careful not to offend."

"Why should anyone be offended by what I said?" asked Jessica. "Are you offended, Sergeant?"

"Yours and my feelings are of no consequence, Jessica. Didn't university teach you what to say and not say?"

"I thought I could express my feelings in Molong."

"You can't express those feelings in a cave."

Jessica turned to Lynne. "Would you have been offended?"

Lynne looked at the sergeant, but if she hoped he would save her from answering, he didn't. Lynne turned back to Jessica. "I know you didn't mean anything by it, Jessica, but you shouldn't have said what you said."

"I was hoping that you'd undo what you've done without the threat of sanction," the sergeant told Jessica, "but I will detain you for the rest of your natural life if I must to serve community interests."

Jessica's head slipped a little lower. "I did apologise to Susan and Briony."

"Keep apologising," said the sergeant. "Buy them gifts. Make reparations."

"I've known them since we were little."

"Everything has changed since then," Lynne told her. "You have to change."

"Do I also need to apologise to the waiter?"

"The waiter?" cried the sergeant. "Where were you?"

"The Pickled Pepper Café."

"Lester Cullen? This is worse than the asparagus sauce."

"An old man died after eating that asparagus sauce, because Lester Cullen left it unrefrigerated," said Jessica. "I haven't harmed anyone."

"You created a civil disturbance."

"The waiter caused the disturbance. I'm glad I didn't leave him a tip."

A middle-aged customer pushed open the salon door. The three turned towards her. "Hello, Sergeant Vaughan," she said.

"Mrs Epthorp."

Mrs Epthorp looked at the two women. "Hello, Lynne," she said, before looking at Jessica. "Hello."

"It's always nice when Sergeant Vaughan comes by," smiled Lynne.

"It's always nice to come by." If his words were a lie, they were a tactful lie; the sergeant would always be tactful. He replaced his cap on his head. "Ladies," he said, putting his hand to the rim of his cap and tilting it slightly.

They nodded, as the sergeant looked at Jessica. "Miss Rawlins," he said, in his most formal tone of voice. "Remember what I've said."

Mrs Epthorp spoke up. "What is all this about, Lynne?"

"Nothing important," replied Lynne. "Is there anything in particular you would like today, Mrs Epthorp?"

Sergeant Vaughan left the salon. Drifting back along the footpath, he deliberated upon what he should do and what people should see he was doing. Jessica Rawlins was young; perhaps his conversation with her would deter her from repeating her ill-chosen words, but she'd not been contrite. Lynne Delaney was more mature; she might tell Jessica what happened to Fergus Millane when he said what he said.

"Good afternoon, Sergeant Vaughan," said a woman's voice.

His concentration broken, the sergeant stopped. He focussed his gaze upon the middle-aged woman facing him, carrying a small bag of vegetables. "Good afternoon, Mrs Miller."

"Lovely day today, Sergeant."

"It is, Mrs Miller," he smiled. The sergeant lied before he breached the peace.

The sergeant returned to the police station. He hung his cap from the stand by the door.

"How did it go, Sergeant?" asked Constable Tarrant, bringing the sergeant a freshly brewed cup of hot tea.

"She said it at the Pickled Pepper Café," the sergeant lamented. "Lord knows what she's done." Sitting down in his chair, resting his elbow on his desk and his head in his hand, he used the fingers of his other hand to check his computer. Jessica Rawlins had no police record. "What happened at university to make her so disruptive?"

The sergeant thought of seeing her at her home that evening, when the night was dark and nobody saw him, but more might happen through the afternoon. She mightn't be at home that evening. Briony Keyte, Susan Hodgeson, Lynne Delaney, Lester Cullen, and anyone else at the Pickled Pepper Café that day might repeat Jessica's words. They might've already done so. They might've mentioned the sergeant. If he were unable to correct her, he needed to refer her to someone who could. The tea in his cup cooled in his hand.

Briony was at the ladies-wear shop, telling prospective customers of the beautiful dresses. Susan was at the post office, franking stamps on letters and parcels with ink impressions of the town before placing them in their respective sorting bins; a post office truck would collect the white canvas bag containing items addressed to leave Molong at six o'clock that evening. At the end of the day, they would hide in their workplaces until Jessica left Bank Street.

At the Pickled Pepper Café, customers drank coffee. Lester Cullen whistled the theme music to a television programme as he liked to do, knowing enough to smile at his patrons until they left the premises. His parents owned the café and prepared the meals, while he listened as best he could to customers' conversations. The woman with blonde hair in a bun had been polite, unlike the man in a suit who'd changed his order but insisted Lester misheard him, or the woman wearing a canary yellow jacket who'd spilled her coffee on the table and blamed Lester for filling it too high in the cup. Their expenditure kept him in his job and condemned him to suffer his ignominy in silence, but the woman in a white blouse and uniform was an employee as menial in her work as he was in his. Never again might he have the chance he'd had that day to be like everyone else. Besides, her two friends had expected him to eject her.

"Jessica," said Lynne, when only she and Jessica were in the salon. Jessica stopped sweeping the floor. "We don't mention people's backgrounds, not where anyone can hear."

"Do you mean their race?" asked Jessica.

"Did you talk about people of other backgrounds at university?"

"My friends and I talked of many things, things we debated," said Jessica, searching her recollections. "Lecturers and tutors never did."

"Were those things you talked about really so important?"

"We thought they were at the time," reflected Jessica. "At the Pickled Pepper Café today, I wasn't saying anything against anyone. I was telling the truth."

"It's not that simple," said Lynne. "You weren't here when Fergus Millane described the man who stole his car as being black."

3

THE BOYFRIEND

The sheltered noticeboard on the Village Green, at the corner of Bank and Gidley Streets, invited visitors that never came to meetings of local clubs. The Molong Advancement Group normally met at seven o'clock in the evening of the second Wednesday of the month, in the old railway station. The Molong Historical Society normally met at the same time in the museum. Nobody attending one attended the other.

The secretary of the Molong cricket team removed the last of his notices from the completed competition. The secretary of the Molong football team affixed a schedule of home and away matches for the coming competition; the team would practice every Monday afternoon at the Molong Oval. Some young men who'd finished school the previous year would join the team, replacing the older men who'd retired since the last competition. If they still dreamt of representing Western New South Wales in the Country Cup competition, those dreams would fade further each year. The amateur performers of the Molong Players would soon begin rehearsing their new production.

Along the lower end of Bank Street, public bars poured cold beer the children only smelt. Behind the Freemasons Hotel was an open courtyard, below a huge canopy to shield the patrons when the sun was too much a curse or rain too much a blessing. Through clear days and warm evenings, they sat at the wooden benches along the wooden tables. They ate their long restaurant meals and shorter counter foods, while slowly drinking local beers and Hunter Valley wines.

That Tuesday evening, Jessica had dressed out of her working clothes into a comfortable light dress, with a white leather belt around her thin waist. Her curling blonde hair released from its bun hung over her shoulders. Derek Saxby still wore his business shirt – a shirt Jessica had bought him – and trousers.

Through their courtyard conversation, Jessica told him about her strange lunch, the rude waiter, and the sergeant visiting the salon: a slowly cascading tide of misunderstanding. "Susan, Briony, and I were just talking," she complained. "Why should everyone care so much what I think, what I feel?"

"You're smart enough to know what's important and what isn't," Derek told her. "Before you say what you think or feel, check to make sure you should. Say whatever they want you to say and don't say whatever they want to keep quiet, the way the rest of us do, and get on with your life."

"Why's everyone concerned about the sensitivities of foreigners who might never come?"

Derek laughed. "They're not concerned about the sensitivities of foreigners. They're concerned about the sensitivities of white people."

"What if I'm telling the truth?"

"Telling the truth is the worst thing you can do. If you're lying, people don't worry so much."

It was all very difficult. "I never expected my friends to report me to the police."

"I won't report you," he smiled.

Jessica resumed sipping her wine. "I'm not going to Susan's pottery show opening Saturday night."

"I went to an arty opening once. That was enough."

"Don't let anyone else hear you say that."

Again, Derek laughed. "Your friends know the person you are."

"Which friends: Briony and Susan?"

"Me." He rested his hands on the timber table.

She studied his eyes not quite as blue as hers, believing them. "Thank you," she smiled, as she placed her wine glass on the table and her hands beside his.

He moved his hand to hers, holding hers. "You're important to me, Jess, you say I'm important to you, and now I'm about to move into my new house, my very big new house." His home would soon be a brick bungalow with four bedrooms on Riddell Street. "It might be time for you to move out of that hall."

Jessica lived frugally, repaying her student loans and university debt more quickly than she was obliged to repay them. She paid little rent to reside in the old Molong Hall, converted into a home with more bedrooms than she needed. The owners, wondering whether to sell it, leased it through Derek's real estate agency.

Slipping the side of his index finger under the tips of her fingers, Derek raised her hand close to his lips. "You could have your own room, your own space," he told her. "No charge." His coarse lips kissed her soft skin. "*My* home can be *our* home."

"Derek!" bellowed a familiar voice, entering the hotel courtyard. Jessica pulled her hand away. Derek stood up.

Jessica's Aunt Nora, dressed in her next-to-best clothes (she reserved her most formal dress for family weddings), reached Derek. They hugged, while Jessica watched them from her seat.

Her Uncle Norris, dressed in his one suit, tie, and jacket because Nora instructed him to wear them whenever they went out of an evening, stood behind her. His body was full with the muscles born of manually working their farm a few miles from the town, but his long face hung with the weariness of work. Like Nora, his skin was parched from the sun Jessica carefully avoided.

"How are you, Mrs Twomey?" asked Derek.

"Please, call me Nora." If Nora's voice appeared educated, then they were other people's educations.

"Mister Twomey."

"Please," interjected Nora, "call him Norris."

Nora sat beside Derek. "I'm so glad we saw you here, Derek," she said. "Your parents must be very proud of you."

"I think so, Mrs Twomey."

"Nora," she corrected him, before her voice became tentative. "Your mother, now would she be in the Country Women's Association, Derek?"

"I'm sorry, Nora."

Jessica had heard her aunt ask no end of people if they could invite her to join the association, although she was free to join without invitation. She wanted to be invited, but members of any association rarely invited people who wanted to be members to become them.

Uncle Norris drew Jessica's attention. "I never knew why you had to go to Canberra," he told her, "or why you're going to London. We never needed to travel so far."

"We never had the money to travel so far," interrupted Nora.

Derek looked at Jessica, altogether irrelevant to the table conversation. "If there is mining near Molong again," said Derek, "it will bring more money to the town."

"We didn't want Jessica to go away last time," Nora told Derek, although she hadn't said so to Jessica. "Now that she's back, we want her to stay."

Derek poured wine into glasses for Nora and Norris. He prepared to pour more wine into Jessica's glass.

"Not for me," said Jessica. He filled his glass and left the bottle beside hers, although she wouldn't change her mind.

Appearing at the table, holding out a round tin and dressed in a long black robe and clerical collar, was an old priest. Old eyes languished in his wrinkled sockets. Thin tufts of white hair seemed ready to float from his head. Only his thick bushy eyebrows were certain to stay. "I'm collecting money for medical research," he told them, "praying we can help Eugene Gallagher."

Derek removed his wallet from his pocket. Norris started to get his wallet but Nora slapped him on the hand. She removed her purse from her handbag. Derek slipped five dollars into the tin, before the priest turned to Jessica.

"I'm sorry," she told him, "I've got debts to pay."

"Jessica!" her aunt chided her. "Please, Reverend, you may have five dollars from Norris and me," she said, pushing a note into the tin, "and five dollars from my niece." She pushed in a second note.

"Thank you, all of you good men and women," said the priest.

"It's a delight having a church to help people," said Nora.

"We've never even seen Eugene Gallagher," replied Jessica.

The priest leant close to her. "I assure you, good woman, he exists."

After their meals, Derek walked with Jessica slowly back along Bank Street, their arms around each other's waists. Derek was tall enough to make Jessica seem small walking so close beside him. "Through everything I learnt in my three years at university," she told him wistfully, "through every conversation with my friends about the world and people in it, I never stopped believing I would again be in Molong." They turned into Edward Street.

From outside, Jessica's home looked every bit a hall. Parked in the driveway was an old pale blue small sedan, which her aunt and uncle had lent her until they needed it again. The grass around the house was long grown before Jessica arrived and had grown without mowing since then. A path through the back yard led to a rotating clothesline, drying her clothes. Derek pushed open the gate and followed her over the white-pebble path and up into the front door alcove.

"I could save you from paying rent altogether," Derek reminded her, as Jessica opened her handbag and removed the door key. "You can move out again if it's not what you want, or have a place to keep everything if you still go to London."

"I am going to London," insisted Jessica, opening the door. "I just don't know how long."

With its high hall ceiling, they stepped into a large single space comprising a lounge room, dining area, and kitchen. White Venetian blinds adorned the windows, although Jessica set the strings adjusting them so the horizontal slats were pulled high, admitting all the light she could.

The timber floor shone with its polish better than it normally shone as a hall. Former tenants had abandoned the worn sofa, matching armchair, and small wooden coffee table in the lounge room. Jessica might've been the only person in Molong without a television set, but she and her student friends sharing a home in Canberra had rarely watched theirs. Hanging from the walls were two old pictures: a lady riding a horse and the farm where her late grandparents lived.

Standing on the coffee table was a vase, in which stood fresh yellow lilies Derek had given her. Beside it were a glass kitten and a small red onyx figure of a tiger. The kitten had been among her mother's possessions; Jessica thought too often of the mother no longer hers, although a year had passed since her sudden death. The funeral had been a rare trip for Jessica home to Molong from university, after her aunt and uncle made the arrangements.

Jessica boiled some water in a kettle in the kitchen area. Derek remained in the lounge area, where he picked up a page of a schoolgirl's handwriting from the coffee table.

"Wendy Allchin gave that to me, last night," she told him as he read, of a girl in her final year at the Molong Central School for whom Jessica was acting as a mentor. If Jessica tried to teach her a little of what she could become, then the schoolgirl taught Jessica a little of what she used to be. "Wendy wanted me to know what's on her mind, after I said all I thought about when I was her age was my schoolwork, and boys."

"Boys?" asked Derek, looking away from the page of paper.

"Wouldn't you rather I thought about lots of boys," she smiled, "or one boy in particular?"

He looked at her long enough not to mention it again, before looking back at Wendy Allchin's words. "These are all the things Ms Ollerenshaw wants her to think about," he said, of the school principal they'd shared, and indeed every student at the Molong Central School had shared for as long as Jessica remembered.

"She's not so bad," said Jessica, carrying two mugs of instant coffee towards him.

He returned the page of writing to the coffee table and took a mug from Jessica. "Thank you, gorgeous," he said, as he sat reclined on the sofa with his long legs crossed.

Jessica sat beside him, sipping her hot coffee and loosening her shoes from her feet. "What are you doing tomorrow?" she asked him.

"The Hammonds are thinking about selling their tomato farm again, so I said I'd go and talk to them. They've done this before, putting it on the market for a ridiculously high price and then giving up and not selling it, but I'll pander to them for the time they actually sell it."

"I won't be having lunch at the Pickled Pepper Café."

"Your best meals are with me," said Derek, as he placed his mug on the coffee table and moved closer to her on the sofa. She stared into his warming blue eyes, resting her mug on the table beside his and closing her eyes, while he gently kissed her lips. "Wouldn't this be easier if we shared a home?"

Jessica opened her eyes and pulled away. "I'm not at high school anymore," she told him.

Derek sat upright. "Is this about London, Jess? Did you come back to become so involved?"

"Of necessity, I have to think more about everything than people who know what will happen with the rest of their lives."

Derek resumed drinking his coffee. "Are you any closer to knowing what you want?"

"When you talk about us living together, I don't mind. I hope we do, someday, but living together now might be a convenience to you that it isn't to me. I don't want to spend my life being your girlfriend to then wake up one morning and realise I was only ever a tenant."

4

THE MAYOR

Wednesday morning, after her toast with raspberry jam and glass of pineapple juice, Jessica dressed into her other clean white blouse and skirt. Her hair again bound in a bun, she sat at her small girl's dressing table and applied blue shadow to her eyes, black liner around them, and red gloss to her lips. Like the rickety bed behind her, the dressing table had been in her childhood bedroom.

Reaching Bank Street, Jessica recognised the elderly widow hovering at the kerb, shaking over her wooden walking cane. Jessica took her hand and helped her to the street. "There you are, Mrs Kincaid," said Jessica.

A young man not long out of school bounded up. He took Mrs Kincaid's other hand.

"Do you know my grandson, Lachlan?" Mrs Kincaid asked Jessica. "I can manage now, thank you dear."

At the higher end of Bank Street, away from the stores, restaurants, and bars, was the repeatedly refurbished old town hall, with its imposing ivory walls and grandiose arch-topped windows. Tucked beside and behind it, at the end of its own long path, was a modern glass-front annex.

The most elegant office in town was the mayor's. Paintings of streets, trees, and waterways throughout Cabonne shire, bought from local galleries, hung from the mayoral office walls. Hanging from other walls through the building were paintings mayors had received from other councils, portraying much the same streets, trees, and waterways in other country shires.

Standing in his office that morning, looking at himself in a full-length mirror, was the mayor. Hector Xiedergrain was a tall man, with a grand head and hair: a thick, aged, waving white mane. The reflection of his pale-coloured suit without a tie seemed inadequate.

Quietly watching him was his personal assistant. Mildred Thompkins was amicable, but relentlessly methodical.

"Cabonne Council should have a mayor in robes," he told her. "Mayors in Sydney do." He nodded a little as he spoke. "A long, red robe lined with black velvet, fur, better not make it real fur, and lace frill."

Mildred took notes of his words. A small pad of paper was never far from her.

"The mayoral hat should be black," he continued. Reflected in the mirror, his chest puffed out a little. "The mayor should have a sterling silver chain of office – gold plated – comprising four dozen shields on wreaths. Gold-plated pendants should represent each of the councils that became Cabonne Council, recalling our heritage. Larger than them should be the ornately enamelled council seal."

When he'd finished, the mayor stepped back to his wide mayoral desk and bonded red leather desktop. A studio portrait photograph of him with his wife and their adult children stood where visitors to his office couldn't help but see it. The two chairs facing him across his desk were set low so he would always be higher than anybody sitting there. The mayor sat in his bonded red leather chair with the desk between him and his visitor when he commanded the authority of his office, projecting his power over people and moving them to do what they should do for the sake of the shire. He sat congenially with them on the two pale-cushioned sofas in a corner when he wanted to befriend them.

He looked towards Mildred. "What is good for the mayor is good for the people," he said, yet again. "For the people of

Cabonne, their council should spare no expense to dress its mayor as soon as it can."

Mildred stepped from his office. She closed the door after her.

The first of the papers for the next council meeting, prepared by the staff to inform the eleven other councillors, lay on his desk. Hector would check them before staff distributed them, and browse through them again before the meeting a week from Monday. The mayor only allowed motions on the agenda that the councillors would pass with reasonable debate, without the disruption of people's passions. They were normally motions about home extensions and shopfronts, although the coming meeting would consider one about the council increasing funds for cemetery maintenance.

With the mayor still thumbing through the meeting papers, a knock came through his office door. A moment later, the door opened. Entering the mayor's office, his cap in his hand, was Sergeant Vaughan: one of the few people the mayor had instructed Mildred to admit directly to him without asking the purpose of their visit.

"Sergeant," greeted the mayor. "I trust you're keeping well."

"Mister Mayor," said the sergeant, closing the door behind him. "I've been awake all night. My wife said I should see you."

"Have you tried drinking warm milk?"

"You've always told me you wanted to know of any threat to good order," the sergeant reminded him. "Well, we had some trouble yesterday at the Pickled Pepper Café."

"Not the asparagus sauce?"

"Jessica Rawlins, a young girl not long back from university, said something at lunchtime the whole café could've heard. She complained about immigrants taking over."

"She said that?" said the mayor, standing up from his chair.

"She admitted it."

"Who knows about this?"

"Briony Keyte and Susan Hodgeson reported her words to me."

The mayor sat back down again. He scribbled those names on a writing pad. "People won't come to Cabonne if they hear of this type of thing."

"Lynne Delaney knows," the sergeant continued. The mayor continued scribbling. "She operates the beauty salon where Ms Rawlins works. Lester Cullen at the Pickled Pepper Café knows, but we don't know who else was there."

"You need to find out, if we're going to keep this thing to ourselves."

"I could ask Lester Cullen."

The mayor returned his pen to his desk. "We can't contain reports about this," he realised. "Charlie Quinn will found out soon enough, if he doesn't already know; much depends upon a journalist's first impressions. Will this Rawlins woman apologise?"

"I don't think she understands what she said."

"That makes it worse," said the mayor, standing up and leading the sergeant towards the door. "Keep an eye on her, will you, Sergeant?" The mayor let the sergeant step out first. "You tell anyone who knows about this that council is dealing with it: crises affecting the shire stop with the mayor. You let me know when you learn something more."

With the sergeant walking away, the mayor looked down at his secretary, scouring computer sites for information about mayoral robes. "Mildred," he interrupted her. She promptly looked up. "Get me Charlie Quinn, here, in person."

Back in his office, the mayor tried to imagine the unimaginable: the face of the woman whose indiscretion had so stirred the town, but couldn't picture in his mind anything but an archetypal effigy of a young woman. They all looked much the same.

Standing in a corner of his office was a television set, on which the mayor watched news bulletins about him. A small cabinet door concealed a tidy collection of liquor, which he often opened to entertain guests with the subtle show of a secret confided in them; Mildred ensured that at least one bottle of Jameson Irish whiskey always stood on a shelf. The day was too early for most men to drink whiskey, but the mayor poured large servings into two crystal glass tumblers he set on the coffee table. He then waited in a sofa beside them.

Mildred appeared at the door. "Charlie says he doesn't make house calls."

The mayor edged forward, but anger wasn't going to bring the journalist to him. The mayor only asked Charlie Quinn to join him in his office when he was most appreciative of something Charlie had written or not written the previous week, or was working hardest to persuade him to write or not write something the next. "Tell Quinn, I'm doing him a favour."

Mildred stepped out of sight. She soon returned. "He said you never do him favours, but he'll wander by when he's next up this way, and in the mood."

The mayor scoffed. "He'll come by if he's not the first man of the day propping up the bar in Freemason's Hotel."

Perhaps it was an indiscreet glance from Mildred, or perhaps they caught his eyes anyway, but the two whiskey glasses he'd set on the table were reason for the mayor to stand up and walk past them. Mildred stepped back out of his office.

The mayor paced around his office for several more minutes. He checked his gold wristwatch; the time was nine thirty. Quinn might realise the young woman's thoughtlessness didn't warrant mention in his newspaper, but a week without anything else to report might allow her words to appear.

Resigned to waiting, the mayor slumped back at his desk. He tapped his fingers repeatedly on the taut leather bonding, until they became too much a reminder of him waiting. A nerve in his forehead irritated him, and he scratched it. He took his favourite ink pen in his hand, lent down to a low drawer of his desk, and pulled it open. He again pulled out the brochures he'd compiled about mayoral robes, chains, and hats.

Sergeant Vaughan stood on the footpath in Bank Street, on the far side of the road from the Bliss Beauty Salon. The awning above the footpath shielded the salon windows from the brightest reflections. Jessica Rawlins was in the salon, washing a customer's hair hanging over a basin. The customer's head lay backwards, supported in a cushioned rest. Lynne Delaney was filing the fingernails of another customer, sitting in a chair facing her. The sergeant couldn't recognise the customers so far away.

The sergeant walked across the street towards the salon, when Lynne turned to face him. He smiled when he knew she'd seen him. She smiled, as the sergeant stepped over the kerb onto the footpath, but still couldn't identify the woman whose hair Jessica was washing. He proceeded along the footpath a respectable way past the salon before stopping. He talked to people, walked along and across Bank Street, and discreetly resumed watching the salon. Again, Lynne turned towards him, but the sergeant couldn't see if she smiled.

At about eleven o'clock, the sergeant observed Jessica step from the salon onto the footpath, her salon white blouse and skirt conspicuous. She walked more slowly than she might normally have walked, suspiciously slowly, perhaps, thought the sergeant, towards Barnsy's milk bar. She came out carrying a milkshake, of a flavour the sergeant couldn't determine, sipping it through a straw as she returned to the salon. The sergeant used his mobile telephone, in which he'd recorded the mayor's private number, to report everything he'd seen.

Those two glasses of whiskey on the coffee table in Hector Xiedergrain's office stood poised to collect dust, if ever there was dust in that office. Soon after midday, the door suddenly pushed open without anyone knocking. The mayor looked up from his desk, saw Charlie Quinn sauntering towards him, and switched on his smile.

Charlie was dressed in another of his open-necked, day-old, cotton working shirts in some shade of grey. His trousers were another slovenly pair in some shade of brown. His clothes of sizes too large for him left space around his waist, arms, and legs making them comfortable to wear. Hanging from his head was his fading bush hat; he might've been the only man not to remove his hat in the mayor's office. It couldn't hide his thin strands of hair greying before their time, counting the years too quickly approaching his forty-fifth birthday. The creases in his face would become wrinkles before he ever retired.

"Charlie!" said the mayor, standing up. "I know you don't like to drink, but let me share this with you." The mayor's hand on Charlie's back, he ushered Charlie ahead of him to a sofa. Mildred shut the door.

Charlie slumped into the sofa, collecting a glass in his hand as he did so. "We're friends are we, Hector?" he asked, before tossing a swallow of whiskey into his mouth.

The mayor sat in the second sofa, leaning nearer to Charlie than Charlie was to him. "I remember," said the mayor, "when the only tourists in Molong were lost on their way somewhere else, taking rooms in the Telegraph Hotel. Now we have a motor inn, bed and breakfasts, and homesteads just out of town. All we need, Charlie, is a few more flower beds and we'll be winning a Tidy Town award."

"You read the *Molong Express*."

The mayor stilled his tones. "I've been wondering all morning what you might do with this," he reflected, "but you might be interested in a little incident at the Pickled Pepper Café."

"We've done several stories about the asparagus sauce."

"Don't quote me telling you this, Charlie. I don't have her exact words, and I'm not sure how much of it might be defamatory."

Charlie drew a long breath. He lowered the glass in his hand, as he slowly exhaled.

"Lunchtime yesterday, Jessica Rawlins, a difficult young woman, complained about immigrants."

"Jessica Rawlins?" asked Charlie, turning his head away. "She went to the Australian National University."

"She can't have learnt anything. She works in a beauty salon now, cutting women's fingernails, drinking milkshakes."

"She seemed so sweet."

"That's what we all thought."

Charlie looked again at the mayor. "What have immigrants said?"

"We're in enough trouble without them getting involved."

"Who heard her?"

Hector returned to his desk and picked up the paper on which he'd scribbled the names. "Briony Keyte..."

"She's Volunteer of the Month."

The mayor began to relax. "I thought the name was familiar."

"You awarded her. What volunteering did she do?"

"You better ask Mildred." The mayor returned to the sofa

where he reclined, crossing his legs. "Our Volunteers of the Month say what we want them to say, if they want to get more awards." Resting his hands with the notepad on his knees, he read the next name on his list. "Susan Hodgeson."

"An exhibition of her pottery opens Saturday night."

"That's her pottery, is it?" smiled the mayor. "I'll speak to Jade's Gallery, but there's your story, Charlie. We'll make Susan Hodgeson's pottery the biggest triumph of global inclusion since Noah packed a pair of every animal into his ark."

"Noah didn't pack a pair of every people."

"Jessica Rawlins was an isolated incident," insisted the mayor, feeding Charlie the words he wanted to read in the newspaper, "unprecedented in Molong."

"So was Fergus Millane."

"Don't worry about him; he hasn't left his farm for two years. This council and community categorically opposed what he said and we categorically oppose what Jessica Rawlins said."

Charlie drank more whiskey, finishing the glass. The mayor walked from his desk to the liquor cabinet and picked up the whiskey bottle. "We'll get this mine up and running, Charlie, and we'll get that new supermarket, if Ms Rawlins leaves us alone." He poured some whiskey into Charlie's glass and a short serving into his. "Write about the Wing Hang restaurant serving good food for as long as anyone can remember."

"What's your favourite meal?"

The mayor sat back in his sofa. "It's hard to find time to eat out."

"I'll talk to Jessica Rawlins," said Charlie, bringing more whiskey to his mouth. "If there's a story here, and I think there is, then I'll run with it."

The mayor wouldn't risk asking whether the story would be on the front page of the newspaper; he only asked Charlie questions to which he already knew the answers. "You and I," he told Charlie, "we stood together when there was talk of a bypass keeping highway traffic out of Molong. You make my response your lead for any story about Jessica Rawlins, instead of the words of a silly young woman who, and this is off the record, might've been intoxicated at the time."

"Do you know that?"

"No blood tests were performed," said the mayor, sipping more whiskey, "and I don't know whether she has a history of mental illness."

Charlie slipped more whiskey into his mouth. "Send me a note before three if you've any quotes you want ascribed to you."

"You let me see anything you write before printing. I can help you, I can add something useful."

"Are you reviewing all my articles now, the advertisements, the page numbering?"

"Just send me anything about Jessica Rawlins. I won't leave this office 'til I hear from you."

"You keep me informed of everything you know about her."

"By the end of the day," said the mayor, "you'll know more than I do."

Charlie finished his drink. "Anything else happening I should know about?"

"You tell me. Can I get you more whiskey?"

"Later," said Charlie, standing up from his chair. "I have a story to write."

Mildred was still at her desk when they stepped from the mayor's office. "I'm sorry, Mildred," said the mayor. "I should've let you go."

"Thank you, Mister Mayor." She quickly collected her handbag from the floor, stood up, and hurried out to lunch.

The mayor watched Charlie leave, as Councillor Sewell came towards him from the councillors' room. Jack Sewell was about Hector Xiedergrain's age, but not quite so much like him as to keep them apart. The councillors most interested in sharing the mayor's whiskey often joined him in his office.

"Pest of a business going on, Jack," said the mayor, leading Jack into his office and returning to his glass of whiskey.

Jack helped himself to a glass from the mayor's bottle. "Charlie's not very good when you tell him to do something," said Jack, sitting where Charlie had sat.

The mayor told Jack what he knew of Jessica Rawlins. "Journalists love this sort of thing," said the mayor, finishing his exposition. "The rest of us rail all we can to progress indigenous people and immigrants, disadvantaging white people, and don't get a whisper on page twenty-two, but one silly woman says something offensive and they're over it like rats. We all look bad."

"Words left unanswered can fester, even inspire," said Jack, as if the mayor hadn't known. "We better foreshadow the questions people will ask, and prepare our spontaneous replies."

"As soon as Quinn's newspaper comes out tomorrow, we'll want people, particularly women, since this troublemaker's a woman, to write letters to him. I don't want them saying they know us, but they live in the shire. They can say that she's brainless, mad even, and nobody agrees with her: nobody. We'll want people with children, young children, worrying about losing their jobs. They fear for the future because of what the confounded woman said. The public relations people can help but the letters should be their words, if they're up to it."

5

THE JOURNALIST

He'd learnt journalism from his father, who'd learnt it from his father, but Charlie Quinn was looking for something more than reporting when he'd learnt the newspaper from his boyhood hometown was for sale. Founded in 1875, the *Molong Express* was published every Thursday, with as many notices and advertisements as articles among its twenty or so pages. Most people in and around Molong browsed through it sometime through the week. Cabonne councillors read every article, searching for mention of themselves and each other. Other people who read everything in any newspaper didn't know why they did, but always had.

Television news and the daily delivery of other newspapers made local newspapers in any country town unsuited to reporting national and international news, although Charlie sometimes sold articles about the town and shire to the *Land and Central Western Daily*. Still, there was no better way to know what a club, society, or school in Molong or the surrounding towns was up to than from the reports they submitted to the *Molong Express*. Nowhere were the Molong shows and Bank Street fairs better recorded.

His heart and pulse racing, Charlie strode from his meeting with the mayor back down Bank Street. Like the mayor at the fore, his blood rushed into what he was doing. Not since Fergus Millane had Molong experienced anything like the incident at the Pickled Pepper Café. Charlie's convictions of political and social responsibilities swelled through his head.

Unlike mere mayors, Charlie didn't condemn Jessica Rawlins for the words from her lips. He condemned her for the ideas in her head; he could only rebut ideas that people made public. Contemplations emanated in the context of beliefs, and she'd stumbled headlong into revealing hers.

Charlie knew that no sensible person felt as Jessica felt, but not everyone was sensible. He would mould people's thoughts and feelings, before they had them. The journalist would extinguish opinions politicians only suppressed.

His means were words and pictures on a newspaper page. His audiences were people who read those words and people with whom they spoke. They'd want to know what Jessica Rawlins said and the circumstances of her saying it. They might've never met a racist and not known what to expect of one. More than just satisfying their curiosity, Charlie would report something important.

The *Molong Express* had moved around the town over the years, but the Gatekeepers Cottage, near the old railway station across the Mitchell Highway, didn't need a sign to say the newspaper was there. Hanging crookedly from the interior walls were certificates of appreciation from local schools and clubs. Behind dusty glass in wooden frames were yellowing front pages from the end of the Second World War, describing not so much the war's end but the town's celebration.

Sitting at her desk was Agnes Plavin, a short and stocky woman with strict spectacles pulled close to her nose. Agnes sold advertising space and kept the accounts. She checked everything Charlie wrote; her diligent eyes saw spelling, grammatical, and other mistakes that he and his computer missed. She brought her queries to his attention and corrected what she knew to be errors without troubling him. Collating stories, photographs, notices, and advertisements into classifications and neat columns, she refined the newspaper layout into what she knew was best.

Agnes knew more about keeping the printing press than Charlie knew, although he learned more about it every time it stopped operating and they worked together to reactivate it. Agnes often talked of retiring to spend more time with her husband, but she'd raised the newspaper as surely as she'd raised her children. Her family could fare better without her than could the *Molong Express*.

"Delete that editorial I gave you," said Charlie, striding past her. "Keep the first page free; relegate everything about vintage farm machinery."

"Something from the mayor, Mister Quinn?" Charlie had stopped trying to persuade her to call him anything else; she'd been calling the proprietors of the newspaper by their surnames too many years to change.

Charlie kicked aside his tattered brown suitcase on the floor. His grandfather had bought the desk in a flurry of optimism after the Melbourne Olympic Games in 1956, before years of pens and ink, typewriters and ribbons, and cold beer bottles stained and scratched it. What had changed was Charlie's portable computer, lying there. Time, he, and Charlie had worn much of the upholstery from his chair, exposing the greying white cushion underlay and rusty steel springs.

Charlie thumped into the chair, pulling it into his desk. Pulling his hat from his head, he tried to dump it at the side of his desk, but his hat fell to the floor. Agnes set a mug of thick black instant coffee on his desk, which he promptly began to gulp. Enthusiastically, he learnt everything that could be learnt about Jessica.

Agnes examined electronic images of past editions of the newspaper stored on computer discs. "This was the article about Jessica Rawlins going to university, Mister Quinn," she told him, "with an accompanying photograph."

"Ah," he cried, standing up from his desk and moving closer to her computer screen. He'd have liked her to be ugly, and hard, but she would've been pleasantly attractive to somebody not knowing what she'd said. She could even have been beautiful, not obviously a demon. "She can't have aged much in three and a half years."

Agnes examined more computer discs. "Ida Rawlins died suddenly when she was fifty-three years old," Agnes read aloud, "the loving and beloved mother of Jessica and her brother, Bede."

"We don't want sympathy for her," said Charlie at his computer. "What are the names of the beauty salons in Molong?"

"Should I know, Mister Quinn?"

"Jessica Rawlins works in one."

"Bliss," replied Agnes.

"Is that a salon?"

"I might be talking about my day, Mister Quinn."

Charlie pushed his chair away from his desk. From the shelves behind him, amidst the papers and books he'd been sent, he pulled out a telephone directory.

"Should I make an appointment for you, Mister Quinn?"

Charlie was already thumbing through the pages. "That'll be all, Agnes."

He tried not to be gruff, but wasn't prone to easy conversation with people concerned in his work. He asked questions of people better than he conversed with them, saving his thoughts for the words of his newspaper and for people he sometimes believed.

Charlie dragged a large pad of writing paper across his desk. He pulled a pen from the several pens standing upright in a black plastic holder. A small audio cassette tape machine recording their conversation might discourage a young woman from speaking, so he left it alone. His right hand dialled the telephone number of the Bliss Beauty Salon, before picking up his pen poised to write. His left ear at the telephone listened for the first sound of Jessica's voice. His small pad of notes from his meeting with the mayor lay where he could easily refer to them.

The telephone answered. "Bliss Beauty Salon, Lynne speaking."

"Does Jessica Rawlins work there?"

"May I please ask who's calling?"

"Charlie Quinn, the *Express*."

The line fell silent. Charlie recognised the complete quiet of a hand placed over a telephone mouthpiece. "Mister Quinn," her voice abruptly returned. "Lynne Delaney speaking, I am afraid Jessica is busy at present."

"I'll call back."

Charlie sat at his desk, tapping his fingers on old timber. The time was not long past two o'clock. Still holding his notepad and pen, he grabbed his hat and bundled outside.

Soon he was on Bank Street, where he pushed open the door to the Bliss Beauty Salon. Charlie's eyes trained upon the young woman in a salon assistant's white uniform, sorting nail files and scissors on a towel on a table. The person who'd so inflamed a town's passions, achieving notoriety far beyond her merit, was slightly shorter than he'd imagined, with a woman's body and hair wrapped in a bun but a little girl's timidity and caution. Her face was much the same as it had been in the three-year-old newspaper photograph, in spite of her powders, gloss, and colours. Charlie could hardly help but analyse her.

"Can I help you, Mister Quinn?" asked Lynne.

Charlie's eyes remained set on her young assistant. "You're Jessica Rawlins."

Jessica turned away. She continued sorting the nail files and scissors.

"I want to ask you about an incident that allegedly occurred yesterday at the Pickled Pepper Café."

Without looking at him or speaking, Jessica shook her head. She sorted those nail files and scissors back and forth.

Charlie needed her too much to abuse her. "I've been told what happened," he told her.

Jessica again shook her head. For all her flaws, she fascinated him.

"I'm afraid, Mister Quinn," interjected Lynne, "we're very busy today." There were two other customers in the salon, their hair cocooned within huge dryers and concentration immersed in magazines. "Perhaps you can call again another day?"

"My deadline is today."

"I'm sure you can wait until next week's edition."

Charlie was civil with people who were civil toward him, and was often civil with people who weren't. He turned towards Lynne. "Can I have a few minutes of your time, Ms Delaney?"

"*My* time, Mister Quinn, and it's *Mrs* Delaney."

"I presume you're aware of the incident at the Pickled Pepper Café."

Lynne hesitated before replying. "It was a private matter outside working hours. Jessica doesn't speak for the salon, or for me, Mister Quinn."

They'd been polite to him; most people were. "I am reporting it."

"I can't see why."

"Do you want to comment?"

"I was actually planning to contact you about placing an advertisement in your newspaper for the salon."

Charlie knew what she was doing. "I can ask Agnes to speak with you about that, Ms Delaney," he told her. "I keep the stories apart from the advertising, unless it's a special feature."

"*Mrs* Delaney," Lynne repeated, "but perhaps I can talk to you about a special feature?"

Charlie tilted his hat towards her. "Thank you for your co-operation."

Stepping back on the footpath outside, looking around as he pondered what to do next, Charlie slowly noticed Sergeant Vaughan across the street, watching him and the salon. Charlie wandered over to him. There, he reached up to speak in his ear. "You can go now, Sergeant."

"I don't take orders from journalists, Charlie."

Charlie laughed. "What can you tell me about Jessica Rawlins?"

The sergeant checked his cap was straight on his head, although it always was. He walked away.

Charlie entered the ladies wear shop where Agnes had told him the Volunteer of the Month, Briony Keyte, worked. He waited while she folded a new blouse to place into a customer's cotton bag. They both watched the customer leave, before Charlie stepped up to the counter. "Can you tell me exactly what happened at the Pickled Pepper Café yesterday afternoon?" he asked her.

"You know about that?"

"You ate lunch with Jessica Rawlins," said Charlie, checking his notepad, "and Susan Hodgeson."

"I should never have accepted her invitation," gasped Briony. "We were talking about the mine and wonderful Chinese people when Jessica, and I'm embarrassed to have to repeat it, complained about immigrants taking our homes."

Charlie transcribed her words. "Was anything else said?"

"She wanted us to be racist too. I said we never would. Susan and I left the table and the waiter, thingy-thingy, had to ask that she leave."

"Have you spoken with Ms Rawlins or the waiter since then?"

"No."

"Has anybody else spoken with you about what happened?"

"We reported her conduct to Sergeant Vaughan."

"Is she being charged with an offence?"

"I hope…" Briony started to say. "That's not for me to say."

"Have you a photograph of Ms Rawlins?"

Briony took her time deliberating, before almost certainly lying. "I don't know where I could find one. We were never too close."

After completing his notes of her words, Charlie paid heed to the expensive clothes and millinery. "Does Jessica Rawlins shop here?"

"I know I ought to be able to serve people and disagree with them about something but I can't, not about this," said Briony. "I couldn't bear to let her in the shop."

Her answer was more than Charlie expected. "Is there anything further you'd like to say, Ms Keyte?"

Briony began fidgeting with a wooden ruler on the counter. "All I hope," she said finally, in her sweetest, most sincere tone of voice, "is that all the people of the world live together in peace."

Walking away, Charlie heard her slap the ruler on the counter. "Yucky, yucky, yucky," Briony muttered to herself. Charlie turned around. "Nothing," she smiled, hurriedly returning the ruler to the counter, wiping the corner of her eyes without smudging her make-up. She slipped through a curtain out of sight.

Pointed there by the Jaye's Gallery manager, Charlie could've been any customer entering the Molong Post Office and approaching the young woman behind the counter, until he introduced himself. "Charlie Quinn, *Molong Express*," he told Susan Hodgeson. "I believe you were party to an incident at the Pickled Pepper Café yesterday."

"I'm sorry, who were you?"

"I'm a reporter."

"I don't think I can help you."

"What did Jessica Rawlins say?"

"Somebody must've told you."

"You were part of the conversation?"

"I never said anything wrong," said Susan. "As it was, I probably should've thrown my drink over her, that's right, or even my meal, but I did go straight to the police."

"What can you tell me about Jessica?"

"She was just an acquaintance. If I'd known what she was like, then I would never have gone. I never knew her too well. I certainly never knew she was like that!"

"Will you see her again?"

"No, never," snapped Susan. "Dreadful woman, I never liked her."

"Could I borrow a photograph of her?" asked Charlie. "I could copy it from your school yearbook."

Susan hesitated. "I've lost it."

Charlie studied her, imagining her rushing home at the end of the day to hide her school yearbook and photograph albums. There was no need to tell her he knew.

After leaving the post office, Charlie sat in an outside seat at the Pickled Pepper Café. The people there for lunch had long gone. The few people around him sat with afternoon refreshments. The waiter moved among the tables whistling something or other, setting a menu before Charlie and brushing some crumbs of toast from the table to the ground.

Charlie began scribbling the words in his notepad that might end up in print. "*Council condemns local girl*," he wrote, before scribbling it through.

Not just the mayor's words for the council, the words of two friends who'd known her the best were most telling. "*Local racist condemned*," he wrote. Charlie assumed that everybody disagreed with her unless somebody told him otherwise.

He developed the words of his conversations about Jessica into paragraphs, amending and correcting them. Melding the testimonies of each participant with his senses of the setting around him, the smell of coffee in the air, the rattling of old cars coming up Bank Street, he described the incident a day earlier as if he were there. He felt like he was.

Venting something from within him, defining himself, Charlie drafted his editorial comment, comprehensively refuting her. "*The extraordinary incident at the Pickled Pepper Café (page 1)*," he wrote, "*reminds us to be vigilant against any form of division. We don't need to understand what leads a person to be intolerant, but we can demonstrate our contempt for her (or him) by politely telling her that she is deeply offensive. She might then realise she's alone.*"

He and Agnes would settle the budding edition of their newspaper throughout the afternoon, while the mayor in his office fretted whether Charlie would diffuse the crisis or inflame it. Charlie smiled, laughing a little at old Hector Xiedergrain. If he quoted anything from the mayor's forthcoming press release then he would juggle it wherever he wanted amidst all other text. Agnes would send Mildred Thompkins what Charlie composed, so the mayor and council public relations officer could pore through it searching for chances to reduce its effect and make more retorts, but Charlie wouldn't change anything he'd written. Only Agnes could do that.

"Are you ordering anything?" the waiter interrupted. He'd stopped whistling to face Charlie.

"You were working yesterday, Lester?"

"You're not still asking about asparagus sauce?"

"Three young women ate lunch. One of them said something."

Lester threw up his hands in recognition and relief. "You're making too much of it."

"I won't mention the café."

"You'll make her a celebrity."

"I could make you the celebrity. Did Jessica Rawlins complain about immigrants? Did her friends want another table? Did you ask her to leave?"

"I don't know her name. She might've been joking."

"If I don't write what happened," Charlie told him, "someone else might talk like her, someone like Fergus Millane."

Lester leant against the table, dipping his head, before looking up to face Charlie. He reluctantly nodded. "You can mention the café, two goat cheese salads for the other two, a penne marinara for what's-her-name, but please don't mention asparagus sauce."

6

NEWSPAPER STORIES

His hat back on a corner of his desk in the Gatekeepers Cottage, Charlie stood beside Agnes at her desk. After completing the layout of each newspaper page on her computer screen, they would set the printing press in the printing room to work. The cranking cogs and tumbling wheels would drop pages of newspaper into piles the machine then folded. They'd produce a few more than usual that evening before Charlie loaded them into his truck to deliver to newsagents, grocery stores, and petrol stations around the shire. More copies would be mailed to subscribers as far away as Sydney.

Agnes kept a handful of copies in the cottage. When everything was done, she stored a clean copy of each edition in a cardboard box. Away from there, in an old shed nobody noticed, cardboard boxes filled with past editions stretched from the floor to the ceiling, covering what once were windows.

Susan Hodgeson was in the post office, hoping she'd given the man from the newspaper the right answers. Rattling about in her brain were other answers she could've given, which she would provide if he spoke to her again. He should've given her more time to reply. She might've said too much. She could've lied to him about having been in the Pickled Pepper Café, but the policeman knew she was there.

Briony Keyte was in the ladies wear shop, just hating Jessica Rawlins. She hated her more than she'd ever before hated anyone.

Jessica was in the Bliss Beauty Salon, preparing to polish Mrs Emery's toenails. She'd need to still her hands better than she could still her fears inside her head, of what the journalist might write.

"Have I told you of my plans for a fishpond?" asked Mrs Emery.

Jessica looked up, trying to realise what her customer had said. Lynne turned towards them, too obviously ready to speak. "You have, Mrs Emery," smiled Jessica, forgetting about everything else for a moment, "but please, tell me again."

Lynne smiled, as only Jessica could see. Mrs Emery spoke, while Jessica thought again about the newspaper. Lynne turned back to her customer's hair.

Their last customer left the salon before five o'clock, when only Lynne and her young charge remained. "You were right not to say anything to Charlie Quinn," she told Jessica. "Journalists can publish your words to the world without writing what you thought you said."

"So can friends over lunch."

"We should be careful what we say, Jessica, even among friends." Lynne stepped aside to her small reception desk and her large book of appointments. "Listen," she continued, turning the page to the following day. "We're not busy tomorrow: Mrs Winterbourne, Miss Mornington, the Cavendish sisters. Would you like me to take care of them and you rest at home? I can call you if I need you."

"Are you worried what the newspaper might say?"

Lynne laughed. "I know Charlie won't mention the salon, but we can both keep a little space from the Pickled Pepper Café."

"Working might pull these past two days out of my mind."

Lynne studied her, as she studied Lynne. Jessica, hoping against hope, didn't have the power for theirs to be a battle of wills. Finally, Lynne nodded. "You decide," she said. She might even have smiled.

Jessica returned to her home. Leaving the front door behind

her a little ajar for Derek, she raised her hands to her hair, removed the pins, and released her hair from the bun. Her hair fell down to her shoulders. In her bedroom upstairs, she dressed out of her working clothes into a casual blouse and slacks.

She was sitting at her dressing table brushing her bun from her hair when Derek's reflection appeared in her small mirror. He brushed his hair with his hands.

Standing up, her kiss to him was unusually brief and distracted. "I've had another strange day," she explained, not quite believing her words. "The journalist from the *Molong Express* came to the salon. He wanted to speak to me about what happened yesterday at the Pickled Pepper Café."

"What happened yesterday?"

"My conversation with Briony and Susan," she explained, "the waiter telling me to leave."

Derek was slow to respond, before cautiously speaking. "What exactly did you say to them?"

Jessica repeated what she'd told him the previous evening. Her words hadn't changed.

"That was all?" asked Derek.

She nodded. "It was a conversation in a café," she told him. "I never thought anything would come of it."

"They take everything so seriously, don't they?" smiled Derek, kissing her lips. "Charlie Quinn got wind of your words and wanted to hang a little human interest off a story about it."

"Why do people with power to do anything dedicate their time to me, in my little life away from them?" she asked. "Can't they just ignore me, the way they ignore everyone else?"

Derek placed his arm around her. "Journalists decide how important you are."

"We might end up with a good laugh about it," said Jessica. "The newspaper novelty might be another trivial notoriety, much like the report of my setting off to university, but I'm not sure I'll keep this one in my pink glory box under my bed."

They held each other's hands as they walked downstairs, where Jessica prepared the meal they ate together. She didn't normally buy newspapers, instead browsing through Derek's copies at his real estate agent offices or home, waiting for him.

"I'll bring you a copy of the newspaper, tomorrow night," he told her.

Parting for the night, they kissed briefly; her eyes remaining open. He wasn't enough to keep her from thinking about morning.

Lying in her bed, Jessica dreaded resolution and the coming dawn. Tireless images of the coming day's newspaper and people reading them shuffled through her restless dreams.

In the morning, Jessica hurriedly dressed for the day, wrapping her hair in another day's bun. Impatient to wait for the bread to toast, she quaffed her orange juice. She rushed her dabs of skin powder, mascara, and eyeliner, leaving a little too much eyeliner behind before wiping it neatly to style. Her heels made running difficult, but she bustled as best she could, almost skipping, along Edward into Bank Street. Her pace quickened as she approached Trethowan's Newsagency.

Wondering how long it would take her to find her name through the newspaper pages, Jessica burst in and looked around for the *Molong Express*. The long racks of colourful magazine covers weren't likely to help. She looked to the counter, where a customer was being served and another patiently waited. Stepping beside them, she looked down at the piles of black, white, and grey newspapers with their punishing big banner headline: "*Molong Girl Sparks Uproar*."

"Huh," she gasped. Dominating the front page was the same photograph of her once smiling face published three years earlier, the one in her glory box.

Jessica stepped forward and pushed a customer a little to the side as she reached down and grabbed the top copy. "*Patrons eating lunch at the Pickled Pepper Café in Bank Street, Molong, on Tuesday were outraged to hear local salon worker Jessica Rawlins complain loudly, 'There are too many immigrants, don't you think?'*"

"Huh," Jessica gasped again. Her face and eyes heating, tears poised to break from her eyes.

There, printed before her, was every detail of a story that never quite occurred, but for the sunny weather, two goat cheese salads, and her penne marinara. She didn't recognise the players in public print, in what other people saw, not even the fictional character unjustly labelled with her name.

Nor did she recognise the two women styled as her two former friends and a Volunteer of the Month. *"Ms Keyte and Ms Hodgeson promptly reported Ms Rawlins to the police, who have not revealed whether they intend to press charges against Ms Rawlins. 'I probably should've thrown my wine or even my meal over her,' said Ms Hodgeson. This newspaper is not aware of any prior arrests or convictions of Ms Rawlins, either in Molong or elsewhere."*

The mayor was also involved. *"Cabonne Council mayor Hector Xiedergrain was quick to condemn her. 'In no way does this silly girl represent the view of every other resident welcoming people of all colours and creeds to our home,' he said in a statement."*

The final sentence was true. *"Ms Rawlins refused to speak with this newspaper."* More than ever, she doubted who she was.

Still holding the newspaper, Jessica turned to run away. "Miss," a voice called to her, as another man put his hand out to stop her. He pointed her back to the counter, where a middle-aged man beckoned her attention. "That'll be a dollar fifty."

Jessica looked blankly at him. She tried to understand what he had to do with the incident at the Pickled Pepper Café.

"The newspaper," he explained, pointing to the copy she carried. "The *Molong Express* costs a dollar fifty."

She looked down at it, wondered whether she really wanted to buy it, and reached for her handbag. Grappling with her purse, she couldn't find the coins to comprise exactly one dollar and fifty cents. She pulled out a two-dollar coin, rushed it to his outstretched hand, and hurried away.

"Miss," called back the voice, "your change." Jessica continued rushing outside.

She scarpered to the Bliss Beauty Salon, still locked from the night. Lynne had not yet arrived.

Jessica could've entered the salon; she had a key. Instead, she hurried across the street to Derek's real estate agency. The only person there when she burst through the door was Derek sitting at his desk, with the *Molong Express* laid out before him. "Jess," he said, standing up.

"Derek," she rushed between empty desks into his arms, dropping her newspaper to the floor. "Oh, Derek, my darling," she cried. "It's worse than I feared it would be, worse than I could've imagined."

He led Jessica into the client meeting room, where nobody from the footpath could see her, and set her in a chair. "People who know you know you're a good person," he said, before recovering her newspaper from the floor outside that room and closing the door behind him. Her newspaper on the table, Derek pulled another chair as close to her as he could sit, taking her hands in his. "People who don't know you won't read anything into it."

Jessica struggled to speak. "It makes me sound awful," she spluttered. "I'm not like that."

"It's nothing personal, Jess. Charlie Quinn and the mayor want to assure everyone that nobody else would say what they think you said. I'm sorry they did it this way."

She looked back at him, wiping some tears from her face. "You know what I said. I was talking about us becoming a minority, but not the way the newspaper says I did. My Chinese friends at university would've understood."

"You have Chinese friends? We can tell the journalist about them."

"They wouldn't have made any difference. I said a little something in a private conversation and now everyone's turning my life upside down. I don't know what will fall out: it might be me."

Derek took one hand from hers and rested it around her shoulders, pulling her a little closer to him. "Some things people don't want to hear," he told her. "Some feelings they don't want discussed."

"All Molong knows what I said at the Pickled Pepper Café."

"You shouldn't have said what you said."

Jessica sat up, pulling away from Derek and looking at him. "You're not blaming me, are you Derek?"

He gently placed his hand on her hair, almost stroking it. "It's not so much a matter of blame as a matter of fact."

"I've been away."

"We don't even know if any Chinese are coming, even if the mine goes ahead, and whether they'll bring their families and stay. We don't know much at all."

Jessica slumped against the table, looking away from Derek. "I didn't realise I could make so innocuous a remark, and have the world crash down upon me."

Derek lent forward and, reaching across her vision, kissed her lips, before pulling back. "You could give the newspaper an explanation," he told her. "If anything in the newspaper's untrue, Charlie Quinn will print a retraction."

"When, next week, after everyone's decided everything about me?"

"By then, they'll have forgotten. They'll be all caught up worrying about who left the sprinkler running all night on the lawn."

Jessica looked back at him. "They haven't forgotten Fergus Millane."

His eyes remained upon hers, before finally falling away. Derek slowly exhaled.

Hers was a point she hadn't wanted to make; she'd wanted his comfort to be correct. "Lynne won't like me being called a salon worker."

Derek laughed, looking up again. "There's an advertisement for another salon two pages in, I noticed. It's tucked in the corner but for Lynne, it'll shine from the heavens. People reading about you will think of it."

Jessica smiled. "Poor Lynne," she said, as the names of every beauty, hairdressing, and other salon in the town ran through her mind. There suddenly seemed quite a few.

"You should take up Lynne's offer for a quiet day at home," said Derek, standing up. "You're her star employee."

"Wait," said Jessica. "Is anyone else here?"

Derek opened the meeting room door a short way before turning back to her. "They've arrived," he whispered.

Jessica turned around, assuring herself there was no other door from the room, before looking back at the door by which Derek stood. She could only leave the premises walking past Derek's colleagues. If she were lucky, they'd all be looking down at her desks or in other directions from her, but Jessica wasn't lucky. Besides, they never seemed to look at their desks, except to read the *Molong Express*.

"I can walk you out," said Derek.

Bracing herself, Jessica drew a full breath. Puckering up her chin, sniffling a little, her fingers were already too damp to dry her face.

She removed her mirror from her handbag. In reflection, the blue shades and black lines around her red eyes blurred where her tears had been, seeming to bruise her. With a tidy, small handkerchief, she wiped the wetted colours of cosmetic from her eyes, leaving not quite enough powder on her cheeks or blue shadow to her eyes to hide most of her feelings. Black liner around her eyes emboldened her long lashes as did the red gloss on her lips, creating the image behind which she hoped she hid. She repacked her handbag, bedding it down.

Jessica picked up her newspaper, folding it to hide the front page, and looked back to Derek. "You're coming over tonight, aren't you, Derek?"

"Of course, I am."

"I love you."

"I love you, too."

She smiled, where nobody but Derek saw her. That might be her last smile before seeing him again.

Derek kissed her on the lips, a little longer than he'd previously kissed her that morning. "Are you going to the salon?"

She shook her head. "I'll be at home."

He pulled the door open and stepped through it. Jessica followed him.

Two men and a woman at their desks looked up. Lying on each of their desks was the *Molong Express*.

"Jessica," said Sophie Fulbright, in her first year out of high school.

Derek started towards the door. Jessica followed closely behind them, trying not to notice the three looking at her.

"I saw you in the newspaper," said Sophie louder. She'd always been nice to Jessica.

Derek momentarily turned around, his eyes at hers. She stopped, her eyes lingering upon his, beckoning his advice. Derek shook his head, but still Jessica turned to Sophie. "I only meant to say that Chinese people value their countries," said Jessica.

"I think everyone wants people with special skills who'll work and invest here," said one man, as much in conversation with Sophie as Jessica, "provided they're not staying forever." His words were all very civil, his tone all very ordinary. Jessica was at a loss to recall his name.

The other man whose name Jessica could never recall joined in. "I think," he said, "any Chinese building the mine would return to China afterwards." He looked at Jessica. "Do you know much about Chinese?"

Jessica remained unsure whether to answer, whether to be party to such a conversation. Derek's colleagues might've been polite. He might've asked them to say what they said. Weary of the experience carrying her along, she was unconvinced of anything. "I better go," she told them.

7

A FAMILY AFFAIR

Out along Peabody Road, several generations of Norris Twomey's family had owned the farm on which he and Nora lived. The single-story timber house had never been particularly comfortable and was becoming increasingly worn, with the plaster ceilings flaking and walls yellowing. Norris painted the outside walls every once in a while, when crop prices were high enough or harvests good enough, but they seldom were. Rain rarely peppered the sloping corrugated iron roof. When it did, the speckles filled every corner of the house.

He or Nora drove into Molong several times a week, and every so often as far as Orange, to buy groceries or materials for their farm. They bought the *Molong Express* and *Land* newspapers every week and the *Central Western Daily* whenever they thought of it; national newspapers didn't report any news relevant to their lives that the *Land* didn't also report. Norris checked the advertisements of his fellow farmers selling used farm machinery, while their friends told Nora most of the things important to her, some of which made their way to the *Molong Express*.

Norris was repairing the fence along a paddock and Nora was in their home that Thursday morning, when a frantic knock came through the door. Nora opened it to see her amply framed neighbour Meryl Brown, practically jumping around. Nora had no time to speak before Meryl did.

"Have you seen the *Molong Express* today?" asked Meryl, bustling into the house as she normally did and carrying a newspaper in her hand. Her voice was no less rapid. "It's your Jessica. I must confess to being in quite a state of shock, all weak at the knees. She's all over the front page."

Meryl must've been mistaken or confused; she can't have seen Jessica since Jessica's return from university. "Our Jessica?" asked Nora.

"She has them all in a flap over a comment she made. Did she tell you about it?"

Meryl sat in her usual place on one sofa. Sitting in her usual place on another, Nora tried to comprehend what Meryl was saying. She often did with Meryl.

"I couldn't believe it," Meryl continued, "but I saw her photograph and I thought to myself: 'That's Norris and Nora's niece.' Seamus was with me and he saw it. He couldn't believe it either."

"Believe what, Meryl?"

"It all happened on Tuesday apparently, according to the newspaper. When did you last talk to her, Nora?"

"It has been some time now," replied Nora, trying to remember anything Jessica said in Freemasons Hotel, Tuesday evening. "What did she say?"

"I thought to myself: 'I know that Norris and Nora would've taught her not to say anything she shouldn't say, even if her mother never did.' Your sister had no control of that girl, none at all. You taught her, didn't you Nora?"

"We did Meryl, we did. What did Jessica say?"

Meryl shoved the newspaper towards Nora. The front page was aloft.

"Oh, dear," exclaimed Nora. She read the article, imagining every member of the Country Women's Association poring over those words. "Is that all?" she asked, rather than turn the newspaper page.

"Isn't that enough? Your Jessica has created quite a storm."

"I am sure there is a perfectly innocent explanation," said Nora. "Newspapers make mistakes."

"I'm sure you're right, dear." Meryl's voice softened with her insincerity.

"Let me get to the bottom of this, Meryl. I'll call you."

"You must," said Meryl, reaching out to recover her newspaper. "You don't want this tainting you." When people felt free to hate and ridicule a person, they felt free to hate and ridicule that person's family, including her aunt.

Nora's hand pressed down upon the newspaper, not because she wanted to keep it but because she knew Meryl's plans for it; Meryl was never happier than she was when she had something to say. Meryl wasn't going to leave her house without it. Nora returned the newspaper to her.

"And please Nora," said Meryl standing up, "if there is anything that Seamus and I can do to help, please let me know, please. If I find out anything more, anything at all, I'll be sure and tell you."

"I know you will Meryl, and thank you for coming by, Meryl. Thank you, again."

Having ushered her out the door, Nora watched Meryl return to the road. Instead of turning back to her home, Meryl proceeded along the road to the home of another neighbour, her newspaper at the ready.

Nora contemplated telephoning Jessica at her work, but didn't know how to ask her what was happening. Grabbing her purse and keys, she hurried from the house to Norris' utility truck.

She drove into town to Trethowan's Newsagency, where Jessica's face blazed from a pile of newspapers. Her niece was the hottest property in town, the villain who smiled.

Nora felt the newsagent studying her, recognising her, as she stared down at the newspaper. "I had no idea, really, no idea," she told the newsagent, paying him for the newspaper before she needed to touch it. "It's all a mistake."

Her newspaper gripped in her hand, Nora rushed back to her home, away from the town and people. The newspaper across their round eating table in the kitchen, Norris read the article.

"Funny seeing anyone from our family in the newspaper," he said. "I still remember that article about her setting off to university."

"It puts all of us in a dreadful pickle," complained Nora, shaking her head. "Meryl Brown is having a field day, working her way along Peabody Road, telling everyone she knows. She'll be showing the newspaper to all of them, saying she's spoken to me. When she's done with them, she'll have her telephone list, and her electronic mail. She might even get hold of a telephone directory before she's finished. Jessica's scandal is ours: yours and mine."

Norris looked at his wife. "What's wrong with what Jessica said?"

"What's wrong!" replied Nora, emphasising every word so he'd know he'd been a fool for asking. "What's wrong Norris Twomey is she said it, in public. Do you want to live like Fergus Millane, holed up on his farm, and don't go telling me again we should visit him?" Nora looked around at the home she could easily hate, much like Fergus Millane's old home before the fire. Only Fergus and his animals ate the food Fergus raised, aside from the small amounts he sold by the roadside far from Molong. "Whether we agree or even Meryl Brown agrees with Jessica, we don't decide what people can say."

The telephone on the table by the lounge room wall rang. It was the only telephone in their home.

"Don't answer it!" snapped Nora.

"It might be something important."

"That's why I don't want you to answer it, not until I know what to say."

Norris and Nora watched the telephone ringing, with Norris sometimes glancing at his wife. "What if Jessica's calling?" he asked her. "The newspaper could be wrong."

"Newspapers aren't wrong, Norris. Newspapers are right and people are wrong. Besides, this is Jessica. She always thought what she wanted to think. Worst of all, she thought she could say it."

The telephone stopped ringing. Nora looked back to the newspaper, reminding herself of what confronted her.

The telephone again started ringing. Thinking that the person who'd dialled the number of their home the first time redialled it was better than thinking a second person was calling them. "If we had a telephone answering machine," Nora told Norris, "then we would hear the person leaving a message, know who was calling, and know what that person wanted."

"Anyone who wants to talk to us will call back," replied Norris, as he'd so often told her. Friendships and associations were more her interest than his.

The telephone continued ringing. "I do worry that we will miss a call from Bede," said Nora of her nephew, Jessica's brother.

"I can answer it and tell anyone other than Bede that you're out?"

"Don't!" The telephone stopped ringing. "One of us will have to speak to Jessica, when I get clear in my mind what to say. One of us will have to teach her a few things she should've already known about getting on in this world."

"I wonder what Derek thinks of this," considered Norris.

"He would be appalled," snapped Nora, "absolutely appalled. I had thought we'd see Jessica in the newspaper because of her wedding, but the newspaper won't print her picture again, not after this."

"She might be so famous that her wedding photographs are on the front page."

"Well, I don't think there'll be a wedding anymore, not with a nice boy like Derek. She should've thought about us before saying anything, she should've thought about Derek, and she should've thought about herself."

The telephone rang a third time. Nora tried to ignore it. Finally, it stopped.

Nora retreated into preparing cups of tea so as not to dwell upon her dilemma, but tea and the passing of time failed to relax her. Norris browsed through the rest of the newspaper, before returning to the paddocks.

She cleaned her already clean home: mopping already clean floors and vacuum cleaning already clean rugs. The telephone often rang. She continued ignoring it. They'd go to bed at nightfall that day, rather than shine lights that would tell neighbours they were at home. If Norris insisted upon watching television, he could do so in the dark. Nora closely inspected the curtain fabric, finally satisfied other farmhouses wouldn't see through it any light from the television set that night.

A loud knock came through the door. Nora turned, standing still.

Another knock came. The visitor would've seen Norris' truck parked in the carport, but might think they were working on the farm.

Nora waited. Finally, the sounds of footsteps departing let her relax.

Suddenly, there at the window beside her, appeared Caroline Potter. "Nora," she called out, hurrying to a rear door.

Nora hurried to open it and admit her, away from outside. "Caroline," she said, "how lovely to see you."

"I've been trying to call you all afternoon."

"I've been into town."

"You should get a telephone answering machine."

"We will, Caroline, just as soon as we find a reliable one."

"I saw Jessica in the newspaper today," said Caroline. "You must've been horrified."

"Norris and I didn't know anything about it," Nora told her quickly, before slowing her voice. "We don't see her very often since she came back from Canberra."

"It's something she would've picked up at university," mused Caroline. "Young people think they can say what they like at universities."

"Oh, I don't think that's the case, Caroline."

"You can't properly control them when they leave home, can you?"

"Her mother should never have given her permission to go."

"Who would've thought it, but I suppose it can happen..."

"Not in our family, Caroline; I thought not in our family. Nothing like this has ever happened before; Jessica never said anything to me that she shouldn't be saying."

"I don't know what you can do now, Nora. People want to

know what you think. They want to know if you say the same things that she says."

"We don't say anything we shouldn't say; Norris and I have always been like that," said Nora, becoming exhausted, fending off comments she would've made to any other woman in her position. "We try to keep out of trouble Caroline, and try to keep our niece out of trouble. You know that."

"Oh, I know Nora, I know, but I don't want the newspaper saying about you what it says about Jessica."

Nora was no nearer to knowing what to say than she'd been when Meryl Brown first showed her the newspaper. Finally, she ushered Caroline Potter out, closing the front door after her.

Relieved to have weathered one conversation but dreading the next, Nora laid the telephone handset on the table by the receiver. Any person dialling the telephone number of their home would hear the busy signal and, Nora hoped, wait, without visiting. The person could wait for a week.

Soon, another knock came through the door. Norris was in the laundry, replacing a broken hinge on a cupboard door. Nora sighed, unable to think of any room in the house where a person couldn't peek through a window. Peeking through the bathroom window would require a stepladder, but there was a stepladder behind the house. Besides, she didn't want people to think that she was hiding.

Nora brushed down her dress with the back of her hand. In the mirror by the door, she checked her face to see her hair was neat. She opened her front door.

Before her stood a man wearing a dishevelled grey hat and sloppy shirt and trousers. "Charlie Quinn," he said, "*Molong Express.*" Nora immediately seized up, gripping the side of the door. "What can you tell me about Jessica Rawlins?"

"But you've published your story?"

"I'm preparing stories for next week's edition and for the news services."

"Please, Mister Quinn. We're ordinary people, extraordinarily average. Her mother tried her best, we all did, but we had no idea she would say such a thing. We don't know what happened to her."

"Where's Jessica's father?"

"Him?" she scoffed. "He left a long time ago, not nearly long enough."

"Has Jessica had any problems before this?"

"No, none at all, never."

"Have you any comment to make about what she said?"

The conversation persisting, Nora felt obvious to anybody watching the house. She pulled the door fully open and stepped back.

Charlie entered her home and lounge room, whereby Nora closed the front door behind them. He paused by the telephone handset lying on the table.

"We're having problems with the answering machine," explained Nora, quickly replacing the handset on the receiver.

She didn't invite the journalist to sit down. He remained standing.

"Are you a parent, Mister Quinn?" asked Nora, trying to seem calm. "You might understand what this is like for us, but Jessica's young and misguided. We love her through whatever she might do, but she needs help, help we can't give her. We see very little of her and she has little to do with us, but people need to know her family didn't make her like this. We aren't to blame."

"Was she a moody child?"

"We wonder how much she kept from us."

"Did she have friends, other than Susan Hodgeson and Briony Keyte?"

Nora relaxed with questions about Jessica rather than about her, but any people whose names she gave the journalist might speak about her as much as they spoke about Jessica. "Susan, Briony, and Jessica were very close at school," she said. "I hope I haven't said anything I shouldn't have said."

"Does Jessica have any hobbies or other interests?"

"Let me think. She is mentoring at the school," said Nora. "I don't remember who told me that."

"Mrs Twomey..."

"Nora," she corrected him. "Charlie, may I make you a cup of tea? Would you like to sit down?"

"Would you mind if I spoke to you again?"

"No, please do," she smiled, her fingers playing with her hair. "I'm usually here."

"Thank you, Nora. Thank you, very much."

"My pleasure, Charlie, and oh, Charlie, would you happen to know anyone in the Country Women's Association?"

8

SCHOOL

The boys and girls of the Molong Central School sat dutifully in their classrooms. The boys dressed in their blue shirts and grey trousers, the girls in their white shirts and blue skirts and slacks, all wearing black leather shoes. Waiting for them under shelter outside the rooms were their satchels, along with the regulation hats they were compelled to wear every time they went in the sun.

In her principal's office sat the memorable Ms Evelyn Ollerenshaw. Wearing her low-hem dresses, sensible flat shoes, and woollen cardigans on colder days, she remained careful in her appearance and proudly staid in her grooming. For half a century, she'd been at the school, briefly leaving it after being a pupil for the education she undertook to return there a teacher. Save only for the dark-rimmed glasses she acquired with age, she was a constant, child and adult, when the children had changed. The trappings of age made her no less aged and ageless.

Several years had passed since she'd stood before a classroom, moulding children into adults. "There is no clarity of thought without clarity of word," she'd instructed her pupils, teaching them classical rules of English grammar when younger teachers didn't. Her voice was precise, and she raised her chin to elongate her neck and throat every time she spoke. She wrote stories for her nieces and nephews that none of them read and knitted socks that none of them wore, but the children she'd taught to speak continued speaking into adulthood as she'd taught them to speak.

Ms Ollerenshaw had suffered a final promotion through seniority to become school principal. Her first day in the role, she'd brought from her home and hung high from a wall of her new office a painting of her long passed away aunt, Rachel Hume. A pupil aspiring to be an artist had portrayed Miss Hume, a school headmistress, standing forthrightly with dark oils and shadowy tones. Her academic gown had the silken colours of university learning, while her black mortarboard rested at a gentle and proper angle on her head. Her attire embodied a principal's authority over staff and students, towering over them as they sat or stood before her niece Ms Ollerenshaw.

The only thing out of place in Ms Ollerenshaw's office that Thursday afternoon was the man in the sloppy shirt and trousers standing before her. She remained in her chair while he remained standing, his dishevelled grey hat in his hands before him much as a dishevelled school cloth hat had often been in his hands standing before her when he was a boy. To Ms Ollerenshaw, very few of the children who'd come through the school ever became anything else, even when they presented themselves as parents of the same children in a new generation. Charles Quinn had been obstreperous when he was young.

"I don't read newspapers, Charles," she told him, "except to converse with people who do. Don't you recall? They're vulgar."

Charlie placed a copy of the newspaper on her desk. He pointed to the photograph of Jessica Rawlins.

Fresh again in Ms Ollerenshaw's mind was her pride when the Australian National University offered Jessica the chance to study there; Ms Ollerenshaw telephoned her at her mother's home to congratulate her. That memory quickly faded, reading what she would soon hear repeated. "Foolish girl," muttered Ms Ollerenshaw, making time to determine what to do. She couldn't scold Jessica with detention after school for what she'd said at a café.

Below her aunt's watchful eyes, Ms Ollerenshaw considered her responsibilities. The school was her father and mother, son and daughter. Nobody had besmirched it as Jessica threatened to do, not since Fergus Millane.

Ms Ollerenshaw pushed the troublesome edition of the newspaper across the desk back towards Charles. She wished he'd pick it up, taking it from her sight, but wishes were for children. "You'll recall Charles," she told him, "her words are unacceptable at this school."

"There's a lot of interest in Jessica: what she was like, how she came to be racist. She was a student at the school."

"I would need to check my records, Charles," said Ms Ollerenshaw, before realising she should remember the names of all students. She should tell journalists what they would discover anyway. "I do recall her."

"Was she was ever in trouble?"

Ms Ollerenshaw considered her reply, wondering whether to say what she knew. Boys and girls were impressionable, and the school was responsible for making them good men and women, but Jessica had never so much as been mentioned for disciplinary reasons, let alone sent to Ms Ollerenshaw's office, unlike her brother. He might've been the bad influence upon her, but he'd also been a student at the school. Jessica should've made no impressions on her, so she couldn't have realised what she was like.

"If Jessica had committed any misdemeanours," answered Ms Ollerenshaw, "I would have disciplined her. If there was anything unusual about her, I would have corrected her. She must have become wayward after she left school. She might have fallen in with the wrong people, something like that. You must have seen it happen."

"What about her involvement with the school now?"

Ms Ollerenshaw could remove Jessica from the Plan-It Youth Programme before Charles Quinn was any the wiser. "We would never have anyone of such ill repute working at our school," she told him.

"I understand she's a mentor."

Ms Ollerenshaw edged around in her chair. "Please, Charles, you have two little boys here. Must you mention us at all?"

"Why give me the impression she's not a mentor?"

"Don't blame me for your impressions, Charles." If Charles didn't think she was a liar, then he thought she was incompetently unawares. "We have a ten-week mentoring programme for children in year ten. Once a week, Jessica sits with a girl much like Jessica once was, trying to inspire her to complete her studies."

"What's the girl's name?"

"I will be talking to her to ensure Jessica hasn't said anything improper."

The school could no longer mould Jessica, but could ensure that students still in its charge wouldn't iterate her indiscretion. Jessica might inadvertently inspire a girl to think as she thought or speak as she spoke. Other educators would want her to act. Parents of other pupils might object to Jessica being on school grounds. The school's student welfare priorities demanded tolerance.

"I had already decided to ask Jessica to resign," said Ms Ollerenshaw.

"Before you'd read my article?"

Charles Quinn wasn't going to faze her. "I would ask the same of anyone saying such things. I would ask the same of you."

"What will you do if Jessica doesn't resign?"

Ms Ollerenshaw tired of conversation with somebody to whom she couldn't dictate. "We are dealing with precious little lives," she told him. "We do not want the children to suffer."

"I could quote you condemning what she said, expressing the school's regret you never identified the problem."

"We are trying to protect the children. We don't want them asking questions."

"I'd like to speak with Jessica's teachers."

"I must return to pressing matters, Charles," she told him, pointing her hand to the door. "I hope we can see you at our pantomime. I shall arrange tickets for you and your wife."

"I..."

"Charles," she snapped. "You are dismissed."

Somewhat sheepishly, Charlie returned his hat to his head. He stepped back out of her office.

Ms Ollerenshaw released a long slow breath. "Horrors me!" she whispered, not so loud that anyone heard.

She turned to the computer terminal at the side of her desk. Archived in the school computer system were past students' reports. Jessica should have been a poor student, to have gone onto say what she said at the Pickled Pepper Café. Instead, her reports were of a girl close to, without ever quite being, the best in her grade. She'd played hockey and netball, as many girls did. Ms Ollerenshaw's school principal comments were no less complimentary of Jessica than her teachers' comments had been, according to her place in the cycle of kind words Ms Ollerenshaw inscribed whenever she had nothing specific to say.

Jessica or her family might have kept copies of her school reports, but Ms Ollerenshaw couldn't do anything about them. As best as she could, she deleted Jessica's reports from the computer records.

Access to student records was restricted to the few, but Ms Ollerenshaw took her wad of keys and entered the room in which files of past students were kept. The oldest boxes were destroyed each time another year of boxes was brought there. The boxes still in the room included those from Jessica Rawlins' time at the school.

Having checked that only one file was marked for Jessica, Ms Ollerenshaw flicked through it. A medical certificate reported that she'd suffered a severe viral infection in her ninth year of school, for which she'd been absent for several days. Occasional letters from her mother excused her from school for stomach aches and other minor ailments. There were no notes from teachers or counsellors.

Ms Ollerenshaw read every word she could about Jessica. Adults being the products of their childhoods, Ms Ollerenshaw felt certain Jessica as a child should've exhibited antisocial behaviour, attitudinal disorders, or other tortured failings to have become what she became, to have spoken as she spoke at the Pickled Pepper Café. A teacher detecting something untoward should have advised Ms Ollerenshaw, who would have informed the girl's parents, but Jessica's files didn't record anything pertinent to her problems.

Some teachers preferred not to record everything they noticed. That didn't absolve them all of their culpabilities.

She closed Jessica's file, relieved a little that it revealed no evidence of Jessica's defective character. Ms Ollerenshaw's failings might have included not noticing the signs upon which she failed to act.

Ms Ollerenshaw wandered into the administration area. "Tanya," she said.

Tanya looked up from her desk. She was quite a bit younger than Ms Ollerenshaw, with children at the school.

"That room in which we keep the old student files is awfully full," Ms Ollerenshaw told her. "Why not destroy some of the old boxes, clear up some space a little? Say, up to three years ago. That should help, should it not? Can you please do that right away?"

At another desk was the main school telephone. Tending to calls, referring them to others, was a woman not much younger than Ms Ollerenshaw, also with children at the school.

"Ava," said Ms Ollerenshaw. "Please ask everybody calling today for any member of staff, or student for that matter, for the caller's name. If Charles Quinn calls, please transfer him to me, and ask the person with whom he wanted to speak to see me, too."

Ms Ollerenshaw started towards her office, before thinking one more thing. She turned back to Ava.

"You better call Jessica Rawlins to come by my office today," she told Ava. "Make it after five o'clock, when all the children have gone, or after ten, when I've gone."

Ava didn't react. Ms Ollerenshaw rarely tried to be humorous; she was not very good at it.

Ms Ollerenshaw contemplated issues best in her office, such as what she would do if Jessica didn't resign from her mentoring role. Around about five thirty, when the other people of day had left but the cleaners had not yet arrived, Ms Ollerenshaw sat at her desk with her hands locked together, beneath her painting of Miss Hume. A knock on the office door broke her concentration; her eyes blinked regaining it. "Come in," she called out.

Jessica Rawlins entered. She wore not the blouse and slacks she normally wore to mentor a student but a long woollen dress too much like Ms Ollerenshaw's long dress. Whatever make-up she'd worn that day, she'd washed from her face; Ms Ollerenshaw never wore make-up. Jessica's hair hung straight and was strangely staid for her, more like a schoolgirl than she'd previously looked in Ms Ollerenshaw's sight since returning to Molong.

"Please close the door, Jessica."

She closed the door. She then stood waiting for Ms Ollerenshaw to tell her what more to do.

"You may sit down."

Jessica sat in the timber-framed chair facing Ms Ollerenshaw. The other chair, with padded cushions, was for adults.

Ms Ollerenshaw lent forward, resting her elbows on her desk and clasping her hands near her mouth. She stretched her neck and head a little bit higher as she would to discipline an errant schoolchild. "Do you like mentoring, Jessica?"

"Yes. Do you?"

Ms Ollerenshaw sat even more upright. She slowly sat back in her chair. "Do you know why I wanted to see you, Jessica?"

"I could guess."

"Many of our parents will have read the newspaper article, Jessica. Many of our students will read it. It puts the school in a precarious position."

"I was thinking aloud."

"You shouldn't think aloud where anyone might hear you, Jessica. People want harmony more than debate. They want to surround themselves with people with whom they concur, assuring them they are correct. They don't want ambiguity, uncertainty, or anything to learn. Anything that threatens the tenets of their lives threatens them."

Jessica looked down at her lap. "I never meant to offend anyone."

"We're trying to teach the children of this school not to offend people, Jessica, not even inadvertently. You should know that from your studies here. Briony Keyte and Susan Hodgeson know what to say."

Jessica continued looking at her lap. "I've been away," she replied. "I forgot."

"Our community has standards it expects this school to uphold and instil into our children," Ms Ollerenshaw told her. "Our parents expect us to set a particularly good example: a standard higher than others. We can't allow people in positions of responsibility to express what they feel; we have our children to consider. It will not do to have our mentors expressing everything they think."

Jessica looked up. "Is it all right to think if I don't mention my thoughts? Is it all right to think? Shouldn't we be teaching our children to think?"

"We are teaching our children to think," Ms Ollerenshaw corrected her, "as this country expects them to think. Imagine if every student thought differently? Why it would be like everyone having a different numbering system or alphabet."

"No, it wouldn't."

"Nobody could do anything, Jessica. If you must say what you think, then you must learn to think properly."

"Where is the reason, the searching for truth?" she asked. "We all keep agreeing in case someone starts to question."

"We don't seek what we already know."

"Studying at school and university, I learned to learn. Others didn't, but some of us did. I strived to know and understand truth, and to appreciate it when I did. What have we without truth, whatever we choose to do with it? Without facts, we're fools."

"Truth is relative," Ms Ollerenshaw lectured her. "You don't lay it down."

"You reduce truth to mere perceptions and call your perceptions facts, but you don't try to know facts. To know truth, we must be truthful. We must be honest and forthright about what we believe, even if we're wrong. I might be wrong, I don't know, but nobody's willing to discuss it. All I want to do is to learn. I prefer that people explain to me why I'm wrong than leave me in ignorance, but shouting people into silence, or breaking them, isn't persuading them of anything. Imagine if Copernicus couldn't discuss the earth orbiting the sun. I studied science."

"We can't be so arrogant as to turn what everyone believes on its head," Ms Ollerenshaw insisted. "Neither you nor I are Copernicus."

"Neither was he, when he started to think. If a clerk in a patents office in Molong first thought gravity affected the passage of time or that nothing could travel faster than the speed of light, would he have been torn apart?"

"There's no patents office in Molong, Jessica. If you want to revive debate in this country, debate something unimportant: something that won't disturb the citizenry. Talk about strawberries and raspberries, varieties of tea."

"When did you stop thinking?"

"Jessica," snapped Ms Ollerenshaw. "I am your principal!"

She didn't respond. The quiet allowed Ms Ollerenshaw to think without speaking. Words to educate an adult child didn't come as easily to the erudite school principal as did words to educate children. She would talk with Jessica all night and day, if talking might move her. Frustrated with Jessica's failure to comprehend what she knew to be true, too tired to fend any more of the young woman's words away, Jessica made her feel older than she ought to have felt.

"Sometimes we all need to make sacrifices, for the sake of the children," said Ms Ollerenshaw. "Are you willing to resign from your role as a mentor?"

Jessica dipped her head. "Wendy Allchin appreciates it."

"I shall speak to Wendy."

Jessica stood up. She walked towards the door. When she was about to reach it, she turned around to face Ms Ollerenshaw again. "If next week's newspaper fixes everything, may I mentor Wendy again?"

"Public mores never change," said Ms Ollerenshaw, before finding a little sadness to express, "not for the better."

Jessica nodded, before turning around, opening the door, and departing. Leaving everything as she'd found it, Jessica closed the door after her.

Alone again in her office, sitting in the chair of principals better than she was, Ms Ollerenshaw wiped her face with her hands. Having failed to persuade Jessica to be what she wanted her to be, Ms Ollerenshaw can't have been the scholar she'd once presumed she was. She couldn't answer Jessica as her schoolgirl teachers who'd taught her would've answered such a critique, but Ms Ollerenshaw had no call to say to them what Jessica said to her. She was no wiser than any other person who condemned Jessica without listening to what she thought. She'd become too clever to think, too important to feel.

When she knew Jessica had gone, Ms Ollerenshaw picked up her briefcase, locked the doors of her office and the building, and started towards the car park. Standing almost idly by her car was Charles Quinn. When she reached him and her car, he stepped graciously aside.

"I tried to lie," she told him. "I am not very good at it."

"I had an English teacher who told me the only people proficient at making untruths are very poor at speaking the truth."

She smiled a small comfort, fondly recalling boys and girls she once knew. "The truth about Jessica Rawlins won't harm us any more than my failure as a liar," she told him. "At school, she was bright and personable, a good girl for the most part, but she talked too much in class."

Ms Ollerenshaw returned to the house in which she lived alone: the house in which she was born. Having become accustomed more to contemplating the students she'd taught than the student she'd been, her black academic gown hung and her mortarboard cloaked in scholarship lay in a cupboard.

Along the shelves of her home was every book she'd owned through her lifetime of study, teaching, and reading: rows of bound covers with names of master works and those that tried. Was the truth beyond knowledge, she wondered, a notion in philosophy that mortal man and woman could never dissertate, or had she merely abandoned the quest?

Ms Ollerenshaw checked every title among the books in the shelves, but didn't know where philosophy had gone. Finally, when the night was late and her back had become sore, she pushed open the creaking door to a dusty spare room. Among the possessions she'd inherited when her aunt died was a small leaded light bookcase. The tape that once sealed the doors had yellowed. It peeled away in her fingers. The door seemed to moan as she pulled it open, but stored on those shelves were the philosophy books. Books of thought had languished in the dark.

Her old woman's fingers touched one book's binding, the dry dust crumbling against them. She opened a book and, pleasing the dead woman's portrait again she felt sure, began to read. *"Our topic is the essence of truth..."*

The souls of renegades had long ceased to elucidate anything men and women heard, since they'd all moved beyond good and evil to being only good. Ms Ollerenshaw needed time away from responsibilities confronting her to consider Jessica's words; she had most reason to wonder and least chance to do so in her school woman's office, where the only principles to know were those in which everyone believed.

9

THE SALON

Friday morning, Lynne Delaney lay awake in the sheets of her bed, staring up into the white plaster ceiling. Her dark hair spread long on her pillow.

Her husband Trevor appeared at the door, returned from his morning walk. She was the reason he kept his body trim, exercising more than he would've exercised without her.

Lynne sat up, holding herself upright with her long arms. She'd retired to bed the previous evening before he'd returned from rehearsals with the Molong Players.

"Charlie Quinn from the *Express* telephoned yesterday," he told her.

Lynne's shoulders drooped. Dropping her arms, she fell back on her bed.

"He wanted to know about Jessica," continued Trevor. "I told him to speak to you."

"He won't."

Trevor sat beside her, placing his hand on her waist. "You know we support you, darling," he said, "but Winifred Mulligan told me she'd be embarrassed going to that salon of yours."

"Mrs Mulligan likes the discretion of being beautiful without people knowing she attends a salon."

"Jessica's making a stir," persisted Trevor.

Other customers had shied away from the salon the previous day without explanation. "I've tried to keep the salon out of it," said Lynne.

"Darling, people who don't know already will discover she works for you. They don't want to be caught up in it. They don't want to be embarrassed."

"I feel like we're becoming the victims of all this," said Lynne, turning to her side.

"I like Jessica," said Trevor, placing his hand on her back and caressing her, "but you have to think of the business."

"I blame myself," said Lynne. "I should have convinced the newspaper to leave her alone. I could place a statement in the shop window, saying she doesn't speak for the salon."

"That will remind them she's there."

"What more can I do, short of dismissing her?"

Trevor caressed her more firmly. "People say Briony Keyte is lovely," he told her. "She might like working for you."

Lynne turned around to face him. Trevor's hand fell away. "Jessica doesn't deserve that."

"You don't deserve what's happening to you. You've put so much work into that salon."

She placed her hand on his shoulder. "I've sometimes thought you didn't like me spending so much time working."

"I want you to choose what you do. I don't want Jessica forcing choice upon you."

Lynne lay back on her pillow. "The salon was so happy a place," she lamented, "not just for customers, but for me. It hasn't been since Sergeant Vaughan walked through the door three days ago."

"You shouldn't have to put up with this," said Trevor, lying beside her.

Lynne lay silently. The silence didn't help. "Maybe the trouble is that I don't like her so much now," she said, "but I've never dismissed anyone from my employ. I don't hate her enough to do that to her. When all is said and done, I don't hate her at all."

Trevor reached across and kissed her gently on her cheek. He then rolled back on his pillow.

Lynne didn't eat breakfast that morning. In her white blouse and skirt and with her dark hair again high on her head, she went early to the salon. She was wondering whether to relieve Jessica from another day working, when Jessica arrived.

"Good morning, Lynne," beamed Jessica. She stood freshly showered, made up, and smartly dressed in the white blouse and skirt conspicuously that of the salon as if it were any other day. A light yellow hat concealed her hair.

"You're early, Jessica."

Jessica hung her hat on the stand near the door, revealing the bun in which she'd wrapped her shining blonde hair aloft. "I want to get a good start," she said. "The new day has to be better than the last." Opening her handbag, she removed two sandwiches she placed in the small staff refrigerator.

Each time the telephone rang, Lynne answered it. Jessica watched her, until she mentioned a customer's name.

If their customers in the salon noticed any similarity between Lynne's young assistant and the woman in the newspaper photograph, they didn't blight their time there by mentioning it. They didn't risk attracting attention.

Eleanor Winterbourne rarely noticed any of Lynne's young assistants. The aging heiress of one of the best farms around Molong enjoyed an instinct to think only thoughts she could speak freely. "What one says is so terribly important," she said in her affected English accent, her voice fluttering with every syllable of a long word, while Lynne tended to her hair. "I don't think issues about which people can be emotive are necessary. Better to let them lie."

"Indeed, Mrs Winterbourne," replied Lynne, glancing at Jessica wiping a bench top.

"Were she in polite society, she wouldn't have talked about it."

"Quite, Mrs Winterbourne," said Lynne.

"She obviously doesn't have any friends, not if she could say such a thing. She really isn't our sort of a person, is she dear?"

"No, Mrs Winterbourne," said Lynne, again looking obliquely at Jessica, "I suppose she isn't." Jessica turned away.

A woman Lynne didn't know entered the salon. With Lynne

engaged, Jessica left her cloth at the side of a sink and went to the woman.

"I'm the mayor's secretary," the woman smiled. "Mildred Thompkins."

"I'll be with you in a moment," Lynne called to her. Very quickly she was with Mildred and Jessica, leading them away from Mrs Winterbourne.

"The mayor would like to see Jessica," said Mildred.

"No," snapped Jessica.

"Shush," said Lynne, keeping an eye on Mrs Winterbourne watching them. Lynne smiled at her. Mrs Winterbourne smiled back.

"The mayor..." said Mildred again.

"It's about the Pickled Pepper Café," Jessica interjected, "and I don't want to talk about it."

Mildred stepped back. "He won't like this," she told them.

Lynne looked at Jessica. "Would you like me to come with you?"

"I've got my job to do," insisted Jessica, returning to the sink and recovering her cloth. She resumed wiping the sink clean.

Lynne turned back to Mildred. "She is a nice girl," Lynne told Mildred, "kind to everyone she meets. She's always done everything I've asked of her."

"You have a word to her," replied Mildred. "Try to slip a bit of sense into her. Surely she knows she can't go around saying whatever she likes, not anymore."

"I'm only her employer. Her boyfriend should say something, or her aunt."

"I'm surprised they put up with it," said Mildred, turning to leave. "She has come to be rather a nuisance."

Lynne continued watching Jessica while tending to Mrs Kitching, who read newspapers but forgot everything she read. "I heard from my son in Melbourne," said Mrs Kitching, as she always did, before repeating to Lynne all her son had told her.

When Jessica saw old Mrs Ibbotson struggling to open the salon door, she helped the elderly widow up over the step. With more movements than most women required, Mrs Ibbotson settled comfortably into her chair beside Mrs Kitching in hers.

"I do want to look my best for my friends, dearie," Mrs Ibbotson told Jessica, under Lynne's continuing watch. "Now, dearie, I don't want you asking how many years it's been since *we* were at school."

Jessica dutifully nodded, while she manicured the old woman's nails. Mrs Ibbotson studied her with the faraway whimsical look Lynne often saw in older women gazing at younger ones, except that this look became rather quizzical.

"I'm sorry, dearie," said Mrs Ibbotson. "You look familiar."

Lynne answered, while Jessica looked up. "She would've been here last time you were here, Mrs Ibbotson."

"It has been a long time," smiled Mrs Ibbotson, looking back towards Jessica. "What was your name, dearie?"

Again, Lynne interjected. "Are we tending to your hair today, Mrs Ibbotson?"

Jessica combed and brushed Mrs Ibbotson's hair, never far from Lynne's watchful gaze. With a pair of fine scissors, she carefully cut away the worst knots, while Mrs Ibbotson stared at a picture on the wall. "All the models in the photographs are so very beautiful," the old woman remarked.

"They are, Mrs Ibbotson," replied Jessica.

Mrs Ibbotson commented upon other items around her in the salon, until the only item left to observe was the reflection in a mirror of the young woman tending to the back of her head. "Aren't you the one in the newspaper?"

Lynne turned around, but Jessica replied before she could. "It's all a misunderstanding."

"Ooh," said Mrs Ibbotson, looking away.

"Can we get you a magazine to read, Mrs Ibbotson?" asked Lynne.

Mrs Ibbotson looked tersely at her. She nodded.

Jessica brought her the *Women's Weekly* magazine, published monthly, which Mrs Ibbotson slowly opened. She sat silently, while Jessica finely cut her retreating hair. Mrs Ibbotson read the magazine twice rather than ask for another one, while Jessica prepared her hair for not just a single dinner party on Saturday, but for the weeks and months she was alone. When she was ready to leave the salon, Jessica helped her walk to the reception desk. She left her with Lynne, before quietly sweeping cut hairs from the floor.

"I hope you're pleased with everything today, Mrs Ibbotson," smiled Lynne, preparing to tell her the cost of the visit.

"Yes, yes dearie," she answered, before dropping her already soft voice so only Lynne could hear her. "Personally, I don't mind what she said, but I don't like confrontation."

"None of us like arguments," said Lynne, walking with Mrs Ibbotson to the door.

"It's not your fault, dearie, but it is your misfortune."

The door to the salon opened and a middle-aged man, whom Lynne didn't recognise, saw them. He carried the *Molong Express* newspaper in his hand and glanced at the front page. He looked at Jessica, seemed to satisfy himself that hers was the face in the photograph, and departed.

Through their time for lunch, Jessica sat at the rear of the salon, facing away from the windows and footpath. In her hands was another glossy magazine for women that didn't mention her, although Lynne noticed her eyes spent little time on the pages. Lynne brought her a milkshake from Barnsy's, borrowing a metal beaker because Jessica preferred drinking milkshakes from metal beakers. When she finished, Jessica checked the make-up on her face. Lynne had nothing to say.

At three o'clock, old Miss Carpenwood arrived. The retired postmistress came to the salon at least once every month, when she felt the centre of all attention for the too short a time she was there. Lynne always allowed more time in her appointment schedule than the hour for which she'd asked because, towards the end of each appointment, she became reluctant to leave. She always asked for more than she'd initially contemplated.

That afternoon, when she arrived, Miss Carpenwood took one look at Jessica and froze. All joy fell from her face. She only talked with Jessica or Lynne to complete the care for which she'd asked, their conversation stilted.

"Is everything satisfactory, Miss Carpenwood?" Lynne asked her.

"I am not feeling myself, Lynne."

In truth, Lynne knew, she felt too much herself. Miss

Carpenwood didn't feel beautiful, as the infamy of the young woman kneeling at her pedicured toes surpassed every sad dream of fame she could imagine. Without feeling pampered as she normally felt in the salon, her time there was tiresome. She felt as unimportant as she felt every other day of her life.

When the tasks for which she'd reserved her appointment were complete, Miss Carpenwood didn't ask for more. "Thank you, Lynne," she said simply. "Thank you, Jessica." She was the only customer that day to recall Jessica's name.

"Can we make a time for your next appointment, Miss Carpenwood?" asked Lynne.

Miss Carpenwood walked away without reply. Lynne watched her leave, aware that the failure of her time to be important made Miss Carpenwood feel worse than she'd felt before she arrived. Her coming days and weeks would feel worse without the comfort of a coming trip to the salon.

When the last customers had gone, Lynne and Jessica prepared to seal the salon for the day. The telephone again rang. "Good afternoon. Bliss Beauty Salon, Lynne speaking."

"Tamsin Davenport, Lynne. I'm sorry to trouble you, but would you mind telling me: that woman in the newspaper, Jessica Rawlins, does she work with you?"

Lynne sighed. "Yes she does, Mrs Davenport."

"Oh," said Mrs Davenport. "Look I am sorry, Lynne, I am scheduled to see you tomorrow morning. Would you mind if I deferred that appointment? I'm feeling poorly."

"Not at all," said Lynne, as she erased Tamsin Davenport's name from the book of appointments on her desk. "Can I fix another time for you?"

"It's a little bit difficult for me to get there at the moment."

"I understand Mrs Davenport." Everything had become a little difficult.

"Let me call you again may I, Lynne, when I have my diary with me?"

Their conversation finished, Lynne turned to Jessica. Jessica was ready to leave, her handbag over her shoulder. Only her hat remained on the stand. "Mrs Davenport called to cancel her appointment," Lynne told her. "She said she was feeling poorly."

"I hope she's all right."

Lynne rehearsed her words through her mind before speaking. "She is concerned about your appearance in the newspaper."

"I never meant to involve you," said Jessica. "I never meant to involve me."

"You have put everyone in a very onerous position," said Lynne, a little more the mistress than she liked to be. "If it weren't for the salon I wouldn't mind what you said, but our customers don't want to be reminded of anything distasteful. They need to feel good when they come here, and they don't want your notoriety pressed upon them."

"I am really sorry."

Lynne wanted one of them to think of something clever to say. "What is Derek's response?"

"We're keeping quiet."

Lynne nodded. "Have you thought about your plans?" she asked. "When are you headed for London?"

"I've been thinking more about newspapers."

"Don't you think you might be happier somewhere but here, Jessica?"

"No!" cried Jessica, shaking her head.

"I am thinking of you."

"No, you're not."

"What else can I do Jessica? What else can you do?"

Jessica slumped onto the chair closest to her and rested her head in her hands. "Do you want me to talk to the journalist," she asked, her voice slowed, "the mayor?"

"I know you're a very intelligent young woman," said Lynne, "but I'm afraid you don't understand what's happening here. I can't afford to lose so many of my customers because of what you said. They might agree with you, or disagree with you, but they don't want other people deciding what they think because you file their nails. Friendships are important, Jessica, but I can't let liking you ruin my business. This town has more beauty salons that it has people speaking their minds."

"Is that what this is, business?"

Lynne sat down in the chair beside her. "Isn't that much clear to you?"

"I like it here," sobbed Jessica, looking around.

"I can pay you through to the end of next week."

"What will you tell people?"

"That you resigned, that it was your decision. I can tell them that you're leaving because you want to leave Molong, if you like."

"I have nowhere to go."

"I can say you're looking for a change."

"If you were the customer at somebody else's salon," asked Jessica, "where I was the employee who'd said what I said, would you not go there anymore?"

"I'm not a customer," said Lynne. "I'm a beautician trying to keep my business afloat, while it's sinking around me."

"So that if I remained, we would both lose our jobs?"

"That's right," Lynne smiled.

Jessica dipped her head. "I still don't understand what all the fuss is about," she said, starting to weep.

"I know, Jessica," said Lynne, placing her arm around Jessica's shoulder. "I am sorry it has to turn out this away."

"I'll come back with your uniform," said Jessica, "after I've cleaned it."

Lynne started to say Jessica could keep the white blouse and skirt, before realising that anybody who saw Jessica wearing them might recall Lynne's salon. "Whenever is convenient, Jessica."

Jessica stood up from the chair. She adjusted her handbag on her shoulder.

"Take some headache tablets," said Lynne. "You will feel better."

"I don't take tablets." Jessica recovered her yellow hat from the stand and placed it on her head, hiding her face. She opened the door.

"I hope everything picks up for you, Jessica."

Looking towards her, from beneath the rim of her hat, a sorrowful smile raised the corners of Jessica's mouth. The face that had seemed so beautiful each morning was defeated.

Jessica stepped through the door and onto the footpath, letting the door close behind her. Lynne watched her walking away, breathing a short relaxed relief that her chore was over. Jessica walked beyond the window frame, like a bad actress exiting another person's stage.

Lynne typed into her computer the words of a notice advising passers-by of a job vacancy at the salon, printed it, and affixed it to the window by the door. She drafted an advertisement for the new job, which she would place in the coming edition of the *Molong Express*. Customers could draw their conclusions about the reason Jessica no longer worked there. Lynne wouldn't agree or disagree with any of them.

Uncommonly late in the day, the telephone rang. "Hello, Lynne," said the woman at the far end of the connection, "Hazel Yardley calling."

"Good afternoon, Mrs Yardley."

"My apologies Lynne, but I won't be able to make my appointment at eleven o'clock tomorrow."

"I am sorry, Mrs Yardley, although that might actually make things a little easier for me. You see, I'll be the only person here tomorrow since my assistant, Jessica, resigned."

"She has gone, has she?"

"Yes, today."

"I might be able to get there sometime tomorrow."

"What time would be convenient, Mrs Yardley?"

"Shall we say eleven o'clock?"

"That would be perfect."

Their conversation over, Lynne hung up the telephone. "What bothers me most," she whispered, where no one else heard her, "is knowing Jessica is right."

10

THE BROTHER

Eucalyptus trees spread across many a country town across New South Wales as if the town wasn't there. Few other trees on earth so defied their habitats, forming forests of high canopies shading the ground, scattering over roads, fields, and paddocks, congregating along creeks and rivers. Bark peeled from the smooth trunks, while dappled among the crooked branches were clusters of long leaves, which fluttered in the swirling sporadic breezes without obvious direction. They fell sporadically throughout the year and grew again in isolation, lost among the group. The shades of grey and green didn't vary. However hot the summer days and cold the winter nights, there were no seasons in the trees.

Only the creeks and rivers changed. They could be so dry that it took an old man's memory to remember they'd been there, or flood like oceans on the march. Rarely flowing rivers going nowhere could still gush from time to time.

Weaving near the old railway line, Molong Creek flowed fervently that Saturday. Jessica's mind was further from the tone of her town than it could be anywhere else in Molong, resting beside her brother, Bede, on a red tartan rug. The shaded grasses never cut were thick and fallen over, making them lush and comfortable. Her blonde hair hung freely from her head, never again in a bun. Her floral dress without a hint of uniform was another break from a bad week behind her. She'd cleaned the clothes from the salon the previous night and, without making a sound, left them in a bag on the doorstep of Lynne's home that morning.

Beside them was Jessica's wicker picnic biscuit, in which were her Camembert cheese starting to run and crisp Vita-Weat biscuits. Bede would open his bottle of wine when he was ready.

The creek was a place they'd often come when they were young, without the wine and cheese; Molong offered many places for children to hide and play. The little weir produced a larger waterfall: a curious piece of human neatness in that haphazard, weaving waterway. Being there made Jessica the adult feel younger than she felt anywhere else. Amidst the trees, townspeople couldn't see them, and Jessica couldn't see townspeople. It was her best venue for respite outside her home, somewhere safe in which to sit hidden from view. If the creek connoted something she had lost, it might convince her she could yet retrieve it.

Saturday was a working day for a real estate agent like Derek, showing people around properties for sale. Bede's pregnant wife, Gemma, was at home in Orange, picking away at chocolates Bede had bought her that morning. It was time for Bede to sit with his sister and talk between them about her extraordinary week, since her lunch in the Pickled Pepper Café. If it seemed the creek was ready to burst forth into a torrent, it was because Jessica and Bede had seen torrents there before.

Five years older than his sister, Bede's face and jowls were strong. His blue eyes were firm and blond brows thick. His blond hair was coarser than his sister's soft fibres, and slightly long and thick because he thought too rarely of cutting it. He wore the clothes, and occasionally the ties, that his more fashionable wife chose for him. He'd finished school with academic grades good enough to get a job working at a health care company in Orange, and studied business two evenings a week for a year at the technical college before becoming a manager at work. His and Gemma's home in Orange was already large, but they'd extend it if four bedrooms proved inadequate.

As much as Bede being with her, the creek flowing unperturbed by anything she said made Jessica feel safe enough to talk. "I don't know anything anymore, Bede," she told him, shaking her head. "I was still deciding what to do with my life when suddenly I'm struggling to survive."

Her brother read the article in the *Molong Express*, while Jessica waited. The trees had been massive when she was small, watching her older brother and other boys climbing the trunks and branches where adults couldn't see them. The trees should've become taller since then, but they seemed smaller than her memories made them. Jessica watched the leaves shaking in the breeze, expecting one to fall. None did, but they couldn't hang forever. She'd spent too little time there.

After Bede put down the newspaper, Jessica told him about the school and salon. "My mentoring and job were never more important than they've become since I lost them," she sighed, her head drifting low. "I'm no longer a good inspiration for the girls of the school or good for business at the salon, which a week ago I must've been. I feel most sorry for Wendy Allchin; they didn't have enough mentors already. Schoolchildren are important, and my time I would've spent with her seems pointless without her. Suddenly I'm a problem, and the easiest thing for everyone is for me to disappear."

"Do you want to stay with us in Orange?" asked Bede.

Jessica giggled, nervously, with thoughts of other times. "Do you remember your last year of high school, when those two girls with the longest hair in your form were bullying girls in my form?"

"I can't remember their names," said Bede, "but they were pretty popular among people their age, until they tied you to a chair with a rope."

"You and Hayden Saville untied the rope, and then held those girls down while Gemma tied their long hair together into plaits, twined like ropes."

Bede smiled. "They screamed and carried on, didn't they?"

"The mother of one of them ended up having to cut her daughter's hair to free them from each other," laughed Jessica.

Bede laughed with her. "The school punished Hayden,

Gemma, and me more than it punished those girls, and we had to sit through sessions with the school counsellor. I think I'd have preferred the olden days when children were caned than sitting through sessions with a school counsellor."

"No one bullied me again," said Jessica, rubbing her hand in the deepest reaches of grass, feeling secure.

"We can't tie the hair of nasty people together, anymore, Jess."

"There isn't enough hair to go around."

Bede pulled himself up from the ground, stepping towards the creek. "Part of loving someone," he told her, "can be privately disagreeing. Expressing your feelings publicly isn't worth the anguish you're suffering."

Jessica followed him. "The time has passed when silence can save me," she said, picking up a long stick she trailed in the water. "Do you think I'm wrong in what I said, not that I really said anything? We're the only races in the world so willing to become minorities?"

"Nobody cares, Jess, not anymore. You're the minority, now."

She threw her stick into the creek. "Without a hometown and homeland, we're homeless."

"We're something, we're here!" Bede rolled his arms through the air, leading her eyes across the grasses and waters to the bridge across the creek.

"Can't I think you're completely wrong and you think I'm completely wrong, without us liking each other?"

Bede lent against a tree. "You think too much."

"I don't think enough, before I speak. Now, I'm unable to leave this peculiar little way I lead my life."

"You assume other people are like you," Bede told her. "We're not as intellectual as you are; we don't see shades that you see."

"They're only words. Other people's words won't hurt me if I don't let them hurt me."

"We do let them hurt us, don't we?" said Bede, stepping forward and gently hugging her. "People think you have motives for saying things you don't."

She closed her eyes, feeling wiser and more ignorant than she was, and younger than she needed to be. "You're the only person who judges me for anything more than one remark at a silly cafeteria, which I never liked anyway. I wish I believed what people expect me to believe."

"I'm on your side whatever you think, and I'll support you whatever you do, but we'll keep it to us."

Jessica pulled away from him, opening her eyes and facing him. "Keep it to us?"

"I can't let my boss know you're my sister, you understand. I've got a wife and unborn child to consider."

She began to sniffle. "Does your boss know what's happening in Molong?"

"He doesn't know what's happening next door, but these things have a way of getting everyone's attention. We need to be careful, that's all. I wouldn't be looking after one part of my family if I wasn't looking after another, would I?" In their disparate homes and lives, his only afflictions were Jessica's. "You weren't around through Fergus Millane."

She sniffed some tears into her nose and wiped some tears from her cheeks. "You only love me because I'm your sister," bemoaned Jessica, taking no compliment from him doing so. "I'd love you if you weren't my brother, just from knowing you."

"Opinions are the most superficial reason to decide whom to love, family the most profound. I love my children before they're born. They can think whatever they think, and I'll stand with them whatever their crises."

"You just won't tell anyone."

"I'll tell Gemma."

"Telling your wife just makes the rest of us less your responsibility."

"Some people don't look after anyone," said Bede, stepping to her again. "No one looks after them."

Jessica dipped her head. "I don't look after you."

"If I lost everything and you had practically nothing, then I know you'd share your practically nothing with me."

"Looking after people isn't always sensible."

"There's not much good sense, anyway," Bede assured her. "I don't know what you'll do or be, but it'll be more than me."

"I won't stay with you in Orange," she told him. "With our little one coming, Gemma needs you more than I do."

Interrupting them were two small boys running through the grass: a ginger-haired boy shouting words Jessica couldn't understand, chasing another boy. The ginger-haired boy tripped and fell, when Jessica reached forward and helped the boy to stand.

"You're the woman from the newspaper," he told her.

Jessica turned to Bede. Bede didn't respond.

"My Dad says I'm not to tell anyone what he said about you."

Turning away from him, Jessica slumped down on the grass. The creek was never more inviting.

"Don't be sad," said the boy, standing beside her. "My Dad likes you."

Jessica, seated on the grass, looked up at him. She didn't recognise him.

"He thinks you're great."

"Come along," the other boy called to him; he had stopped and turned around. The boys resumed running.

Bede and Jessica looked at each other. "If you can't be silent," he told her, "then all that remains is unashamedly arguing your point of view. You were always the one who admitted wrongs the rest of us would've denied. Don't start admitting wrongs you've not committed. Try to teach people to understand your views and to respect your right to say them, even if they never agree. If you're fortunate, you'll persuade them. If you're very fortunate, they'll persuade you."

Jessica quickly stood up. "I need to know more than I do," she told him. "Come on."

She bundled her rug together, collected her picnic basket, and led them the short way to what been a railway station, when passenger trains stopped at Molong; only goods trains still set abuzz the railway crossing lights and bells roared through regardless. Horizontal timber planks formed the station house walls, below the corrugated iron roofs and decorated eaves, all nicely painted.

Occupying the old station was the community library, offering books concerned with contemporary social issues about which everyone agreed. It was Jessica's chance to learn, and decide she'd been wrong or learn more to argue her case. Among the newspapers in the reading area there'd be the current edition of the *Molong Express*, although she had no heart to see her name in print again.

The library was closed. It was closed every Saturday, open Mondays, Wednesdays, and Fridays for two hours before lunch and three hours afterwards.

Bede remained behind her while Jessica pressed her face to the screen over the window. Handling some books inside was a woman wearing a long-sleeved black blouse with a collar covering her neck, black dress, and black stockings. Her black leather shoes had low square black heels. Her black hair was wrapped in a bun higher than Jessica's blonde hair ever was. A black cord around her neck was affixed to each end of large gold spectacles through which she peered.

She saw Jessica at the glass and shook her finger in the air. She came to the door near the window and opened it. "We're open on Monday," she whispered; the library was closed but was still a library.

"Do you have any books about Confucius?"

The woman stepped back. "Nobody's ever asked about Confucius."

"Confucianism values uniformity, homogeneity," explained Jessica. "Do you have any books about Asian philosophies?"

"If you want books about religion, ask a church." The woman could have closed the door then, leaving Jessica outside. Instead she remained at the open door, studying Jessica. "What is your name?"

Jessica froze. "What's yours?"

"Ms MacNee. Do you have a library card?"

"Yes," declared Jessica, for that moment not an interloper, but she dared not take her card from her handbag. Hoping she didn't have to say anything more, a sudden distraction would've been useful then. None came.

Ms MacNee drew back her breath. Her thin lips tightened in the faintest hint of a scowl. "I saw your photograph in the newspaper."

"All I was trying to say was that Chinese people wouldn't want to be a minority in China."

Ms MacNee almost raised her voice. "Before you start abusing anyone, bear in mind this is Aboriginal country, not ours."

Jessica fell silent, before gently she spoke. "Can you imagine Chinese people saying the same thing about Tibet, Taiwan, or even Singapore? We made Molong."

"You're disrupting the concentration of other users of my library."

"The library's closed."

Ms MacNee's lips tightened still more. Her scowl became thinner in new degrees of her demeanour, staring Jessica down.

Anything to read could help lead Jessica through those days. When she'd been younger and risked being lonely, Bede consoled her before her loneliness swelled. He'd told her about a book he'd read when he felt confused, without direction. She'd listened to him talk about the book only to hear him talking about himself and never contemplated reading it, until she stood before Ms MacNee at that open library door. "Can I please borrow *Catcher in the Rye*?"

"My library will *never* stock *Catcher in the Rye*!"

Jessica had infuriated the woman without fury. "You used to stock it," she told her.

"I burnt it. It's a very narrow, masculine, white view of growing up. Why would any woman want to read it?"

"Some girls read it," replied Jessica, although Ms MacNee was surely no less disdainful of those girls and the women they became than she was disdainful of Jessica. Few traits could be as masculine to Jessica as the treatment meted out to her in recent days. "The school library used to stock it."

"The school library burned its copies, too." Her thin lips curved slightly in a rare trace of a smile. "We had a marvellous bonfire that year."

Jessica thought of all the things she knew because she'd read the books of which the library wanted her to be unaware. "What books haven't you burnt?" she asked.

Ms MacNee's smile vanished. "We have some excellent books

about the experiences of indigenous girls," she told Jessica. "They are the books you should read."

"Do indigenous girls come to the library?"

"I can cancel your card," she told Jessica, in her most forthright librarian decorum. They stared briefly at each other, before Ms MacNee stepped back. "Good day," she said, in the friendliest tone of voice she'd used. The door closed in front of Jessica.

Standing in the life in which she stood, Jessica wondered what the catcher in the rye might have made of the time in which she lived. She was becoming too old to learn but wasn't old enough to know.

Jessica turned around to Bede. "Why was that woman even here on a Saturday?"

11

THE SHOW

Paintings of scenes from their shires allowed country people to see inside their homes what they saw outside them. Without reputations to bolster them, amateur artists abided by the norms their teachers imparted to them in classes. Mimicking innovations in stroke, style, and colour made them conventions; the artists' brazen signatures became the only means to differentiate their works. They gave paintings to relatives living elsewhere and sold some to strangers from strange places.

Early that Saturday evening, two dozen men and women gathered for the opening of Susan Hodgeson's first pottery show in the rearmost room of Jayes Gallery. It was the largest room, with high white walls and ceilings and trim blue carpet almost shining. The women wore their long dark dresses and men their open collar shirts, some with fashionable jackets. Briony Keyte nonchalantly wore another gorgeous gown, her high cheek bones and red lips glowing. A raffle at the door supported research into the human immunodeficiency virus, while Eugene Gallagher sat alone in his family home. His parents were guests in the gallery.

Susan's pottery stood on tables and in glass cabinets. Around the walls were a few large photographs of her at her mother's pottery wheel, along with little flags from a multitude of nations. In place of paintings people hadn't bought were a picture of the Forbidden City in Beijing and another of the Great Wall of China, although seeing them there so starkly made the mayor wonder if Mildred Thompkins should've chosen subtler images.

Dressed in a pale suit that seemed hopelessly inadequate without mayoral robes, hat, and chain, Hector Xiedergrain stood taller than anyone else in the room. Beside him stood Susan, in her blue-green dress and overly styled hair.

Watching them was the mayoress, wearing a long flowing mauve dress that nobody recognised. Presenting herself better than she thought she deserved, Mrs Xiedergrain sauntered about civic functions enjoying and despising her status.

Lynne Delaney stood beside her, more modestly dressed. "Susan's wearing a beautiful blue dress," whispered Lynne.

"I think it's a little bit more a green than a blue," replied Mrs Xiedergrain.

"Well, it's blue-greenish, isn't it, as much one colour as the other?"

"Turquoise, isn't it."

"Yes, turquoise."

"That's right, turquoise."

Turning to the formalities, the mayor's voice bellowed with the certainty of a man accustomed to being heard. "Shall we sing the national anthem?" he told his audience.

Every adult in the gallery stood still. Wearing their school uniforms and shining black leather shoes, the boy and girl captains in their last years at the Molong Central School stepped beside the mayor. The boy captain held up the red flag of China. The girl captain held up the dark blue, white, and red Australian flag. The mayor placed his right hand over his heart, as Mildred Thompkins pressed the button beginning the recorded rendition. The music stirred throughout the gallery as the mayor in his loudest voice and all the voices with him conscientiously sung, "Australians all let us rejoice, for we are young and free..."

When the anthem finished, the mayor declared the exhibition open. "But before I leave you to this celebration of our world," he said, his voice slowing to bring tension to a climax, "we have a special award for our potter tonight." The audience studied Susan's face for a clue. "Susan Hodgeson is our next Cabonne Council Volunteer of the Month!"

Susan gasped, holding her long fingered hands to her blushing, white-powdered face. Her mother stepped forward and hugged her, as Susan began weeping profusely. The mayor clapped loudly, driving the audience to clap with him. The ritualistic, feverish applause meant much less to him than the corners of his eyes watching the only person in the audience not clapping. Charlie Quinn simply observed.

The mayor presented Susan with a certificate, before he kissed her cheek. He then drew the shapely young Susan close to him, his long arm enveloping her and his large hand covering her shoulder, posing for the cameras. Susan's eyes flinched but his were unaffected; every photograph of the opening would include his face. Charlie's camera flashed brighter than any other.

The clapping eased long enough for Susan to wipe some tears from her face and speak a few words. "All I hope for from my pottery," she said, turning her head seductively around and to her side, "and from my award, is that all the people of the world can live together in peace." She smiled, and her bleached white teeth shone in the artificial light.

Speeches complete, Briony stepped towards Susan. "That's what I said when I was Volunteer of the Month," complained Briony.

"Now, ladies," said Hector. "It's what all our winners say."

Briony gritted her teeth. "What volunteering do you do?" she asked Susan.

"What volunteering do you do?"

"I'm nice to people."

"You're nice to Mildred Thompkins."

"She has a right to buy clothes."

"Please ladies," interrupted Hector, stepping between them and placing his hands on their shoulders. "I'm sure Charlie Quinn will report the wonderful work you've both done: saving abandoned pets, bringing meals to the elderly."

Charlie took several photographs of the three of them together. The proudly grinning mayor remained unchanged.

"Something for the news services, Charlie," said the mayor, as Charlie turned away. "I have a friend you should meet," he told Briony and Susan, his arms still on their shoulders.

He took them towards a short man in a dark pinstriped suit and waistcoat, standing motionlessly near a wall. The pinstripes accentuated his ample, low-lying belly, from which the chain of a gold fob watch hung. His poorly dyed hair tried to hide its growing grey, without much success. In his hand was a glass of Champagne.

The mayor's arms fell away from the two women's shoulders to shake the man's hand. "Ladies," he told them, "this is Rudy Gellner: the only man in the room not born in Cabonne. Rudy's a most eminent banker visiting us from Orange."

Susan smiled. She offered him her right hand.

"Congratulations, Ms Hodgeson," said Rudy, cautiously shaking her hand.

Briony offered him her right hand. He shook her hand, too.

"These girls are right behind us with the mine, Rudy," said the mayor. "We've got developers who'll build more roads and houses, good houses, complementing each other. We'll get them the land, arrange water and electricity, and you can finance it all. We'll get a new shopping mall for the town; let the old buildings fall down."

"Are you asking me for my views of town planning?" asked Rudy.

The mayor leant close to the banker. "On the other hand, Rudy, you close your branch and we'll take all our business away."

The banker stared past him and the young women. He mightn't have been listening, but the mayor couldn't let that deter him.

The mayor continued. "People go to cities for jobs – we know that, Rudy – but here, we have air we can breathe, clean water. We can walk the streets at night and all the streets by day. This place is as good as it gets, Rudy, as good as it gets: perfect earth, Rudy, perfect earth."

"Congestion is whenever the postman delivers the mail," remarked Rudy. "Don't people worry that an influx of new residents might be detrimental?"

"Maybe once we had people like that," reflected the mayor. "Today, people want more people with whom to share their good lives. More people mean more money, if you like."

The banker looked up at the mayor. "I heard about your problem."

"We don't have problems, Rudy. We have issues to address."

The banker looked back to Susan and Briony. "You had somewhat of a lunch with that Rawlins girl."

"She's awful," said Briony, "positively dreadful."

"You both came over very well," said the banker, "very sophisticated."

"I saw a programme about that sort of person on television," Susan enthused, preparing the mayor to hear her wisdom. "I can't remember what it said."

The mayor continued looking at her. Unusually for him, he was uncertain how to respond.

"I really like Chinese art," added Briony.

"Oh, so do I," said Susan. "It's so, so... I can't get the right word."

"Oriental?" asked the banker.

"We can learn so much about Chinese food from cookery books," Susan added. "Peking Duck, Dim Sims...Sushi."

"I really like Chinese people," said Briony, "like the one in *Anna and the King of Siam*."

"They're good at tennis," said Susan.

"I wouldn't even notice a player was Chinese," boasted Briony.

"I saw one play in the Australian Open," explained Susan.

"You were in Melbourne?" asked the banker.

"I saw him on television," explained Susan. "He seemed very nice." Her head turned away. "Come to think of it," she mused, "Chinese people did applaud him more than they applauded anyone else." She turned back to Briony. "You don't think Jessica might be right?"

"Never you mind," the mayor interjected, before addressing

Rudy more than anyone else. "I don't like people categorising people into one group or another. I don't like anything that encourages people to argue. I don't like anything divisive."

Briony's voice became stern. "I think the Volunteer of the Month award is divisive."

Susan was brighter. "I think the Volunteer of the Month award unites us."

The mayor pulled Susan and Briony close to him, again placing his arms around them. "You must understand, Rudy, we're a community here. We want what's best for everyone, and we'll all work together to make this mine happen. Stability brings prosperity, instability brings poverty."

Rudy looked at Susan and Briony. "You run along, girlies."

Susan and Briony looked up at the mayor, who released them from his arms. He looked around until he saw Councillor Sewell. "Jack," he called out. "Look after our favourite daughters, will you?"

Jack led them away. Only the mayor remained with the banker.

"Rudy," said the mayor, leaning forward and resting his hand on his shoulder as if imparting a great secret to him. "Ask your questions of anyone in this town and you'll hear what I'm telling you: not a single person in or around this shire is anything less than a hundred percent behind what I'm trying to do, welcoming all people and all that they bring."

"Do you know why we stop racism, Hector?" asked the banker. "Do you know we cared so much about that farmer of yours a few years ago: uneducated filth? Do you understand, Hector?"

"I understand, Rudy," nodded the mayor.

"Anything that deflects people from thinking about people in commercial terms is not good for business, Hector, not good."

"We have laws to deal with abuse, Rudy."

"I'm not talking about anything as blatant as abuse, Hector. I'm talking about that little sense of people being of a race, religion, or anything else, that creates camaraderie to anything but their jobs. The bonding, the spirit should be here." He tapped his finger on the small silver badge on his lapel and emblem of the Commonwealth Bank, which the mayor hadn't previously noticed. "When my grandparents brought my father to this country in 1938, they were a lot of things. Me, I'm a bank person, Hector: nothing else, a bank person."

The mayor listened closely, shaking his head, imparting all the sense of understanding he could for Rudy to see. "I'm the mayor."

Rudy pointed him to the Australian flag left on a table. "We wheel out the flag when we're trying to sell, but don't let it get in the way of business or television time. Is this clear to you now, Hector?'

The mayor nodded repeatedly. "It is Rudy, it is."

"Good." The banker winked. "Banking is busy, Hector."

"I know, Rudy, I know."

Appearing with them, with a glass of sparkling mineral water and wearing the same loosely fitting black dress, black stockings, and black leather shoes with low square black heels she wore whenever the mayor saw her, was the librarian Ms MacNee. Her black hair was, as always, seized up in a bun. "Mister Mayor," she addressed him, before looking at Rudy. "Mister Gellner."

"You know each other?" asked the mayor.

"That woman from the front page of the newspaper came to the library today," Ms MacNee told the mayor.

"That's all we need," sighed the mayor.

"She tried to push her way in," explained Ms MacNee, "when we were closed."

"The gall of the woman," said the mayor.

"She was very rude about Confucius, indigenous children's literature, and Molong."

The mayor shook his head. "Dear, oh dear."

"I'd have liked her to come here to see the indigenous art," said Ms MacNee, looking around at the walls. "Where has it gone?"

"We put most of it away for the night," the mayor replied. "It's all the same."

"It's lovely."

The mayor noticed Charlie Quinn gazing into a glass of cold beer, watching the white head dissipating into amber. "Come join us, Charlie," the mayor called to him. "You should hear what you've done."

Charlie looked up from his glass. A passing waitress with her tray provided the mayor and Ms MacNee with glasses of Champagne and replaced the banker's empty glass, while Charlie ambled towards them.

"Write about this girl tonight and her pottery," the mayor told Charlie. "Give your readers good feelings about their shire."

"And good feelings about you?"

"Your readers want good news," explained the mayor, settling into gentle persuasion.

"Our readers want facts."

"They want some facts more than others."

"Jessica Rawlins makes people who already feel good about themselves feel even better," Charlie told them. "She makes people who don't feel good about themselves at the least feel they're better than she is."

"She'll make them feel worse about the world, Charlie, and it's the world we're trying to save."

"I'm writing another piece about her."

"Don't encourage her, Charlie. What interests the public mightn't be in the public interest."

"People who know her answered my questions, something you never do."

"Doesn't she understand what we're trying to do?" lamented the mayor, shaking his head. He turned to Rudy. "I'll do what I should've done days ago. I'll get hold of her myself, Monday."

"I heard she's seeing Derek Saxby," said Ms MacNee, "the real estate agent."

"Saxby?" said the mayor. "He won't want to get messed up in this."

Rudy nodded, before looking back at Ms MacNee. "Do you still want to discuss funding for those indigenous children, Ms MacNee?"

"Isn't your wife expecting you home in Orange, Mister Gellner?"

He checked the time on his fob watch from his waistcoat pocket. "Banking is busy, Ms MacNee."

Carrying his glass of Champagne, Rudy walked slowly away, as his ample belly required that he walk. Carrying her glass, Ms MacNee slowly followed him, through the smaller room and the front room crowded with everyday things for sale and cards for coming exhibitions. He led them out of the gallery and a short way along Gidley Street to the corner with Bank Street. At the door into the Commonwealth Bank, with Ms MacNee waiting several paces behind him, he drew a long gold chain from his jacket pocket, at the end of which were a dozen or more keys. One opened the door to the bank, and he entered. Leaving the door open behind him, he walked to the branch manager's office, free for him to use.

He stopped by the desk, turning around as Ms MacNee entered the office. "Banking is busy," he smiled, resting his glass on the desk. He removed his bank lapel badge from his jacket and dropped it in the glass.

Ms MacNee giggled, her lips easing. She rested her glass beside his on the desk.

The banker stepped around her and closed the office door, before facing her again. She was taller than he was, even after she stepped out of her shoes and her feet in stockings stood on the carpet.

He placed his hands on her bony waist, when suddenly she raised her right hand and slapped his cheek. He jolted backwards, before laughing and slapping her cheek.

"Ah," she gasped in a muffled shriek, placing her hand against her mouth. He laughed and slapped her other cheek.

Ms MacNee pulled a pin from her hair and the bun fell away, bouncing her dark hair not quite black on her shoulders as the pin dropped silently to the floor. She let her head fall back and her eyes close as he slapped her face again, her head flopping back and forth. He wrapped his arms around her waist pressed against his belly, preparing to bite her neck.

She pushed him away. "Not now," she said, rushing past him towards the closed office door. She locked it.

12

THE REVEREND

Sunday mornings could be times for sleeping late, after Saturday nights too long away from bed. They could be times for brunch, or catching up with laundry or house cleaning. What they hadn't been for Jessica, since she was a child and Christmas came around, was time for church.

Churches featured in most old Australian towns, without modern buildings to conceal them. Nineteenth-century pioneers built a Methodist Chapel in Molong in 1858, before church leaders formed the Uniting Church subsuming it late in the twentieth century. A notice in the *Molong Express* newspaper mentioned a Uniting Church service at eleven o'clock that sunny Sunday morning.

With her straw hat covering her head and dark sunglasses across her eyes, Jessica stood before the brown-brick church amidst open lawns in Edward Street. It wasn't the biggest building in the town but surely the tallest. Seeing the cross atop the wiry steeple, against the sky so far away, a church seemed suddenly a strange place to find books about Asian philosophies.

Jessica needed only to enter the church to ask about books and leave, but church congregations who'd give comfort to everyone might not accommodate her. They mightn't speak with her or might ask her to leave, but they ought to be polite.

She climbed the steps to the open door. Stepping inside, she removed her sunglasses.

A middle-aged woman smiled. Her eyes dwelt upon Jessica.

Jessica smiled. "Do you have a library?" she asked.

The woman lent close to an older woman there. Their faces were strangers to her, but their eyes remained trained upon Jessica. The older woman's eyes sized Jessica up and down. "What do we say?" she whispered to the other, loud enough for Jessica to hear.

"Why have you come?" the first woman asked Jessica.

"I'm looking for a book about Confucius."

"Why have you really come?"

"I want to learn."

The woman continued looking at Jessica, before silently taking the other woman's arm. She led the older woman into the church, out of Jessica's sight. If Jessica were to argue her point of view across the town, then she should follow them, but theirs was no place to argue.

Left alone at the open door of her childhood church, Jessica didn't know what she believed, but small serenity was no less important than deep belief. "Dear God," she whispered, fearing her inadequacy to speak, "please teach me."

Jessica turned, placed her sunglasses back across her eyes, and hurried back down the steps. Her hair under a hat in the hot sun tingled through her head.

Behind the church, away from sight of the main door, was a low brick wall. There, Jessica sat, for the want of anywhere else to go. Sitting in the shade, alone, she removed her hat and sunglasses.

Hearing the church people sing almost in unison about somebody not her, Jessica looked up, but saw only the gold cloud windows with nothing much to say. The few lyrics she recognised, she recognised too late to sing aloud. They might've been a hundred people in the church or very few; it was difficult to tell.

The singing finished. People spoke, but the voices were too

muffled by the time they reached Jessica. The voices singing had music to assist them as voices speaking did not. Sitting in the open air, with the sounds of song and muffled church voices, was more peaceful than Jessica had thought being alone could be.

In the shade becoming warm, Jessica ran her fingers through her hair, lightening it on her head and forehead. An hour or more after she'd sat down, Jessica heard the sounds of people bustling back down those steps towards the street. She quickly replaced her hat on her head and sunglasses to her eyes, covering her face turned away from where people might come. She would wait until they had gone.

They sounds of people leaving had all but passed, when an old man's slow voice disturbed her. "I'm Reverend Athol Underly."

Jessica turned to face an old man with old eyes in wrinkled sockets, staring down upon her: the same priest she'd seen collecting money in a can. He wore no robes that Sunday morning but a pale blue cotton short-sleeved shirt and cream white trousers. Around his neck was a clerical white collar, not as clean and white as clergymen once kept them, but still whiter than anything else he wore. If he was the same minister when she was young, then he'd become shorter than she remembered him being, almost stooping. His tufts of hair had thinned but not his thick bushy eyebrows, all paled to whites and greys. The children who might once have teased him about his name no longer saw enough of him to do so.

"You wore robes at Freemason's Hotel," said Jessica, "last Tuesday night."

"I collect more money for the poor and sick the more I look like a priest."

Jessica again removed her hat and sunglasses. "I wasn't going to hurt those two women at the door."

"Our church mightn't mean much to you, but it means much to us. Lottie worried we'd be forced to close if people thought you were a parishioner. She prayed a little prayer that God would keep you from coming back."

Jessica dipped her head. "Words have never been more important than they've come to be important now."

"Isn't there anything you'd rather do but talk?"

"What more can I do?"

He was slow to respond. "May I sit with you?"

"It's your church."

"It's yours, too," said the reverend, sitting down and adjusting himself on the wall. "Thieves and vandals compel us to lock the doors, but I can always let you in."

Jessica tried to be polite. "I'm sorry I missed your sermon."

"I've given it many times. I'll give it many more."

She smiled and rolled her eyes. "The woman from the library thought you'd have books about Asian philosophies."

"Is that what people think churches are: repositories for books about other religions?"

"And charity tins."

The reverend studied her. "A long time has passed since anybody new came to our Sunday service," he told her, "other than people nearing death who've decided it's time for salvation."

"I might be one of those people." His confidential counsel of sad and dying people without the luxury of judging them should keep him from judging her. "When I was young, I came here at Christmas with my mother."

"You're still young, to people who've come to be my age. What were you expecting to happen after your conversation at the café?"

"I wasn't expecting anything to happen. I mean, I never thought about it. I never expected a small remark, with people I presumed were my friends, to come to anything, but now the town can't talk of anything else."

"They're keeping their peace in their particular way, after you punctured their veils of serenity."

"Nobody says anything against you, in spite of things you believe."

"People can't prosecute us for our beliefs unless we reveal them," the reverend explained, his slow voice becoming slower. "People judge us according to what they think we believe, not what we actually believe."

Jessica remained silent, as she'd too rarely remained. The reverend imparted his tutelage to her.

"I am careful what I say," he continued. "I mention God when my small audience concurs, but not where others hear. If Charles Quinn heard me talk of my faith without speaking as favourably of other faiths and faithlessness, then the newspaper would call me intolerant and people would protest where we're sitting now, calling me a hypocrite for lacking their love. I would lose the little that remains of my congregation. If they think we obstruct their vision of the future, they shut us out from the present, but I can't talk favourably about other faiths and faithlessness. So I say very little, except about helping the poor and sick."

The reverend confessed a faith in reclusion more tragic to Jessica than her momentary indiscretion. "The librarian presumed you'd have books about Confucius," she told him, "because she didn't imagine you'd have any about God."

The reverend slowly nodded. "Any risk of religious belief has become a reason to fault us. My congregations, here and in other towns, are too old, and I am too old, to weather anyone trying to shut us down. This church of mine doesn't let God unsettle people, and my presbytery in His name can stop me. My parishioners can only enjoy whatever comfort they take from me if I can continue coming."

"How can I be heard," asked Jessica, "when I want to say something no one else says?"

His eyes drifted away from her. "As you go through life, my child, you're going to meet people good and bad. Some of those good people are going to say stupid things, but they're still good people. Part of growing up is realising when to speak of what you believe, so you and other people learn something, and realising when silence is better than trouble. Try not to be wrong too often."

"If I were mayor, I'd let people disagree."

"It isn't the mayor," said the reverend, without obvious feeling or opinion. "I knew Hector Xiedergrain when he was a fearful little boy." Jessica wasn't the only adult once to have been a child. "Three boys from the Fairbridge Farm School set his shirt on fire."

In the warmth of a sunny day, even in the shade, Jessica felt a little heat on her, but her predicament remained. "Hector Xiedergrain's childhood doesn't make him any less the mayor, today."

"He's still doing whatever others compel him to do, even if he doesn't realise it."

She looked around the peaceful town and setting. "I'm starting to think people make wars over words when they have nothing else to fight for."

"Are you one of those people?"

"I just want to find my way."

The reverend placed his hand on her knee. "Don't fight it, my child. Don't make battles you can't win. We have too many battles we might win or lose to fight those we can only lose. I, for one, don't want you to lose."

"What more can I lose?" asked Jessica. "What more can happen to me?"

"I knew Fergus Millane."

"What was he like?"

"Headstrong, candid, he said what he thought." The reverend smiled. "He'd pretend the scar on his cheek was the work of a jealous husband, but if anyone believed him he was quick to tell the truth: a falling tree struck him."

Jessica gazed into the ground. "I remember a parable," she said, "about a farmer sewing seed, some of which fell on a path, some of which fell among thorns, and only some of which landed in the good soil."

"You're more knowledgeable than most people about the Bible."

"That might be all I remember," Jessica laughed, looking back at him. "Words can be seeds."

He pulled his hand away. "Words can also be weeds. Disconcert can take root from a single sentence."

She thought about his words, but still did not believe them. "You confide your beliefs to people who agree," she reminded him. "You don't lie, but you don't tell the truth. You don't say anything."

Staring back at her, the reverend's tired old eyes started to moisten. "You and I can't change the world, my child," he told her; speaking again kept his eyes dry. "We must try to keep our little corners."

"I wish I could," sighed Jessica, but the reverend made silence moribund. "Nobody cares if I take offence at what people say about me."

"Worry more about what harms you than what offends you." His words might have been a warning, and Jessica studied his damp eyes for what they revealed. "Those of us not allowed to be sensitive, to find offence where none is intended, must be stoic. If I complained every time I saw people mocking my faith and God, then the newspaper would accuse me of imposing my views upon others. I would lose my small influence. Everything is acceptable except believing otherwise. Let your actions shine more than your words."

"What actions? What can I do but talk?"

"I too was young," he said. "We can give God what is God's, and the Romans what is the Romans'."

"Is this what the people who built your church expected of you?"

"They expected us to endure, as best we can."

"Is this what you once expected of you? You let people, not God, tell you what to do. Aren't we the Romans?"

The reverend looked pensively at her. "I am starting to understand why people find you so unsettling."

"Don't worry," she smiled. "I just talk."

"I became a priest to do more than talk," he sighed. "Now, I don't even do that." He looked back up at the walls of his church. "Am I, my life, so stale?"

He stood up from the wall, flexing his back and arms. Jessica prepared her back, arms, and legs, before standing up too. She pulled her hat back on her head and sunglasses to her eyes, before collecting her handbag. He led them ambling around the lawn.

"A rebel would be as foolish for mindlessly opposing dogma," said the reverend, "as a sheep would be for mindlessly acceding."

"Is that what you think I am," asked Jessica, "a rebel?"

"You're the insubordinate, but you might as well be a rebel."

Ahead of them, on the footpath, was a man walking a dog. Jessica turned to walk away from him, back from where they came. The reverend turned to walk with her. "I know you didn't have to spend time with me today," she said.

"I think I did," said the reverend, "but I'm not sure I can help you. I've tried so hard to save me, and wonder if I have."

"Do you and I talking to each other achieve anything?"

He stopped, so she stopped. They stood facing each other. "The last young person to appear at our church door was eight months ago," said the reverend. "Lottie worried about Eugene Gallagher, too, and his disease. She said her prayer, but not every prayer we ask receives the answer we expect. I visit him at his home, the Ellerslie Cottage on Hill Street, because nobody else will. You might want to visit him, too."

"A gathering of castaways?" asked Jessica.

"Two solitary people would be foolish not to free themselves from solitude in the company of each other. You might appreciate each other's words."

"I'm not one to be a priest. I've got a town to meet."

"You could think of it as offertory."

"I can give you money," said Jessica, reaching for her handbag.

He held up his hand to stop her. "You have debts, I know."

They returned to the church front steps. The church door was closed. "I don't want to be just a talker," said Jessica. "Could I be a candidate at the next councillors' election? Could I be mayor?"

He studied her. "I'll vote for you."

"Will you pray for me?"

The reverend nodded his head, with a twinkle in his eye. "Will we see you in church again?"

"What will Lottie say?"

"I'll hide you."

Jessica wanted to tell him she'd return, but they'd shared too much for her to lie. "There's always Christmas."

"Easter is coming."

Jessica smiled. "I never did find a book about Confucius."

The reverend looked back towards Bank Street and the town centre. "I must inform this woman in the library: the only books in my church honour God." He turned back to Jessica. "I can give you a Bible."

13

THE SUMMONS

The elected representatives of Cabonne shire council held their public meetings on certain Monday mornings, although not that Monday morning. They convened in the council chamber, before a gallery of anybody wanting to be there. The chamber was also available for use by people wanting to address or consult with residents.

Jessica had never before entered the old town hall building, through the iron gate and imposing colonnade façade. She arrived a few minutes before ten o'clock, dressed as well as she dare; a hat would have been superfluous. Several people entered ahead of her, paying accounts, lodging forms and plans, or making enquiries for permission. Jessica didn't sit in any of the empty waiting chairs but remained standing, until she had her chance to speak to the officious middle-aged woman behind the public counter. "I'd like to reserve the chamber for a public meeting," said Jessica.

"I can't allow that, Ms Rawlins."

"You let other people speak there?"

"I can't guarantee your safety, or the safety of people who speak against you."

"That's not fair," complained Jessica.

"It wouldn't be fair on everyone else to let you speak."

An unfamiliar, amicable tone of voice interrupted them. "Is that Jessica Rawlins?"

Jessica turned uneasily around. Beyond the counter end was an open door that had previously been closed, restricted to the people of the council.

Standing there was a tall man with thick white hair. "I'm Hector Xiedergrain," he smiled, stepping towards her and offering her his hand to shake, "the mayor of Cabonne."

They shook hands; his large hand engulfing her little one. She presumed he'd mistaken her for someone else.

"May I call you Jessica?"

His pleasant paternal voice made her speak a voice a little like an adolescent. "If you want to call me Jessica, then I suppose you can," she said. "May I call you Hector?"

He laughed. "I'd like to have a little chat with you, Jessica. Can you come to my office?"

Lynne too had been kind, before relieving Jessica of her employ. The only sanction left for the mayor to impose upon her was to banish her from the shire. She might once have thought he had no power to do so, but she'd once thought many things she'd learned were ill-conceived. He might still smile as they carted her away, but he couldn't send her anywhere she'd not already been. "I guess so," she said.

He led her through the private council space, but left her waiting outside his office while he stepped inside. Keeping her waiting might have been supposed to make her feel fortunate that he afforded time to her. It might've also been so people saw her there and know he was dealing with her.

Returning to her desk was Mildred Thompkins, who didn't seem to recognise Jessica without her salon uniform. "Are you here for an interview?" asked Mildred.

"In a manner of speaking," said Jessica. If her performance satisfied the mayor, then he might allow her to remain in the town.

Jessica began softly tapping the tip of her shoes on the floor, until Lilly looked up and glared at her. Jessica stopped tapping. Mildred looked back down at her desk again.

The door to the mayor's office remained open, while Jessica

edged towards it. Feigning comfort and cohesion in her mind, he wouldn't see she'd ever cried and wouldn't see her cry again.

The mayor was at his desk, a gold pen in his hand, writing on a sheet of paper. He suddenly looked up; she must have made a sound. He opened his large creased hand to show her one empty chair of the two chairs facing him across his desk. "Please," he smiled, "sit down."

Jessica sat as he directed, at the front edge of her chair, as Mildred Thompkins closed the office door. The mayor continued writing, while Jessica sat with her legs tightly held together and her hands clasped on her knees, holding her handbag. The low seat, regal office, and imposing mayor made her feel very small. Finally, he put down his pen and turned over the sheet of paper, ensuring she couldn't read it.

The mayor sat back in his large red leather chair. "You've created quite a stir in this town, young lady," he told Jessica, like a gently scolding father of his wayward youngest child. "Is there anything you want to tell me about it?"

Jessica shook her head. "No," she said, expecting more to listen than to have reason to speak.

"Do you think you said anything wrong?"

More than she'd previously done, Jessica carefully considered her words before speaking. "I don't understand why this is happening to me," she said.

"I'm told you tried to enter the Uniting Church yesterday, but they didn't let you in."

However surprised Jessica was that the mayor knew where she'd been, she knew it was best to leave him with that interpretation. She would leave him with his ignorance.

"Ministers go into maximum security prisons and talk to murderers," the mayor continued, "but not even Underly gave you refuge."

In that instant, she recognised a truth that would serve them all. "I won't be going back this Sunday."

"God Himself doesn't make as much noise anymore as you."

"Should I ask Him how He copes with the quiet?" asked Jessica, sounding more insolent than she'd intended to sound.

"Underly could teach you about goodness, Jessica. He doesn't cause trouble."

Jessica stared back at him, wondering whether she needed his permission to leave. She thought all manner of words she wouldn't say.

"What were you trying to achieve, Jessica?"

"I wasn't trying to achieve anything. I simply mentioned my thoughts and feelings."

"We can't have people saying whatever they like; we don't know where that could lead. It can be incredibly divisive."

"Can't a person have an original thought?"

"There are no original thoughts."

"There won't be again," Jessica muttered, confiding small meaning, "not now."

"That's the intention, Jessica. You're a woman of words, but words are fodder for ideas from which people want to be insulated."

"Words are ideas," pleaded Jessica, her voice dwelling upon every word.

"So we must control one to control the other," the mayor explained. "Ideas create passion and passion creates tension. We're one world, Jessica."

"Aren't we anything more?"

Hers was a question without answer. "This town believes in diversity," he told her. "I won't allow you to impose your opinions upon us."

"Chinese people keep their countries."

"Whatever," muttered the mayor, turning over the sheet of paper on his desk and handing it to Jessica. "I've drafted a statement for you to sign."

Below the council crest was the heading of it being a statement by Jessica Rawlins, along with a paragraph of text. "*I regret and apologise completely for any offence my words might have caused, which have been inaccurately reported and quoted out of the context in which I spoke them. I welcome all immigrants and especially congratulate Chinese people for promoting diversity at every opportunity.*"

Jessica returned the sheet of paper to his desk. "That isn't true," she told him.

"Truth isn't the most important consideration, Ms Rawlins."

"Does everyone believe what you say they believe, or are they too frightened to say otherwise?"

"Can't you see what we're trying to achieve here? If we get this mine up, one of the big supermarket chains might come: Coles, or Woolworths."

"We have a supermarket."

"Coles or Woolworths won't charge me an extra two dollars for credit card purchases below twenty dollars."

"I'm not going to pretend I believe something I don't believe," Jessica calmly insisted, her intransigence growing as she cared less what he thought about her. "I wouldn't do it for me, why would I do it for you?"

"Why can't you get along with people?"

"I am the only person willing to get along with people, without imposing conditions on what they believe."

"We don't need to believe *everything* everyone else believes, but some opinions are so important that people must be...correct."

"What do you do about people you think are incorrect?"

"We do what we must," answered the mayor, as if Jessica should've known. "Values bring us together, Jessica. Values keep us from breaking apart. Among those values is diversity, and we can't countenance any loyalty to one group of people or intolerance of another. We can't tolerate groups any less than the whole of us."

She had nothing to lose by engaging him, and if she persuaded him she was right then she might retrieve her passing life, if that life was worth retrieving. If he persuaded her she was wrong, she would attest her name to a truthful statement of her past error. "There is no diversity in this country," responded Jessica, "not of ideas. Everybody says the same things, about everything important. The worst thing a person can do is disagree. Nobody dares to breach the torturing peace by thinking, heaven forbid! This is not a safe place to proselytise."

"Pro...?" the mayor started to ask, rising from his chair and resting his long arms on his desk. "You wouldn't understand, little girl."

"I don't understand."

"Are you a racist?"

Jessica jolted back. "You wouldn't ask me that question if I were Chinese."

The mayor stood up, turning towards the window. "I know what is best for these people," he said, his voice pained, staring at strangers Jessica couldn't see, even if none of them looked his way. "I give my life for this shire." He turned around to face her again. "Can't you see that, silly girl?"

Jessica looked down at her lap. The clasps of her handbag and threads in her dress were places to lose her concentration.

"Why can't you be like everyone else?" the mayor asked her. "Do you think you're better than we are?"

"Have I any recourse to reason?" she asked, looking up. "Reasoned people can disagree. Preaching your beliefs is no substitute for practicing them. Your diversity is a pretentious lie, an oxymoronic slogan, you can't see beyond your all-consuming catch cries."

"How dare you!" said the mayor, slumping back in his chair. He slapped his sheet of paper onto his desk. "I expect you to show me respect."

"I expect you to show me respect," said Jessica, surprised by her reply.

"I hardly think that's appropriate."

"Other races of the world don't want your diversity," she persisted, certain she was rational and searching for rationality in him. "They're admirable people."

"I admire them."

Worse to Jessica than the likelihood he was lying was the risk he might be sincere. "Would you treat Chinese people wanting China to remain Chinese the way you treat me?"

"You're making this harder for yourself."

"They reflect something more profound than we do."

"We're talking about us," the mayor told her, pounding his large open hand on his desk. "We're saying what is right!"

"You dismiss the great traditions of East Asia," said Jessica, "not only in China but Japan, Korea, Laos, Vietnam..."

"Forget them," he screamed, as he stood up from his chair and towered over her, his face and eyes burning and his mane of white hair alight with rage, striving to strike her further down into hell. "What would they know, those...?"

The mayor checked his temper before saying the word that followed. Their conversation had become about the world, but Jessica alone was not the world. She was less than a fleck upon it.

"I can teach you about rules," he resumed, collecting his pen. "I'm drafting a Diversity Ordinance this council will pass on Monday; this will shut you up." The nib of his pen pressed hard against the council crested paper. "Ours is a welcoming, tolerant town. If you can't accept that, you have to leave."

"Asian people value their racial homogeneity."

"Get away from here," the mayor demanded, dropping his pen on the desk and pointing his long arm, hand, and outstretched index finger to his office door.

"I'm sorry," said Jessica, without considering why she should apologise. She couldn't have said anything except what she had said. Being the only person to see what she saw merely made her more alone.

"Nobody wants you in this town! Are you too stupid to see that? I'll pass every law I need to pass to be rid of you! Get out of everywhere!"

Their argument might've vented something from her in a game of brinkmanship, but Jessica had come there with nothing left to lose and still had lost it. The only points she'd made were those in her defence, begging for a right to be ignored. She hadn't even started to be heard. If dialogue had been her chance for mitigation, then she never had a chance. The breath of hope with which she'd entered the old town hall building was a cruel memory she wished she didn't have. She'd lived moments of that optimism to learn she'd been a fool.

"If I'm to die anyway," whispered Jessica, looking up at him from her low seat, "I'd rather die in reality than a lie."

He continued to glare down at her in her nothingness. His long and mighty hand still pointed to the door.

Jessica stood up, holding her handbag to her side. She stepped to the door and opened it.

Without expression, the mayor's secretary stared at Jessica. "Mildred," the mayor called to her. "Bring me a dictionary!"

14

THE WANING CONFIDANT

A few miles south of Molong, between farms along a short road from the Mitchell Highway, lay Yuranigh's grave. Yuranigh was an Aborigine who'd led Sir Thomas Mitchell on his expedition to Queensland in 1845, but who was killed at the edges of Molong in 1850. Mitchell paid for the headstone and square timber railing.

There, at around about lunchtime, Jessica stood in the empty air of country. The wind was a warm nor'wester, without much to slow its passage. It seemed the only tall trees Europeans hadn't cleared for farms were the trees carved to mark Yuranigh's grave, signifying he'd been a man of distinction.

Into her silence, waiting for Derek, came the songs of hidden birds. They'd have sung since sunrise and would sing until night fell. In the simplicity of their lives without judgement, they wouldn't accept or reject her. They'd only care about her if she threw scraps of bread or other food at them, loving her when she fed them and then leaving her fast alone.

Birds were more honest than human beings had become. Their thoughts unclouded with pretence and arbitrary mores, they didn't suffer orthodoxy or the unorthodox.

Derek arrived a little late. As he stepped from his car, Jessica wrapped his arms around him, resting her head against his chest. Derek kissed her hair.

"Why did we have to meet here?" she asked him.

"Only tourists come here." She stepped back from him, when he kissed her briefly on the lips and she reciprocated. "We can hide if a school excursion comes."

Derek carried two paper bags. Inside the bag he gave her, Jessica found a bread roll filled with cold roast lamb and salad, along with a small bottle of orange juice. "I hope you didn't buy these from the Pickled Pepper Café."

He led her to a timber railing in the shade, where they sat. "The mayor called me to his office after your visit, seething," he said, opening his bottle of juice. "Why can't we just be happy?"

Jessica opened her bottle. "Is this happy?"

He studied the bottle of juice in his hand. "I can get wine."

The two sat eating their lunch, occasionally reaching down to the ground to pick up their bottles and sip. "The mayor says the council will pass an ordinance promoting diversity," Jessica told him, "keeping me from saying anything he doesn't like."

"Politicians are happiest when they're passing laws about something."

"The mayor asked me if I was a racist."

"You said you weren't?"

"I said he wouldn't ask Chinese people such a question."

"Your head's full of the world," said Derek, shaking his head. "Mine's full enough with my life."

"Should I ignore what I know?"

Derek turned towards her. "The Cadwalladers are worried about people finding out they own the home you're living in."

Jessica had never met the Cadwalladers. "Didn't you tell them I was nice?"

"They don't care whether you're nice. Nobody's pausing to know the content of your heart."

"Would the next tenant care about a prior stranger in the house?"

"Your presence in their property now is the problem. The Cadwalladers don't want to be embroiled in conversations to which your name is attached."

"Does that mean you're not coming to my home anymore?"

"I'll come after dark," smiled Derek. "Xiedergrain, in his friendly tone of face, warned me what you're doing could harm the agency; I hate it when that man's so friendly."

Jessica studied his eyes. "You've never told me how you would feel about us becoming a minority in our hometown, in our country."

"My feelings are immaterial, if I don't mention them."

"I won't report you," she said, in the privacy of that wide country space.

"Don't you understand, Jess?" asked Derek, running his hand across his scalp, clasping his hair. "I don't see the point in thinking about things we can't do anything about. I don't feel things when feelings make them worse. Governments aren't going to stop immigration or even cut it back. Your problem is you think you can do something about it, but they're not letting us keep this country, whatever China or anywhere else in Asia does and whatever you or I think and feel about it. It's the same in Europe and America, even Canada and New Zealand. All you and I can do is the best we can with what remains of our tiny, little lives: do our jobs, make some money, and be together, taking whatever slices of happiness we can."

"So you've learnt to censure every thought you can't mention, every feeling you can't express, even if you don't realise you have? You think the things you're allowed to say, or have to say."

Derek sprang from the bench and wandered agitated around the grass, expressing his energy through his shoes on the ground. "You're contemplating things that can lead you to what we're not meant to imagine, Jess. Don't expect the rest of us to miss what we've never known."

"Are relationships better when people never mention their disagreements or when they refuse to have any?"

He stood facing her. "Nobody else wants your kind of attention."

"Nobody else has it."

Derek's hands took hold of hers, his eyes centred upon her eyes. Her eyes dwelt upon his, a little fearful of their attention.

"The only references I want to me in the newspaper are my real estate advertisements," he told her.

Jessica looked away. "I'm not sure our relationship is much like it used to be, when I was comfortably insignificant and we could love each other freely."

"You looking after yourself will make it easier for me to look after you."

She looked back at him. "I don't need looking after. You don't have to say anything if you have nothing to say. You don't have to do anything, but leave my words to me."

He let go of her hands and stepped away again. "You think you can leap into the lion's den, then talk the lion out of eating you."

"I can't get to talk. What about my right to free speech? Don't I have a right to talk over lunch in a small town café without losing my job and home? What about my tenancy rights, my employee rights? The days have passed in which people resolve issues between them without recourse to rights and I'm not conceding my life to save a past that nobody else wants, but a country that espouses the rights of people ought to give my recourse to law. Your friend's a lawyer. He can look at my letter appointing me to the salon. He can check the laws on councils letting people speak. He can check the rules on landlords. He can keep our conversation confidential."

Derek shook his head back and forth, sitting back down beside her. "Lawyers don't run cases like yours, Jess. They sell bakeries and administer estates, but defending mobsters charged with murder wouldn't harm their reputations as much as any mention in despatches of assisting the woman in the newspaper. Stirring a town in which they earn their livelihoods can only hurt them. My friend will nicely fob us off; lots of people walk into law offices, but not all of them walk out with lawyers. You're better keeping Lynne as a referee for your next job application and the Cadwalladers for the next time you rent."

"How can I get a new job anywhere that reads that stupid newspaper? How long will I have a job before the customers stop coming and another friend sends me back to the streets?

Besides, I can't face the chore of trying to present myself proficiently and failing to do so."

Derek rested his hand on her shoulder. "You don't need a lawyer."

"Do I need a counsellor?"

"You need a friend."

"I don't have too many friends anymore," she said, less sadly than she felt.

"I'm the best friend you've got, Jess, but I read about this all the time. Anti-discrimination people, human rights people, aren't going to defend you expressing opinions and feelings they're trying to eradicate."

Tears swelled into her eyes. "What opinion?" she asked him, her voice fading and eyes drifting away. "What feeling? All I did was think aloud."

"Grounds where discrimination might be illegal don't include thinking aloud."

"It doesn't seem fair."

"The world isn't fair, Jess, now less than ever."

A car came along the road towards them. Derek raised his hand to cover his face, motioning Jessica to do the same. She did, leaving space for her eyes to see past.

The car stopped. A man and woman stepped out. They explored Yuranigh's grave, while Derek and then Jessica lowered their hands from their faces, smiling at the strangers who didn't smile back. The tourists photographed the grave and looked around.

"What happens if the Cadwalladers evict me?" asked Jessica.

"The Molong Motor Inn is nice."

Jessica looked away. "I can't afford hotel rates," she said. "Is your invitation to live with you still open? Being a complimentary tenant is better than being no tenant at all."

"I'll ensure you have somewhere to live." The strangers returned to their car and drove away.

Jessica smiled, tilting her head towards his hand. "Can I sue the newspaper for defaming me?"

Derek sighed. "Are you willing to stand in court while lawyers for the *Molong Express* argue the article is true? They'll tear you apart and then the newspaper will report it. Readers will think you're on trial, Jess."

Her last chance for recompense was withering around her. "Some people have more rights than others," she lamented.

"They can do more with them. Rights are matters of money more than law."

Her sad voice softened. "I don't have a newspaper, police force, or council." Her cheek rubbed a little against Derek's hand on her shoulder; his was a human touch she needed. "You're all I have."

"What do you want, Jess?"

Jessica took her time to answer. "I want to go about a normal day, that's all, with a home to rent and a job like the one I used to have. I want enough money to live and contemplate the rest of my life."

He put his arm around her and pulled her close to him. She rested her head close to his. "You want to do more than that," he told her. "You want to talk."

She lifted her head and faced him. He pulled his arm away from her. Slowly, she began to steel herself. "Knowing what I can't do frees my mind to consider what I can," she told him. "If I can't speak to a lawyer or call a public meeting, there's only one person left for me to see, before the mayor passes his new ordinance on Monday."

Jessica collected a long breath and released it. She stood up, collecting her rubbish from the ground to take away with her.

Their parting was brief, as she lent down and kissed Derek on the lips. Preparing herself for more interrogation, she explained. "Charlie Quinn."

15

THE PUBLIC INTEREST

Tuesday morning, compiling the coming edition of the *Molong Express* with Agnes in the old Gatekeeper's Cottage near the old railway station, Charlie Quinn completed his biography of Jessica Rawlins. He repeated much of his article from a week earlier by way of background; readers would've forgotten the details.

Through the door came an unfamiliar knock. It opened to reveal Jessica in a soft yellow frock, her blonde hair freed from that bun. Her make-up more obvious to Charlie that it might have been to her made everything around them rather rustic by comparison.

"Something troubling you, Ms Rawlins?" asked Charlie. Standing near them, watching silently, was Agnes.

"Do you still want that interview?"

Charlie stared. "Are you sure you know what you're doing?"

"I want people not to hate me."

On a table behind him was Charlie's camera and colossal flash unit. "Can I photograph you?"

Jessica looked down, modestly patting the top of her frock against her chest. "Not in the cottage," she said, looking around. "This is your place."

Photographers looked through people, placing them in light

and context. "I can meet you at the salon," said Charlie, although he'd already seen Lynne Delaney's advertisement for a new junior assistant.

Jessica shook her head, looking back at him. "Lynne would prefer you photographed me at *another* salon."

"We could try the Pickled Pepper Café?"

She laughed. "Anywhere else?"

"What about your home?"

Jessica hesitated, before pointing at two piles of a dozen or more letters apiece on Charlie's desk. "What's that?"

"Readers' letters about stories we've published," replied Charlie. "Readers like reading what their fellow readers have to say."

"Are they about me?"

"Do you think people agree with you?"

"If one of those piles is letters defending me, will you publish them? They're stories you don't have to write."

"I like writing."

She smiled. "It's my price for granting the interview."

Charlie wasn't sure if she was being serious. "Are you trying to be famous?"

"I'm trying to be forgotten."

Almost an hour later, with the sun too soon becoming bright overhead and Charlie again wearing his fading grey bush hat, he arrived at Jessica's home. Living in the old Molong Hall could've been a point to make, but Charlie wouldn't let his newspaper readers know Jessica's home address. He need only mention the rented home required repainting of its white wooden front fence.

With his camera strap and camera hanging from his shoulder and notepad in his hand, Charlie pushed open the gate. He explored the front garden for anything unusual to mention in his article. A small flower faring poorly stood in dry dirt; Jessica Rawlins wasn't a gardener. A small frilled-necked lizard huddled in the long grass. Charlie left it alone.

The front door opened without Charlie knocking. "You're early," said Jessica. "Can I get you a cup of coffee or tea?"

With Jessica in the kitchen area, Charlie remained in the

lounge area, examining her home for everything that implied something about her. Sunshine came through the windows and everything was neat. Jessica was orderly. She had little money, or was saving what she earned; he might've liked her, but for what she'd said at the Pickled Pepper Café. The pictures on the wall drew his attention. "Is that you on the horse?" Charlie asked.

"I used to think so."

Two ornaments on the coffee table also caught his eye. "Where was your tiger ornament made?" he asked.

"Macao."

The tiger appeared Chinese, which might confuse the issues if anyone noticed it in his photograph of Jessica. Charlie pushed it and the glass kitten behind a vase, in which was reflected a large window behind him and world outside. "Did you buy the flowers?" he asked.

"Are you asking me if I have a boyfriend? Can I get you some biscuits?"

The kettle boiled, triggering the loud flicking of the button stopping the power from heating the water anymore. The boiling died away.

Soon Jessica was carrying a tray with two mugs towards him. "There you are," she said, setting the tray on the coffee table.

Charlie picked up a mug and sat with it in the sofa. Leaving his notepad conspicuously on the table might lull her into thinking he wouldn't recall what she'd said.

Jessica took her mug and sat in the single armchair, facing him. She crossed her legs, leaving her frock flowing over her knees, exposing her stockings, ankles, and clean shoes. She took a sip of coffee from the mug in her hand.

Charlie had long learned to discount the impressions people made to journalists of being relaxed. "You have a nice home," he said, as if they were in an ordinarily casual conversation, but they weren't in casual conversation. "What happened at university?"

"I completed my degree."

"Why didn't we report it in the *Express*? Molong girl graduates from university?"

"I never thought to tell you."

"Did you receive honours?"

"I qualified to study the extra year, but there aren't many jobs in biology and I don't want to be a schoolteacher."

Charlie sipped more coffee, contemplating questions to ask her and unable to keep them sounding like the inquisition they were. "Why be a hairdresser?"

"A beauty technician," Jessica corrected him, "income."

Charlie smiled. "Why aren't you living with your aunt and uncle?"

"We're used to living apart." Jessica sipped more of her coffee. "The rent here is cheap."

"Do you live alone?"

"Yes."

"Have you a boyfriend?" asked Charlie.

Jessica's round eyes stared back at him: a lull in the repeating inquiries. "Would you mention his name in the article?"

"Do you want me to mention him?"

"You won't if I don't tell you his name."

"Does he agree with your remark at the Pickled Pepper Café?"

"He doesn't contemplate such issues."

Time was starting to waste. "Would you repeat your words now, to me?"

She glanced at his notepad on the coffee table. "Don't you want to write down my answer?"

Charlie dared not admit remembering her words without needing to record them. He picked up his notepad, flicked past the first page on which he'd written notes preparing for that interview, and drew a pen from his pocket.

She placed her coffee cup on the table. "All I said was Chinese people wouldn't want to become a minority in China," she said slowly, allowing Charlie time to write. "I don't see what's so great about us becoming one here."

"What was your point?"

"I can't remember anymore."

"What is your side of it?"

"I don't have a side of it," she said, throwing her arms in the air. "I was having a conversation. It was nothing really."

"Your friends were offended."

"They mightn't have understood what I meant."

"What did you mean?" Charlie leant forward towards her. "Why should you be different, Jessica Rawlins?" he asked her, as she should have asked herself. "Why should you and no one else have said what you said?"

He waited patiently, allowing Jessica to think. "I had friends at university," she answered, her voice calm, reflective, and thoughtful, "good friends, from all over the world, as people do in Canberra. Yee-Gwun gave me my tiger."

Charlie glanced at the red onyx figurine. It remained where he'd tucked it beside the vase.

"Yee-Gwun told me Chinese people like China being Chinese, ancient and modern, evolving as it chooses. She'd welcome me visiting her, even working there, but China could never be mine because I wasn't Chinese. She surprised me, accustomed as I was to our ways, but their ways came to appeal to me; I related better with people of other races when I saw them in their entireties, with families, ancestors, and races. I decided to see England when I finished studying, only because my ancestors came from there. Yee-Gwun said doing so made me more like the Chinese than other Australians, who set off to Asia without thought of their European origins and races. That was all I was thinking in the Pickled Pepper Café."

Charlie sat quietly. He'd not written the details of her reply, but she'd not remarked upon it to him.

Jessica smiled. "Yee-Gwun invited me to a Chinese dinner," she said, "She told me that traditional Chinese mores say guests should leave after dessert, or when dessert is being served. I asked her whether that was because dessert was so unpleasant. She laughed."

"You know more about China than do most people in this country," admitted Charlie.

"That might say more about Australia than it says about me."

"Do you know Fergus Millane?"

Jessica shook her head. "People keep mentioning his name."

Charlie saw a thousand thoughts whirl around behind her

eyes, when all he wanted was one. "How do you feel about racism?"

"How do you define racism?"

"Don't you know?"

"I don't hate anyone, but if Chinese people can like China being China, I don't see why I can't want Australia to be Australian and England to be English."

Her words were enough. Charlie drank the last of his coffee and placed the empty mug on the table. "You should see London."

"Are you being racist?"

"I think everyone should see London."

Jessica laughed. "I'll be in England, Scotland, Wales, and Ireland for as long as it takes me to learn something of life and me, and governments allow me to stay."

Charlie looked again at the first page of his notebook. The list of more than thirty contentious issues he'd prepared was entrapment, but Jessica was accountable for everything she said. Her views might be normal or unique to her. They could be opinions he'd never before seen in print because people hidden in the populace or out on their farms only expressed them with anonymity. Publishing opinions peculiar to Jessica would be airing what the council didn't want him to air, but Charlie's list mirrored public curiosity to observe the eccentricity of a renegade. It would root out opinions he needed to reform.

"Do you believe in capital punishment?" asked Charlie.

"I beg your pardon?"

"Do you think we should execute murderers?"

"Why ask me?"

"You're being cagey."

"I'm starting to like my privacy," she smiled. "I don't mean that rudely, but I don't have opinions about everything."

"Are you worried about illegal immigration?"

"Have you noticed the levels of legal immigration?"

Charlie folded his notebook and slipped it into his pocket with his pen. He picked up his camera.

"Would you like my photograph inside the house or outside?" asked Jessica.

Charlie looked around the room for a suitable backdrop to the photograph. The yellow flowers in the vase would be too sympathetic for her, although they were starting to wilt. The picture of a lady on a horse was too quaint, in a shire where many men and women rode horses, but the painting of an old small house would characterise Jessica as being lonely. Charlie stood up and walked to a particular patch of floor. "Would you mind standing here?"

Jessica stood where he asked her to stand. "Here?" she asked.

Charlie stood where the photograph would be of her face and body as far as her waist. Examining the image at the rear of his camera, her smiling face was clear. The painting of an old house behind her was blurred, as images of the past should be blurred, but recognisable as being isolated, lost to time. "Good," he told her, as he photographed her. "Let's have a picture more serious."

Jessica relaxed the sides of her mouth. Only her face changed. "Good," he said, "and another one."

Her eyes blinked, when he photographed her again. "I wasn't ready," she said.

"I'll pick the best one."

"It won't make me look ugly," she said, "or silly?"

A loud knock came from the door. Charlie checked his watch. The time was a quarter to twelve.

"I wasn't expecting anyone," apologised Jessica, starting towards the door.

"I've invited Doctor Zachariah Mooney to join us," said Charlie, putting his camera away. "He's a psychiatrist from Orange."

Jessica stopped. "I don't want to see a psychiatrist."

Charlie walked past her to the door and opened it, revealing a short middle-aged man in a tweed jacket and trousers, stepping into Jessica's home. "He writes under the pseudonym the Mind Doctor," Charlie told Jessica.

The doctor took hold of his thick spectacles. "These let me read people's minds," he told Jessica. He then tapped his hand on the large bald area on his scalp expanding from his forehead. "This is the result of me thinking about them." The long symmetrical curls of his thick grey moustache distracted most people's attention from the rest of his face.

The doctor and Charlie sat in the sofa. Jessica remained standing.

"You're racist, Jessica," mused the doctor looking up at her, nodding his head and chin. "I didn't think anyone dared say anything racist anymore."

"Why are you doing this to me?" Jessica asked Charlie.

"This isn't just about you, Ms Rawlins. It's about anyone who thinks the way you think. It's about changing that person before anyone finds out."

"What if that person doesn't change?"

"Doctor Mooney can cure him, or her."

Jessica looked back at the psychiatrist. "I don't want to talk to you."

"Do I represent your father, Jessica?" asked the psychiatrist, fidgeting with the left side curl of his long grey moustache. "Fergus Millane also had a great deal of anger, towards somebody stealing his car."

"Can't you write about me without meeting me, the way other psychiatrists write about people?"

"Feisty," observed the psychiatrist, twirling the left side curl of his moustache between his fingers. He looked at Charlie, speaking as if Jessica wasn't there and more rapidly twirling the curl of his moustache in his fingers. "A woman who would utter one thought she shouldn't express might utter others, Mister Quill."

"Quinn," Charlie corrected him. "Why would someone think what she thinks? How do we treat her?"

"I don't want to be treated," complained Jessica.

"Won't you, can't you, relate as everybody ought to relate?" asked the psychiatrist, rubbing both long curls of his moustache in the thumbs and fingers of his hands. He turned to Charlie. "Anyone who would say anything so offensive clearly needs professional attention, you understand. My article might help your readers spot similar maladjustments in other people, Mister Quayle."

"Quinn."

The doctor gripped both curls of his moustache. "I can make a professional diagnosis," he said, "along with general observations about people of such nature."

"No," said Jessica. "Out you go, both of you!"

Manhandled by Jessica, the psychiatrist let her push him upright out of her sofa. No longer playing with his moustache, she pushed him across the floor back towards the door he opened. Charlie walked after them without interfering, following the doctor outside. Just as Jessica was about to slam the door, the psychiatrist stepped back in her way. "One question," he said. "Do you know the meaning of xenophobia?"

"Do you know the meaning of ridiculous?" She slammed the door on him.

Charlie looked at the doctor. "I'll defer printing this week's edition until your article arrives."

At the old Gatekeeper's Cottage again, Charlie transferred the photographs he'd taken of Jessica into his computer to examine on the screen. Her serious face made her seem scholarly. Her eyes blinking made her seem inhuman; Charlie might use it the following week. The most suitable photograph was the one with her smile pleasant, without credibility.

"We could darken her eyes," said Agnes.

"We don't need to hurt her," said Charlie. "We only need to ensure no one believes her." Charlie expanded the articles he'd already written and embarked upon more she compelled him to write.

"She might have meant well, Mister Quinn," said Agnes.

"So did Hitler," replied Charlie, without interrupting his typing. "We're not going back."

From the computer files of photographs, Agnes extracted pictures to include in Charlie's article condemning fascism. She found images of Adolf Hitler, Benito Mussolini, Francisco Franco, and Emperor Hirohito.

"Not Hirohito," Charlie told her. "He'd be counterproductive."

They scoured news services for items pertinent to issues Jessica raised. The tenets of Charlie's articles required immigrants to be Australian, making Jessica Rawlins treasonous.

"A journalist can merely report the news," he told Agnes, "or refine it, having regard to all the circumstances. We don't want to cloud people's judgements with irrelevancies, risking them reaching improper conclusions."

"Does that mean we only research what we already know, Mister Quinn? What do we do when facts are inadequate?"

"Lies aren't lies when we use them to prove what we know to be true, Agnes. We want our readers to understand issues." Charlie credited words rebutting Jessica to unnamed residents of the shire; they were composites of what he knew people thought. He was, after all, a resident. "Where's the number for that reverend, Agnes? He knows what to say."

Agnes prepared for publication the letters from residents condemning Jessica. Letters supporting her remained in their pile.

"We don't have the room to publish those letters," said Charlie, pointing to that pile.

"The post office can be unreliable."

16

THE GATHERING STORM

Wednesday morning, the door to the old Gatekeepers Cottage pushed open to reveal Mildred Thompkins. "The mayor wants to see the photographs you took of Jessica Rawlins," she told Charlie Quinn at his desk.

"Has Sergeant Vaughan been watching me?"

"Not you," replied Mildred.

"Copies of our photographs cost ten dollars each."

"Oh," said Mildred. "Can't you invoice the council?"

"You'll have to come back with your purse." Charlie turned back to his keyboard.

"The mayor," quipped Agnes, "might want to buy every copy."

"The mayor wants to talk with you, Charlie," said Mildred. "You'll want to hear him."

"When I'm finished," said Charlie, without looking at her, "sometime later."

The time was after twelve thirty before Charlie swaggered through the Cabonne Council building towards the mayor's office. The mayor's door was closed. Mildred Thompkins was not at her desk.

The only other person there was the mayoress, sitting in a chair outside her husband's office. In Mrs Xiedergrain's hand was a Champagne glass, although if the glass came from the mayor's office, the bubbling drink in it was a lesser sparkling wine than Champagne. She smiled, wearing a long elegant but informal dress, eying Charlie's characteristic ill-fitting suit.

"My husband is quite devoted to Cabonne," she told Charlie.

"Your husband is devoted to many things, Mrs Xiedergrain."

She laughed. "Very tactful, Mister Quinn!"

"Is your husband in, Mrs Xiedergrain?"

"Do you think this new mine and developments will be good, Mister Quinn?"

"We're already developed, Mrs Xiedergrain. We have shops, and people who work in them."

"My husband will look after them, Mister Quinn," she said, her voice tailing away. "Men of politics, men of laws, are men of words. You're a man of letters. My husband is devoted to words. He'll give people something small and make them think they have more." If her status afforded her anything, then it afforded her chances to be injudicious.

"Your husband, Mrs Xiedergrain?"

"This is the point in our conversations, Mister Quinn, when you normally tell me that Molong is the same as it was when you left it. Are you an expert again, Mister Quinn?"

"About some things, Mrs Xiedergrain."

She sighed, before taking another long sip from her glass. "This mine he talks about won't affect us," she told him, "however much I might wish that it would."

Charlie removed his notepad from his pocket. It was a poor excuse not to say anything.

"Forgive me, Mister Quinn," she smiled, reaching from her chair towards him and placing her free hand on his. "I didn't mean to embarrass you." She raised the glass in her other hand. "I should never drink mediocre Champagne."

Charlie prepared to push open the mayor's door, when it opened before him. There stood Mildred Thompkins.

"I thought you'd be here," said Charlie.

"I thought you'd join us, eventually," replied Mildred. She stepped back, inviting Charlie to enter the office.

Mrs Xiedergrain stood up by the open office door, where she raised her glass in a toast to her husband he didn't acknowledge.

Mildred closed the door upon her, remaining with Charlie in the mayor's office.

Standing up from his desk, the mayor started towards his drinks cabinet. "I'll get you some whiskey, Charlie."

"Not today." Charlie slumped in a chair facing him. "You knew I saw Jessica Rawlins yesterday."

"Your wife won't hear it from me, Charlie." The mayor sat back in his chair. Spread around his desk were the photographs of Jessica taken by Charlie the previous day. "You're infatuated with her," said the mayor, picking up a photograph with both his hands. "Is she still seeing that boyfriend of hers?"

"She's an attractive girl," said Mildred. "She might want a career in modelling and think this is a way to start."

"Famous people can be controversial," said the mayor, returning one photograph to his desk and picking up another. "Ordinary people can't, or they'll never become famous."

"She might've wanted her name in the newspaper," Mildred suggested, "if she doesn't have much in her life."

"Who wants too much of novelties?" asked the mayor. "Like a publicised mistress, she'll have attention without respect."

"Pictures are people's first impressions," interrupted Charlie.

"Then you shouldn't have photographed her unless she was ugly," the mayor told him. He picked up another photograph, comparing the two in his hands to each other. "At least in the newspaper, they'll be grey and white."

The mayor returned the photographs to his desk. He pulled them into a pile he pushed to one side.

"It's a shame, really," sighed Mildred, as she opened the door to leave. Standing there was Mrs Xiedergrain, waving her hands towards her husband and grinning. Mildred left, closing the door.

The mayor pulled from the side of his desk a red cardboard folder marked for the Volunteer Recognition Programme, except that Cabonne Council spelt words as Americans spelt them. "You've got a story about our Volunteer of the Month Susan Hodgeson," he told Charlie, "with her multicultural pottery."

"What is multicultural pottery?"

"I might need to leave you alone for a few minutes," said

the mayor standing. "I wouldn't want anyone knowing how you came to know about more Volunteers of the Month we're preparing to recognise."

"I could copy any other story I've written about your Volunteers of the Month, changing little more than the winner's name and photograph, and nobody would notice."

The mayor sat back in his chair, pushing the red cardboard folder back to the side of his desk. "No need to play up this racist thing, Charlie. If you must write about it, why not lead with the actions of council? Don't focus on that poor Rawlins girl when you can write about our new Diversity Ordinance; all the councillors are coming in shortly. It proves our position, and the position of every man, woman, and child in the shire, except this unfortunate, troubled, poor lass."

"Would you pass the Diversity Ordinance were it not for Jessica Rawlins?"

"Yes, we would. Perhaps not this Monday, but we'd have passed it sometime. You see Charlie, Jessica Rawlins is insignificant. Don't destroy our town by making one bad egg a celebrity and, worst of all, a role model. We're trying to remove reasons people have to talk about her. Don't make her a pariah or she might be a martyr. We want her to be nothing."

"Are you expecting international news services to read about Susan Hodgeson's pottery?"

"Don't you want a new supermarket?"

"We have a supermarket."

"Do you like the credit card surcharge?"

"You could open an account."

The mayor leant forward in his desk. "Jessica Rawlins could bring us all down, Charlie, drag us all under. She could cost you your newspaper."

"Journalists win awards for these sorts of stories."

"Is that what you want?"

Charlie studied him, letting him worry about Charlie's reply, before relenting. "I don't want the aggravation," he answered, before taunting him. "We don't always get what we want."

"Don't write much about her," said the mayor. "She has only herself to blame, but we don't want everyone to suffer because of one woman's words. Remember Charlie: Stability brings prosperity, instability brings poverty."

"About Jessica Rawlins and racism, I've written seven articles."

"Seven!" cried the mayor, starting to stand. He clenched his fist and thumped it onto his desk. "One girl speaks out of turn and you give her your newspaper! What else are you planning, colour supplements?"

"I'm thinking of the common good."

The mayor waved his hand over the photographs of Jessica on his desk, figuratively flicking them away, before slumping back in his chair. "She's news, Charlie, and I respect that, news that will help you sell newspapers and get you somewhere else, if that's what you want, but news that will damage this town and deter people from coming, except to peer at the oddities and leave without spending money. You and your family are threads in the social fabric we have here. What happens if Fergus Millane or some other malcontent writes you a letter supporting Jessica Rawlins?"

"We don't publish racist material."

The mayor pulled a copy of the previous week's *Molong Express* from the side of his desk. "The front page is always a problem. Can't you put your Jessica Rawlins' articles somewhere else, next to stories about waste management?"

"You'll study every word and phrase, the placing of every comma, about Jessica Rawlins wherever I publish it, trying to understand everything it can mean, gauging every impression she makes."

"Isolate her, Charlie. Pull her apart. Look into her. Everyone has skeletons in the closet, or bones we can make into skeletons."

The mayor reached forward his right hand to shake Charlie's hand, in confirmation of a supposed agreement between them. Charlie kept his hands to himself.

"It's up to you, Charlie," sighed the mayor, closing the conversation.

Mildred knocked on the door, opened it, and poked her head through. "It's one o'clock," she said.

"Bring them in," the mayor told her. "Stay for this, Charlie. You might even report it."

Mildred stood at the door, handing sheets of paper to councillor after councillor filing into the mayor's office. Most of the councillors were men, with ages around about that of the mayor and manners made formal by them being together. They'd come from their farms, stores, and homes to fill every available seat and stand wherever they could, quietly reading the sheets of paper Mildred had given them. Involving all councillors in formulating the new law would ensure their support.

Charlie didn't try to read the words they were reading; the mayor would show him a copy soon enough. Beyond the open door, the mayoress was waving her outstretched arms at her husband, although he still paid no attention. Mildred left and again closed the door.

Joining them was the council general manager, dressed in her business blouse and slacks; Mildred Thompkins was careful not to dress like her. Tall for a woman, although well short of the mayor, Barbara Woodley dutifully followed the mayor's directions whenever she knew they were the right course to take; she knew council's operations and parameters better than any mayor could.

"I'll tell them what's happening, Barbara," said the mayor. "You weigh in if you can add anything."

Eleven men and women sat and stood around the mayor's office, where Charlie had never before seen more than two or three people. Barbara stood reading the mayor's proposed ordinance where she could watch the nine councillors.

"I don't know what was said," started the mayor from his desk, "I wasn't there, but Jessica Rawlins has been sounding off again, this time to Charlie."

"Jessica?" said Councillor McDermott, sitting on the sofa. "She seemed so sweet."

"I've put together this ordinance from what other councils and governments have done," the mayor told them, "taken a word from here, a phrase from there. It puts us at the pinnacle of progress."

Charlie interjected. "You know what a pinnacle is, don't you, mayor? It's the point where you start going back down."

McDermott was shaking his head. "I attended her mother's funeral."

"Talk to her, Garth," the mayor told him. "Convince her to talk about daisies, or not say anything at all, but if you can't convince her to apologise and retract what she said, then I'll have to stand her on the carpet and lay down the law. I've tried to talk with her but you can't reason with the girl; she's not very bright. You know she's seen a psychiatrist, fellow from Orange, but he had to give up on her. If we're not careful with this, it'll get out of hand."

"I don't know her that well."

"Matters got out of hand with Fergus Millane," the mayor resumed. "I've drafted this ordinance to deal with this problem now. You tell me if you think of a better way to phrase it or something more effective we can do quickly, but we don't want discussion and debate upsetting people."

Sitting near the mayor's desk was Councillor Poole. "We don't know what she said, the second time. We don't know what Charlie's going to write."

The mayor glanced at Charlie, who didn't respond. "We oppose any division," said the mayor, "without needing to bog down in detail. Save the partisanship and politics for topics of no importance."

"What immigrants do we know?" asked Poole.

"Do you eat at the Wing Hang?"

The councillor shook his head. He opened his mouth as if about to speak, but closed it again.

"For the sake of the shire," said the mayor, "we need to silence her so she'll never say such words again, to mitigate the impact of what she's already said, and to dissuade other people from speaking as she has. We need to eliminate her words, exorcise them from our world, and reconstruct the world as if they'd never been spoken. The flame she's ignited having been lit, we need to extinguish it."

Councillor Hagarty ventured a comment. "We can't imprison people."

"Are you opposing this measure?" retorted the mayor.

"No," he snapped. "We could establish an intolerance register, naming Fergus Millane and Jessica Rawlins."

"We don't want a register reminding people they exist."

"Mister Mayor," said Barbara. "Are we certain the council has the legislative power to pass this ordinance?"

"Who's going to challenge it, Barbara? What magistrate will be seen to support her? You're quibbling about legal nicety, but this council must be seen to repudiate her. What government in this country wouldn't do what we're doing? None of us can afford to let this thing lie."

"If there's a problem," observed Barbara, "the state or federal government can remedy any deficiency in the law. Do you want to limit the ordinance to public areas?"

"That won't be enough," said the mayor. "Some people might think it's acceptable to make divisive and offensive remarks in offices or at home."

The mayor stood up and began pacing about the floor. "We'll have a law, an ordinance of this council without any sense of dissent, making that absolutely clear. This council will do whatever it takes to safeguard the economic prosperity and social cohesion of this town. Nothing is more important."

The mayor studied each of the councillors in turn, his eyes into theirs. They all remained silent.

"We'll make my motion retrospective to the day she said what she said," the mayor told them. "No court will complain, but prosecuting her is better than not doing anything even if she's acquitted, but she won't be acquitted."

"The police can prosecute her under state and federal laws," added Barbara.

Charlie spoke up. "Do you want my opinion?" he asked.

"Naturally, Mister Quinn, council considers everything you say."

"If you prosecute, you revive her. You make her the victim you're trying to keep her from being, and give me reason to write more about her."

The mayor nodded. "People tell me her parents divorced when she was young," he said. "Her mother is dead. Nobody knows where her father is. I'm inclined to give the girl a chance to apologise, do some voluntary work, and nip this thing in the bud."

"Will that be real voluntary work," asked Charlie, "or the sort that makes someone Volunteer of the Month?"

"If she again says anything wrong," continued the mayor, "then we'll bring the law down upon her, but only if she compels us to do so. I think that's generous, but we have to be fair to everyone, not just Jessica Rawlins."

The mayor allowed them more time to consider the proposed ordinance. He gave them time to say nothing.

"So, we're unanimous?" asked the mayor. "We can pass this thing, Monday?"

The councillors all nodded. Some muttered their concurrence.

"If Jessica Rawlins was trying to achieve anything by doing this, she's made a terrible mistake," said the mayor. "She can never amount to anything now."

Mildred normally sent Charlie copies of new ordinances upon the council adopting them, but this one the mayor gave Charlie a copy from his desk. "*The council and people of Cabonne Shire affirm our right to diversity, and prohibit anyone from any expression of a divisive and offensive nature. The penalty for a breach of this ordinance shall be a maximum of twenty thousand dollars and three months imprisonment.*"

"If we can be of any more help, Charlie," said the mayor, "please don't hesitate to call."

17

THE ENCROACHING SOLITUDE

Thursday morning, hurrying along the Bank Street footpath to the newsagent, Jessica passed Mildred Thompkins running to the council offices. She held aloft what was surely the new edition of the *Molong Express* newspaper like a champion's baton, or torch.

Jessica pushed open the newsagent door to see Briony Keyte and Lester Cullen, examining the newspaper. "That's a shocking outfit she wore in the photograph, so gaudy," said Briony, loudly enough for everyone to hear, "and that hovel she's living in..."

"She really has no idea, does she?" said Lester, shaking his head. "No idea."

A boy dressed for school pointed his finger at Jessica. "I know you," he exclaimed. "You're the woman in the newspaper!"

Briony and Lester turned to Jessica, as did every other person there. Jessica would attract more attention by trying to hide than she attracted standing still. "We thought we knew you," Briony told her. "I guess we were wrong."

"You weren't wrong."

"We never thought to ask what you think."

Dominating the piles of newspapers was the banner "*Meet Jessica Rawlins, Racist.*" In more colour than the newspaper normally gave anything was her horrifying, huge photograph.

The familiar image of the painting of her grandparents' house brought the gasping horror to her home, where she'd stupidly allowed it to come.

Grabbing the newspaper, she read her conversation with Charlie Quinn reduced to words painfully inadequate. *"Ms Rawlins explained her tirade at the Pickled Pepper Café by saying she wants Australia to be Australian and England to be English. She admitted she's never been to England, but would rather be there than Australia."*

Every sentence pounded her, wearing her further down. Feeling the welter of the world against her, Jessica turned to see Briony and Lester still watching her. "Why?" she pleaded, willing her tears to stay inside her rather than let a description of her demeanour appear in the newspaper's next edition. "It didn't mean anything."

"It meant everything," replied Lester.

Her eyes fell out of focus gazing downward, thinking about everything, imagining she would cry. Clutching that newspaper, she turned to leave.

"That will be a dollar fifty," called out the newsagent.

Jessica turned back towards him. She rummaged about in her purse for the money, before finding a five-dollar note she slapped on the counter.

"Miss," called the newsagent, as she dashed to the door, dragged it open, and scurried out.

Jessica's shoes clicked on the roadway as she rushed across Bank Street without checking for coming traffic. A car sounding its horn stopped suddenly, jolting her, before she resumed running to the footpath and lunged at the door of Derek's real estate agency.

She burst in to see Derek at his desk reading the newspaper. Tears pouring from her eyes with the freedom she gave them, she scampered to the safe reclusion of the meeting room and collapsed into a chair, burying her face, eyes closed, in her hands.

"It's way over the top," said Derek, placing his hand on her knee.

"The more I try to extricate myself from my calamity, the

worse it becomes," she struggled to say. "They will think I'm a fool and an unjust fool at that. They will think that I hate people. Friends and strangers are holding me underwater, trying to drown me."

"I've got you these," said Derek.

She opened her sobbing eyes to see Derek in the chair beside her, offering her tissues from a box. "Thank you," she said, wiping her tears-soaked skin.

Her dampest tissues tucked on the floor by a leg of her chair and a fresh tissue against her face, Jessica again took the newspaper: that black ink on the grey. She read more about her, her mind, and words she'd said and not said.

"*Residents expect thunderous, rapturous applause from the public gallery this Monday when Cabonne Council responds to Ms Rawlins by unanimously rushing through the Diversity Ordinance. 'Rawlins doesn't speak for anyone but herself,' said one man. 'She's a horrible person.' Ms Rawlins hasn't identified any person who agrees with her views, and nobody whom this newspaper interviewed supported her. She is already planning to leave Australia.*"

"Did the newspaper ask you about me?" she asked Derek.

"Charlie Quinn won't upset an advertiser."

Jessica turned the newspaper page, opening before her a flood of articles across the second and third pages. The words and pictures swelled into a whirlpool the longer Jessica stared into them, threatening as much to suck her in as sweep her away. "I'd throw this newspaper to hell," she said, "but I don't want it there with me."

The psychiatrist's report profiled a crazy woman. Jessica didn't recognise her.

"They're the impressions of the ignorant," she said. "He says I've dispossessed society, but I haven't. Society dispossessed me."

Every article that didn't mention Jessica by name was less gruelling than those that did. An article profiled an immigrant horrifically murdered in Sydney, without identifying her killer. Another article described the racial prejudice suffered by immigrants around Australia, Europe, and America. Among the stories of charming immigrants was a photograph of an Asian child drowned in the surf.

Jessica read every word, presuming it was true. "None of this is news," she said. "None of it relates to what I said."

She turned another page, where an article applauded the two Volunteers of the Month: Briony and Susan. Letter after letter to the editor condemned Jessica: the mob in civilised tones.

"*Dangerous Beauty*" headed the barbed editorial comment. "*It's easy to perceive Ms Rawlins as a pleasant young woman, but her civility masks an idea as dangerous today as it has always been.*" Quinn's kinder words among them only made the cuts more telling. "*Now, more than ever, Ms Rawlins needs to appreciate that for all our politeness, she has no friends in this country.*"

"I was nice to him," wept Jessica. "I allowed him into my home. I gave him coffee, even if it was instant. I offered him biscuits."

"He mightn't realise the effect this is having upon you."

"He knows the power of words. He's a newspaper man. He does this for a living, for money."

"He mightn't read words as he writes them," said Derek. "Are you going to do anything about it?"

"What can I do?"

"Do you want to talk to him again?"

"No," snapped Jessica. "I don't *ever* want to see him again."

Cautiously, she turned the newspaper page, where there came at last articles Jessica hadn't inspired. She turned every page, past all the articles, advertisements, and notices. Among them were advertisements for properties Derek's real estate agency was selling.

A notice from the Molong Uniting Church said the women's fellowship was meeting there at ten o'clock on Sunday. Jessica wouldn't be going.

Jessica closed the newspaper, the back page with its advertisements, before turning it over to see the front page again: that grotesque colour effigy of her, the shadows of a senseless camera smile. "If I'm spending too long looking back at my face," she said, "it's because I'm trying to see the stupidity in me."

"Looking the way you look doesn't help."

"You used to like the way I looked."

"Beauty brings women invitations, but won't help you trying to hide from your publicity."

She might've laughed, in a sorrowful, sad laugh at the cruelty of his compliment. "I wish the photograph didn't look like me, or that I didn't look like it. I might start wearing a disguise."

"Will I recognise you?"

Jessica sniffled. When she knew she wouldn't cry again soon, she used her fingertips to wipe the last waters from her eyes, and saw the trail of black and colour her tears had left.

Derek took more tissues from the box. He wiped her soiled face.

"What are we going to do?" she asked him. "Quinn admitted in his article, in his perverse way, I am nice, but he's decided I'm a social warrior, or he is."

"He's slandering you to stop other people talking, Jess."

"He's maligning me to stop other people thinking. They'll know everyone who dares to contemplate will be shouted down."

She folded the newspaper tightly into something unintelligible, but it was all still obvious. She hid it on the floor below the chair so nobody would see it, but feared leaving it behind. She pulled it out again, slapped it on the table, and began tearing it into strips and tiny pieces. On and on she tore, destroying every hint of a face in the photograph and meaning in the text.

Derek stepped out of the room, soon returning with a wastepaper basket. Into it, he collected Jessica's soiled tissues from the table and floor.

Page after page Jessica continued to tear. If she could not be sure each strip of newspaper couldn't be deciphered, she tore it more. Finally, she bundled the torn bits of rubbish newspaper into a rough, chaotic ball no passing eyes could accidentally read and shoved it into the wastepaper basket. She pushed her refuse ball into the bin as far down as she could, burying it.

Her arms were sore, when Jessica slumped back in her chair. She picked up her handbag from the floor and stood up. "Has anyone else arrived?" she asked.

"I've asked them not to come in this morning until nine o'clock."

"You're sweet," she said, reaching up and kissing him. As she pulled away, she saw a hint of colour she'd left around his lips. "Sorry," she said, her longest fingers wiping his face clean.

Clutching the drier tissues in her hand, Jessica slipped into the staff washroom and closed the door. Standing alone at the washbasin and vanity unit, she cleaned and dried her face. She carefully applied fresh colour to her eyes, brows, and lashes. She moistened her lips with her tongue, reapplying red gloss.

When she finished, she stared into the mirror. There, reflected in the glass, was a performing clown: a saddened face that Jessica once knew. The media man who took her smile kept it for himself.

"I'll take you home," said Derek, grabbing his hat from a stand. He coyly pulled his hat a little further down his forehead than he normally did, before leading Jessica outside.

Not for Jessica was Molong still her serene, childhood town. It gave way that morning to what seemed like crowds of opinionated newspaper readers, all searching for her. The streets were places to flee. The buildings were too few places to hide.

Jessica walked quickly, held up by Derek's hand around hers, feeling the weight of people ordinarily weightless; the forces that maligned her made her weak. She didn't speak, for fear her voice revealed her. She would've cried some more, but didn't want the scores of evil eyes peering at her to know she was aching.

Ahead of them was Susan Hodgeson, carrying a newspaper. She stepped into a store.

Other people might've also recognised the woman walking along the footpath, or wondered if they did, thinking something Jessica couldn't bear to hear. If they did, they didn't say anything aloud.

A man Jessica might've recognised walked towards them. His

height was average, his gait normal, wearing a commonplace checked cotton shirt and denim jeans without a hat. His elliptical face, waving beige brown hair, and pointed nose, might've been familiar. He might've seen her, but continued looking ahead of him without his eyes contacting hers. She stared at the stranger's face, examining it for any message in his expression, while Derek looked down at the footpath, slowing his and Jessica's pace until they passed beside them.

Turning into Edward Street, Derek and Jessica moved a little quicker, but not so quickly as to attract attention. They hurried through her open gate into her home.

"Can you come in?" she asked him, closing the gate after them, away from the town's sight and hearing.

"I have to work."

"Please?"

Diverting her mind from the matters of the morning, Derek sat on her sofa with space for Jessica to sit beside him. Amorously, she pulled his hat from his head and stroked his hair. "I love you, Derek," she told him, taking his hands in hers and kissing him. "I love you loving me."

She pulled her feet up to the sofa behind her and kissed him with a passion for forgetfulness. Derek's hand on her back moved to hug her as she cuddled close to him, finally settling under his shoulder, her eyes closed.

They sat there for several minutes, before Derek pulled away. "I do have to work," he told her.

She opened her eyes. His hat was back on his head. "Can you come over afterwards?"

"I'll come as soon as I can."

"Thank you, my love."

Her arms around him, she walked with him as close as she could to the door. Her right foot rose from the floor as she kissed him. He pulled his hat low on his head, and walked away more easily without her.

18

WILTED FLOWERS

Derek returned to his desk in his real estate agency office, where people other than Jessica and words other than those in a newspaper ought to have held his thoughts. Instead, he again pored through those pages.

When visitors entered the offices, Derek quickly closed his newspaper, leaving only the inoffensive back page showing. His colleagues at their desks did the same.

The problems of Jessica played upon Derek's mind, even while sitting in his meeting room with aging Oscar and Samantha Hammond. Oscar walked with a limp since falling from a truck, although Derek hadn't noticed it until Samantha mentioned it. They were considering selling the farm on which the Hammond family had lived for generations, but which was mortgaged to the Commonwealth Bank and mightn't raise as much money as they'd imagined. "We'd have liked someone within the family to buy it," Oscar explained, "but our daughters and their husbands aren't interested."

"Have you thought about where you'd live?" asked Derek.

"We've lived too long around Molong to live anywhere else."

"Excuse me," Samantha asked Derek. "I know this is a little off the purpose of us seeing you, but Oscar and I were wondering, earlier this morning, didn't we see you with that woman in the newspaper?"

Derek's answer came slowly to him. "You might have."

"She has created something of a storm," said Oscar.

"It does make us a little uncomfortable," explained Samantha. "Not that we mind what she says or wants to do with her life, so much, but it might unsettle things if people know her friend is selling our farm. We need desperately to receive as much money as we can."

"She doesn't have anything to do with the agency," Derek assured them.

"So, you don't know her that well?" asked Samantha.

"She used to work in a salon, I think."

Oscar and Samantha looked at each other, before looking back at Derek. "That should be all right then," smiled Oscar. Samantha also smiled, although most uneasily.

They still hadn't decided whether to sell their farm when Derek walked with them back to the footpath. He was shaking Oscar's hand when a voice interrupted them. "You're Jessica Rawlins' boyfriend, aren't you?"

"No, no I'm not," snapped Derek, to a man a little younger than he was, dressed in a working man's shirt and stained denim jeans.

"You are," the stranger insisted. "I've seen you with her."

"I spent a little time with her, but we were never close."

"Are you sure?"

"I'm sure," said Derek. "We never hit it off together."

The young man pursed his lips, expanding his eyes as if to say he wasn't really convinced. He walked on along the footpath.

Derek looked at the Hammonds. "People presume so much," he told them, with nothing better to say.

"Yes," said Oscar, taking his wife by her hand. Derek watched them walk away.

Inside the agency offices, with their colleagues elsewhere, Sophie Fulbright worked diligently at her desk. Sophie performed the secretarial and administrative work of the agency while she studied real estate at the college in Orange. Her nose and face were sharp, focused upon life ahead of her. She was pretty enough not to think about prettiness, but wasn't yet accomplished. Derek trusted her to protect and develop the business as if it were her own, because she hoped it someday would be.

"If people mention Jessica," Derek told her, "please don't let them think she's my girlfriend. If they've seen me with her, say we were acquaintances."

"I understand Derek," she smiled, "really I do. It can't be helped."

People rarely worked late of an evening in country towns, but that Thursday evening Derek remained at his desk after five o'clock. Sophie remained at hers, after their colleagues had left. A timber cabinet in a corner of the meeting room concealed a small bar refrigerator, in which Sophie maintained stocks of small bottles of beer and cider, large bottles of wine, and soft drinks. Derek removed a bottle of pear cider and poured Sophie a glass of wine. He returned to his nearby desk, twisted off the metal top from his bottle, and sat down. The cider was cold and reassuring.

Sophie at her desk sipped at her wine. She brushed her brown hair from her neck and shoulders. "What's going to happen between you and Jessica?" she asked him.

"Nothing is as it used to be."

"When opinions were unimportant and public pressure unimagined?"

"We can't let the controversy embroiling Jessica embroil this agency."

"Does it make you wonder if you want a girlfriend who attracts that sort of attention?"

"It makes me wonder if I want a friend who does."

"She depends upon you."

"I hope not!" cried Derek.

"So," said Sophie, sitting up, "what are you looking for in a woman?"

Derek swilled more cider from the bottle. "Apart from devotion to me?" he smiled, not really being facetious.

"Apart from that."

Derek lowered his voice. "I never thought about it," he told her, but he had.

"I like Jessica," said Sophie, "was even a little jealous of her, but she could be indiscreet."

"Indiscretion doesn't have to be a problem, depending on what you do with it."

"You sound like you want a woman with whom everyone agrees, or is it enough if she keeps her disagreements secret?"

"You sound like Jessica. I don't know whether she's right, but she is sincere."

"Is loyalty worth losing the customers that feed us? Don't risk what you've achieved, Derek; you have more to lose than Jessica. You have a business to run."

Derek said nothing, shamed by his silence. He swilled more cider.

"My friends and I are eating out tonight," said Sophie. "You can come with us."

"I better see Jessica."

She smiled, more broadly than she usually smiled. "We're eating Chinese."

At about six o'clock, with his hat pulled own on his head and his newspaper folded tightly under his arm, Derek arrived at Jessica's home. She opened the door, wrapped her arms around him, and kissed him passionately. He pressed them inside her home, closing the door behind him, before speaking. "You must have had a good day."

"It's over now." She removed his hat from his head. "I've told you, you don't need to wear your hat this late in the day, and you're wearing your jacket."

"I walked here."

"Where is your car?" she asked, placing his hat on the coffee table among the chairs. He placed his newspaper beside it, but she took it away from him and discarded it in a bin in the kitchen. "Let me take your jacket."

Derek removed his jacket from his shoulders and gave it to Jessica, who took it to her bedroom upstairs before returning. "How are you feeling?" asked Derek.

She brought a bottle of cold cider from the refrigerator and handed it to him, but he placed it unopened on the coffee table. With her shoes fallen to the floor, Jessica folded her legs onto the sofa and nestled beside him. "How was your day?"

"The Hammonds saw you in the newspaper."

"I'm sorry," said Jessica, retreating a little from him. "I hate you getting caught up in this."

"I had to play down my relationship with you, I'm afraid."

Jessica quickly sat up, straightening her legs so that her feet touched the floor to balance her, and looked at him. "Why should you care about the newspaper?"

"I might've lost their account."

Jessica sat dejected back into the sofa, away from him. "It seems rather sad, if only to me."

"Somebody else recognised me as having been with you."

"What did you say?"

"I had to say I didn't know you well, I had no choice. My business occupation needs the goodwill of strangers. There'd be people applauding me if I left you, and I have as much to gain by their applause as I lose by their condemnation. If people think I'm supporting you, they'll damn me. They'll forgive you a certain stupidity, recklessness, or illness, but they won't forgive me. Think of it as another bit of fluff from someone selling real estate."

"It isn't fluff, is it?" asked Jessica. "It's you and me."

"Does honesty with strangers matter so much? We can be truthful with ourselves, but you can say the same thing to people until everything settles down."

"I don't want to say that."

Derek became frustrated with her selfishness. "I'm getting on top of the business now," he told her. "I can't afford to have people keeping away because of my relationship with you. I don't know what else to do."

"What would you have done if we were sharing your home?"

"This isn't the time to think about it."

"You have talked about it, and I've imagined it too, when I thought us loving each other was enough."

"I'm not mentioning it now." Derek collected his thoughts in his brain and bracing heart. "I don't think people should see us together until all this blows over."

"Are you ashamed of me?"

"No," said Derek, "but everything would be easier if we kept a little space."

"What are you telling me?"

"It's one thing for you to give everything away trying to save this nutty-case world, but something else to expect me to give everything away to join you. Do you want to ruin my career, my life?"

"You know I don't," she cried, "but this conversation isn't about what I want."

"We can still talk to each other."

Jessica curled up on the sofa. "What would you do now if you were me?" she asked him.

"I have to be careful with my answer."

"I can keep secrets."

He owed her enough to answer the question from which he was inclined to skirt away. "I wouldn't have said what you said."

"No one but I would've said what I said," she laughed. "Do you want me to renounce what I said?"

"Would you?" asked Derek. "That would be marvellous."

"What would I say?"

"Say you were misunderstood. Apologise for everything. Say categorically Chinese people aren't racist, and you want all the immigrants who'll come. You'll like every one of them."

Jessica fell away from him into the armrest of her sofa. "Why don't you write my words?"

"You're marvellous, Jess." Derek quickly sat up. Beside her telephone on the floor, Jessica kept a notepad. Derek brought the notepad to the coffee table, removed his pen from his shirt pocket, and started to write.

"I can read from it when I talk to the newspaper," she sighed, "or anyone else."

Derek wrote while Jessica lay quietly, ascribing words in quotation marks to her. When he finished, he gave her the notepad.

She sat up slowly to read it. When she finished, she returned the notepad to him. "I studied to learn and think," she told him, with a hint of confrontation, "to believe but then abandon beliefs if I learnt something contradicting them. I have been wrong in my life, often, but I never said anything I knew to be untrue. Some of your words might be truthful, but none of them I yet believe."

"I'm giving you the chance to be reasonable," Derek implored of her.

"Would telling the newspaper I was wrong really make my problems vanish? If I found a Chinaman and kissed him, the newspaper would call me a whore and be right. People would always doubt whether I believed anything I said."

"Jess, please..."

"I love you, Derek," Jessica interrupted, sniffling back another tear, "but in spite of what everyone's telling me, I also love me. I like being me and who I am. I like being the same person wherever I go, adjusting only the subtleties of when I speak and my vocabulary for the sake of courtesy. I wish I'd never said anything at the Pickled Pepper Café, but I've come too far without lying to people to start lying now. I don't think I want a relationship that depends upon me saying things I don't believe, so you can sell another farm."

They stared at each other, waiting for one of them to speak. The home was Jessica's, and she could wait longer than could Derek. She wouldn't fight him, but nor would she compromise herself to make conversation easier for him.

Slowly, Derek stood up from the sofa. "Goodbye, Jess," he said.

"Goodbye, Derek."

"I better get my jacket."

Jessica remained on the sofa, letting him go and waiting for him to leave, while Derek walked back upstairs. She listened to their time together ending: the footsteps through the floor, the opening and closing doors, in hollow requiem. Ahead of her, the unopened bottle of cool cider she'd brought him was losing its droplets from the glass.

Derek came back downstairs wearing his jacket. "I'll get my casserole dish," he told her, proceeding to the kitchen.

Jessica didn't care, but he could've left it there in deference to her. It was a reason for him to return when he shouldn't have a reason.

He picked up his pen from the table and returned it to his shirt pocket. He picked up his hat from the small table by the door.

"Would you like your cider?" she asked him, barely interested in his reply.

He hesitated, without facing her. "I'm sorry, Jess," he said. "Everybody is."

Leaving the cider bottle behind, Derek stepped outside. He tried to pull shut the front door with his hands holding the casserole dish but couldn't do so. He left the door slightly ajar.

Remaining on the aged sofa that wasn't even hers, Jessica's head lay back against the armrest, the fabric warm against her fading face. Her dress wrapped her like a closely fitting sheet in another person's bed. The place in which she lay was large, too large for her. Lying alone where she'd often lain with Derek, remembering his comfort only pained her all the more.

The reasons for their parting were unclear. He might reappear at the almost open door, but she would never again have sufficient confidence in him to risk being with him forever. The man she loved was much less the man than she had presumed he could be. Suffering her notoriety might be easier without his ambivalence loitering beside her. Like the two friends who'd walked away from her at the café, Derek hadn't been worth retaining, but adjusting to life without him was one more burden to bear.

The yellow flowers he once gave her had wilted in the vase. Finally she stood up, collected them, and dropped them in the bin, with Derek's copy of the newspaper. She closed the front door of her home, and returned the cider bottle to her refrigerator.

Other men and women were together, in homes and public places, but Jessica was safer being alone. Nobody could hear her think and if by accident she spoke, then nobody would hear her words. Nobody remained to hear her weep.

19

BROKEN FAMILIES

Jessica's aunt and uncle's farm was somewhere of a sanctuary to which she could retreat if everything became difficult, and everything had become difficult. She could hide there, and think in the framework of a life, not a week.

Wandering wearily downstairs from her bed, Friday morning, Jessica tried to telephone her aunt and uncle. Their line was engaged.

Jessica dressed into her any-day clothes of a blouse and blue denim dress. Driving her aunt's old car, she fled the town for Peabody Road, and the rough dirt of her aunt and uncle's short driveway along which the car bumped and rattled. Vines grew over the carport to make a form of garage, in which was parked her uncle's utility truck. Jessica left the parked car unlocked, as she always did at the farm.

Nora answered the front door. "It's you," she said.

"I tried to call," said Jessica.

Nora stood holding the door. She didn't pull it open.

"Were you going out?" asked Jessica. "Do you have people over?"

"No, no," said Nora.

"I thought I'd come here to unwind," Jessica explained. "May I come in?"

Nora hesitated, before stepping backwards. She dragged the door open with her.

Jessica walked forward. "Thank you," she said, kissing her aunt's cheek.

Nora stepped outside, quickly looking around, before stepping back inside and closing the door. "Meryl Brown didn't see you?"

In her aunt and uncle's lounge room, Jessica kissed her uncle on his sweating cheek; he held his greasy hands away from her so they wouldn't soil her clothes. "I'm sorry for coming over without calling but the telephone was engaged."

Norris looked at Nora. Her eyes remained upon Jessica.

"Derek and I split up last night," Jessica told them. "I might be better off without him."

"I'll scrub myself up a bit," said Norris, stepping away from them to the laundry.

Jessica sat on the sofa, while Nora sat in a single person's armchair facing her. "Have you seen the *Molong Express* this week?" asked Jessica.

"We both have," replied Nora. "It was a great shock to us."

"It was a shock to me, too. Derek wanted me to apologise for everything."

"Will you, Jessica?"

If Jessica had imagined before she'd come what her aunt would do, she'd have imagined them hugging through her pain. Instead, she was defending herself before a woman against whom she hadn't expected to need defence. "I'll apologise if I'm wrong," said Jessica, "but nobody has given me any reason why I'm wrong."

"You're the only person saying what you said," continued Nora. "Are you sure that you're right?"

"No, I'm not sure," said Jessica, raising her hands in the air.

"We don't want scandal around us. We keep out of controversy. Even if you think such things, why did you have to say them? You should've been contrite. You can't expect us to agree with you."

"I don't expect anyone to agree with me. I just expect people not to ostracise me, whatever they think."

"How could you do this to us?" asked Nora, in a tone Jessica hadn't heard for years.

"What can happen to you? The newspaper never mentioned you. I never mentioned you."

"You've made people talk about us in a way we don't want people talking about us. A newspaper article next week, or the week after that, will be about us."

Jessica dropped her head. "I didn't mean to hurt you," she said. "I didn't mean to hurt anyone."

"People want to know our opinions about you and about what you said," Nora persisted, "and then they see you in our car..."

"Do you want your car back?"

"Your uncle and I," said Nora gradually, "we can't afford to be involved."

Jessica struggled to comprehend what her aunt was saying. "I'm your niece. I love you very much."

"We love you, too, but we all need to be careful. We're all trying to deal with this as best we can, but we're not big enough to weather this; Bede's too busy with his baby coming to have you drag him and us into this. We're not as strong as you are. I know this is unpleasant, but we need to leave you to resolve this one yourself, until everything returns to what it was. Don't tell us what you do. We don't know anything."

Jessica dwelt upon her state of mind. "I wish I were stronger than I am," she said.

"Please, darling, trust me," said Nora, becoming resolute. "We can't let you being my niece blind us to what's happening."

"Nothing blinds me to loving you."

"You've started something that nobody controls anymore, not anybody we know anyway. I don't want to lose the last of my family."

Jessica began shaking her head. "Families are supposed to stand by each other in difficult times," she said, beginning to cry. "I would always try to help you."

"Try to help, now," said Nora. "We have a whole town to keep in mind. We have committees to consider, and associations."

"I remember Sam Bottomley having that affair with Lucy Coote. His wife and her husband were the only people in Molong who didn't know about it, but you remained friends with all of them."

"It wasn't our place to judge," explained Nora, "but better for all concerned to let them think they kept their secrets."

Jessica restrained her tears. Words she'd failed to comprehend failed her again.

"People will want us to stand against your words," said Nora. "They will want us to strip you from our lives."

"Is that what you want?" asked Jessica. "Am I so much a demon?"

Nora stared at her, as if wanting her niece to know her reply without her needing to say it. Like and unlike Jessica, she remained silent.

Jessica followed her uncle towards the open laundry door, beyond which he was still scrubbing his hands. Her steps loud enough for him to hear, he turned off the tap. He began rubbing his hands dry in a towel.

"Do you want me to leave?" she asked him. Nora stood beside her.

Norris replaced the towel on a small rack. Without looking at his wife or niece, he walked from the laundry past the women into the lounge room.

Nora and Jessica followed him, until he stopped and turned around to face Jessica. "We're normal folk, Jess," he said, with space between them, "working hard, trying to earn enough money to keep the little we've got. This old place might seem like it's not worth the trouble, but it's all we have. People like us can't afford complication. We can't afford to put our heads up, or we might lose them."

"We worry," said Nora.

"We worry we mightn't be able to buy things we need for the farm and house because we can't sell the crops that we produce," explained Norris. "We worry that when we next experience a flood, or drought, people won't give us the help we need, because they're just as frightened as we are. We worry we'll go hungry, because of what you said."

"I'll apologise," said Jessica. "I'll renounce what I said."

"Thank you," said Norris, starting to move towards her.

His wife cut him short. "When everything is normal again," said Nora, "we can see you." Norris stood motionless.

"I'll apologise," repeated Jessica.

"People need time to forget," Nora explained. "Have you not caused us enough grief already?"

"Not as much as you've caused me," said Jessica. She might cry, but not with them; she'd cried too much in recent days. "How can so much happen to me?"

"You have done this to yourself," replied Nora.

"I know," sighed Jessica. "I had no idea what I was doing."

She continued to stand. That home was the last of her past to lose, but she dared not ask if she might be standing there for the last time for fear of her aunt or uncle telling her the truth.

"I should have remained with my blithe ignorance in my small house in the town," Jessica told them. "A false comfort I could escape here would've been better than no comfort at all."

Norris lowered his forehead, facing the floor. Nora watched him, her jaw clenching and stern eyes narrowing.

"I know I've been a fool," said Jessica, "but who is genius enough to bring me out of my predicament?"

Jessica would gleefully accept any reason to believe that her aunt and uncle alone in Molong mightn't wish never to have known her. They gave her no reason.

"I might as well go then," she said, returning to her handbag on the table where she'd left it. She removed from it the keys to her aunt's car, which she placed on the table. Nothing of hers she wanted to keep remained inside the car.

"I have a whole family to protect!" Nora told her husband, before rushing out of the room.

Jessica thought of saying something, but talking hadn't helped her before then. So short and long a time since she'd arrived, she opened the front door and departed, closing the door behind her.

Stupefied, she trod slowly along the driveway towards the road. She moved quietly, hoping to hear her aunt or uncle call to her from the hard house behind her. She heard a sound and turned, but nobody was there. The sound had been a rogue noise from another family home.

The driveway ended with the gravel and rough asphalt of the sides of a country road. The fields around her were empty, in her parody of a nightmare, through her long trek back to town. The dust and dirt of soil too dry pocked her face.

Trudging along the roadside, a small truck slowed and stopped beside her. The driver was as old as her uncle, with whiskery stubble from his chin and wearing a shirt and trousers worn at the elbows and knees.

Jessica sat quietly beside him, staring forward through the windscreen to the rolling road headed into town. Words were less important than people she had known. With every budding trauma, a time when the loneliness of life had passed became harder to imagine.

His truck parked against the kerb in Bank Street, Jessica stepped outside and closed the door. He reached across from his driver's seat and locked the door. She waited while he stepped from his truck and locked his driver's door. "Thank you," she whispered.

"I hope things get better for you, Miss."

It seemed she should thank him for those words and sentiment, but the day and days had been too difficult. Kind thoughts too late couldn't save her. They would not become her memories.

Jessica lost her gaze before she walked along the footpath, uncertain where to go and how to get there, unable to run. She watched the people of the town and hoped, as she always seemed to hope, they weren't watching her. They didn't turn their heads and admit they were.

One tall middle-aged woman strolling along the footpath, carrying her pink handbag and a frilled pink umbrella, mightn't have noticed the young woman moving cautiously towards her, but for the defensive and almost fearful way in which Jessica studied her. She smiled, as she surely smiled at everyone. Jessica almost smiled in reply, but Jessica did not believe her. She didn't trust her. The two women walked past each other without breaking their gaits.

Jessica's head was sore, and she believed enough of Lynne to accept a little of the advice she'd given her. Jessica stepped into the pharmacy, where the pharmacist's young assistant, in her white laboratory uniform, smiled cheerfully to everyone. As often as not, customers paused to talk with her, going so far as to defer to her a status like that of a doctor.

The few people in the pharmacy stopped talking to watch the woman from the newspaper. Jessica found the cheapest headache medicine; paracetamol tablets cost least in a box of a hundred.

She paid the assistant the money for which she asked. "Thank you," said Jessica, accepting the few coins in change.

On the counter was a small charity tin collecting little money for Eugene Gallagher. Jessica left the tin alone.

Clumsily, too close to falling, she retreated to Edward Street and her home. Unlocking the door, pushing it open, she faced her little hiding space: her last place left to be. She pulled the door closed behind her.

Jessica adjusted the strings so the Venetian blinds dropped down, covering the lounge room windows. The room darkened without daylight, where nobody could see her. No passing birds would know that she was there. She could rest and think alone what she should do, without the distraction of everybody watching her.

Unwilling to trouble Bede, she was alone, wholly alone, for the first time in her life. Helpless to redress her situation, Jessica collapsed into the fraying fabric of her sofa. She would've wept, alone in a town where everyone else had somebody, but she'd cried often in recent days and tears were hard to come by.

Jessica wanted to hate somebody, but didn't know whom she should hate. She'd entrusted one small thought and feeling to Susan and Briony, but knew them well enough not to hate them. Besides, they weren't responsible for her fall.

She couldn't hate people she'd met as people she hadn't met could hate a stranger's name and photograph in a newspaper. She didn't hate people who'd abandoned her, and might've even sympathised with their situation, but she hated her situation more.

It was easier to weep, after all. People hadn't treated her as she would have treated them.

20

OUTCASTS

For the new day, Saturday, Jessica opened the lounge room blinds. The sun was shining, but enough clouds hung in the sky to make her wary.

Not quite surrendering, Jessica tried to think of any last recourse to save the remnants of her life. She didn't need another place to weep, but one to help her salvage something from the wreckage. In her pink-covered diary were the names of people she'd seen too rarely since coming home to Molong.

Jessica dressed in a white-laced shirt and dark slacks she rarely wore, which might distinguish her from the woman in the newspaper. Her face behind piles of pink and powder, her large round sunglasses covered her eyes. Securely on her head, a wide rim straw hat hid her hair; she pulled it down as low as she could. Wide hats and dark sunglasses made most women indistinguishable from each other. Her clothes might make her ugly to anyone who thought the woman in the newspaper was pretty, and make her pretty to anyone who thought the newspaper woman was ugly. Over her shoulder was her handbag.

Pretending the day was two weeks earlier, Jessica opened the front door of her home. The day was warm, as she stepped onto the mat outside her house, turned, and closed and locked the door.

Passing through the open gate, two middle-aged women across the road saw Jessica, hurriedly looked at each other, and looked away. People might've been warier of her than she feared them.

Under her straw hat and behind her sunglasses, Jessica walked with tacit anonymity away from Bank Street; Saturdays in Molong could be busy with weekend visitors. Watching the few people she passed, she could not forget herself.

She knocked on the door of her school friend Agatha's home in Phillip Street. It opened to Agatha's cheerful voice. "Hello!"

"Hello, Agatha."

All cheerfulness fell from Agatha's face. "Oh," said Agatha. "I wasn't expecting to see you."

"Why not?"

"No reason."

"Can we do something today, my treat?"

"I can't," said Agatha.

"What's up?"

"Nothing, I just can't. I can't get involved."

"Agatha!" said Jessica, as the door closed in front of her.

In Gwyn's home in Thistle Street, a curtain moved beyond a window, but no one answered the door. Gwyn's cat might've brushed past the window.

Eric and Polly lived in Kite Street, where Eric answered the door. "We're busy today," he told Jessica.

"Can I see you tonight?"

"We'll be busy, for a while, a long while."

"Is that because of the newspaper?" asked Jessica.

He stepped back. "I better go," said Eric, closing the door before Jessica could say anything more.

Weary of uneasy smiles in broken conversations, all Jessica's deliberations but one dissolved in the fantasies they were. There wasn't any reason why she should have recalled Eugene Gallagher's address from her conversation with the reverend, except that she happened to be in the quiet end of Hill Street, where the houses were few and grasses thick, and Ellerslie

Cottage was the sort of name that stayed in people's minds. She needed to do something with the story in her head.

Red corrugated-iron roofs covered not just the century-old cottage and surrounding veranda, but a well. Eugene had surprised everyone by applying and being accepted to study economics at Sydney University; Jessica remembered sitting in the audience at a special assembly at Molong Central School, which even the mayor attended. (By the time Jessica qualified to study biology at the Australian National University a few years later, the town had become complacent, although the *Molong Express* said kind words about her. The mayor congratulated her in his offices and soon forgot he had.)

In one instant of abandon, his parents said, Eugene contracted the virus too rarely mentioned. It developed in his blood, eroding his natural immunities and making him increasingly susceptible to ailments that didn't trouble other people. Some people who left Molong came back to live, but Eugene came back home to die.

The virus killing Eugene could kill anyone it infected. If Jessica cut herself on a loose nail on which he'd cut himself and left a trace of infected blood, then she might also die. If he hated her as other people hated her, he might wilfully infect her. His killing her might make him a hero among people who'd shunned him, but they would continue to shun him. Her thoughts were ludicrous, but everything had been ludicrous since her lunch in the Pickled Pepper Café.

The gate in the front fence creaked as Jessica pushed it open. It creaked again when she closed it after her. The weatherboard walls had been recently steam cleaned. Under the veranda roof, she needed her hat and sunglasses only to hide her face.

Green plants bloomed from pots beside the front door, concealed by a screen door she pulled open. Jessica knocked, but not too loudly, on the wooden door. In the door were tall thin panes of glass, but she was too polite to try to peer through them. She closed the screen door.

Jessica wondered whether to knock again, or leave, when a shadow moved across the glass. The door handle turned and door opened a short way, just enough for her to see through the screen a man's eyes studying her; his caution was the same as hers would be. "Hello," he said.

"Reverend Underly thought you might like a visitor."

His voice was slow. "Why would he think that?"

"He said you don't get many."

"Why would he say that to you?"

"He thought I might want somewhere to go."

"You're too young to be from the women's church fellowship."

Far from other people, Jessica removed her hat and sunglasses, always watching the eye through the doorway. She loosened her blonde hair with her fingers.

"You look better than your photograph," he said. "What would the neighbours say to see you outside my humble hospice?" He pulled open the door.

Through the screen door, Eugene Gallagher's drawn face unsettled her, but she didn't flinch for fear of offending him. He appeared much older than his age made him, while her good health made her uncomfortable before him. His cotton shirt, denim jeans, and sneakers were by the by.

"On melancholy mornings, I languish in my pyjamas and a dressing gown," he told her, "but if I don't dress each day, I can't feel progression from the night. I then can't tell when another night has come."

She again opened the screen door and stepped into his funeral home. Eugene closed both doors after her.

His lounge room was clean and comfortable, as hospital beds should be, but untidy. A long sofa lounge served as a bed, with a thick white pillow at one end and white cotton sheets and woollen blankets. "We keep the drugs and other medicines in a drawer in my bedroom, where my parents don't always need to see them, but I make this room look sickly so the white-collar priest and a parade of frightened doctors and passing nurses all feel needed."

Jessica stood in the sick bed of his home, holding her hat and sunglasses. If she offered him anything, then she offered him a day to spend differently to every other day.

A television set was playing without sound. Eugene stepped

slowly towards a low glass and timber-framed table by the sofa, picked up the remote control handset, and switched it off.

Her gaze caught a painting on the wall of a portrait in oils of Eugene as a boy. He'd been the innocent, with the cheerful white cheeks and softened smile of a cherub. "The only child and heir of both his parents' families," said Eugene, as if the painting were anyone but him. "The little prince should've lived forever, always to be his parents' joy, but soon they'll bury him, and wonder what they'll do with their big, empty house."

"I shouldn't have come."

Eugene picked up from the table a plate of several white bread sandwiches cut into quarters, which he offered to Jessica. "Do you like salami, cheese, or tomato? My parents are out now, they're always out, but my mother makes too many sandwiches."

Jessica looked hesitantly at the plate. She dared not ingest what a dying man had touched.

"I won't catch anything," he assured her, almost smiling in a joke at the expense of both of them.

"I'm sorry," she said. She held her hat and sunglasses in one hand, uncertain what to do with them, and took a sandwich with her other hand.

"It's an occupational risk, for me. Sit down."

Jessica sat in a chair for one, beside which she placed her hat, handbag, and sunglasses on the floor. Eugene sat on his unmade bed as if it were still a sofa.

"I've nothing more to do in my cosy little cemetery but die," he said, looking around them. "My mother cleans everything thoroughly each day, fearing the microscopic germ or bacteria that would kill her weakened son. My parents sometimes talk to me, but they're wasting their time and mine trying to amuse me, when nothing they say will. We've long exhausted anything to say, since we can't talk about the sorrows in our heads."

Jessica remained content to listen, to hear him talk about anyone but her, to study the man who would be dead. He talked without engaging her, his sounding board, without giving her the chance to talk about her pains and problems. Slowly she stopped wanting to mention them.

"We bide our time we wish could last forever and wish had never started," Eugene continued, "so my parents confine their times at home to another family room. They see their friends in restaurants for conversations they would've made if I were never sick. I read books when my concentration is most kind, but my mind soon falls away, so I have television and radio blurred into sameness, now."

Jessica was slow to realise he had finished. She looked back at the food in her hands. "The sandwich is very nice," she said.

"You've become a celebrity," Eugene told her.

"I liked being nobody."

"So did I."

"People like you," said Jessica.

"They like the *cause célèbre*, but I'm as much in exile as you are."

"They hate me."

"They say they hate you because they're frightened of being seen not to hate you. Defending themselves from what other people think, they're desperate to assure each other they're not like you. They don't think about me enough to hate me."

"They care about you," she said. "All those tins raise money for medical research because of you."

"They convince themselves they're righteous for popping a few coins and notes into a slot," he said, as angrily as the virus allowed him to be, "but they never invite me anywhere. Company means more to me than care."

"People worry about catching the virus."

"I won't kiss anyone, or share needles with people shooting up behind the stage. People will never say it, but the only way to be anything more than a curiosity, a moment of entertainment in a passing conversation, is to be like everyone else. My virus is the charity, not me. I'm a nothing person."

"I wish I were," said Jessica, turning her head away.

"People who were my school friends see my parents in the town and ask them how I'm faring, but they don't ask me. My father obtained a friend's business card with his electronic mail address and we exchanged some words through our computers for sixteen days, until I asked him to visit me. He told me he could pretend I was still healthy through our messages on his monitor, but he couldn't continue the pretence if he saw me. He was very nice about it, but he parties while I sit here alone.

"The person of whom I feel most disappointed is Tilly Peyton: my only girlfriend at school. She doesn't acknowledge my parents when they see her. She's married now, which is good for her, but one moment of her time would cost her nothing, and help me more than any doctor helps me now. I know she'd see me if I were only sick but would recover, but she won't see anybody dying."

"The reverend visits you."

"Dying people too young to die are the lepers of our age, although neither the living nor the lepers will admit it. I help the reverend return to his Biblical roots, when little else about his ministry reflects them. We talk about my life, his life, and other lives. He tries to turn me to his faith, and I joust with him. I might be the only person who talks with him without agreeing with him, and he enjoys it. He knows I won't tell people what he's saying."

Listening to him there, Jessica realised how important listening could be. She didn't understand his situation, but hadn't lied to say she did.

"Sometimes," continued Eugene, "I hope the reverend succeeds in his arguments with me, convincing me to paradise. Lifetimes are a luxury for people who'll still be here tomorrow. Eternity means more to people approaching death. Most often we just talk. We talked about you this week; I can't recall which day. We'll talk about you this coming week."

"I hope what you say is kind."

"The reverend says nice things about everybody."

"He said them about you."

Eugene smiled, for the first time in her company. If he'd assumed a gentle rebuke in her words she'd not intended it. "You're my chance to say aloud majestic words I've been thinking every day but nobody can hear; the reverend, he doesn't count, not when he's heard so many other dying people. I'm not yet willing to talk aloud without somebody to hear me, but I imagine I will before I die." Eugene dipped his head. "I sound like I'm drunk, don't I?"

Jessica became lost again whenever he stopped talking. She watched, waiting for him.

"Would you like to play?" asked Eugene, standing up.

She stared dumbfounded at him. Jessica remained in her chair; he was surely joking.

"We'll wear gloves," he told her, "so you don't make me sick."

For several more moments she stared, before cautiously nodding. She stood up before him.

Eugene removed from a drawer a box much like a box of tissues, but from which he pulled a pair of surgical gloves he placed on his hands. He gave her a pair of gloves she placed on her hands.

"Thank you for not offering to lead," he said to her, as they stood before each other. "Do you know scissors, paper, rock?"

Jessica again stared dumbfounded. Slowly, she raised her right arm.

"Scissors," said Eugene, raising his right arm and dragging it down. Jessica dragged hers down, before they raised them in tandem. "Paper," he said, as they brought down their gloved hands in unison. Again, they raised them and pulled them down. "Rock."

Jessica's fingers formed scissors. Eugene's fist formed a rock. "Rock blunts scissors," admitted Jessica, edging her fingers near his.

"My parents treat me like I'm an invalid," said Eugene, "but I'm not. I'm dying."

She'd forgotten that he was. He could make his fate seem glib.

Eugene raised his hand again, so Jessica did. "Scissors," he said, repeating the game. Their hands came down. "Paper." Their hands rose again. "Rock."

Jessica's hand formed paper. Eugene's fingers formed scissors. "Scissors cut paper," admitted Jessica, reaching her hand near his.

"Why did you come?" asked Eugene.

"Reverend Underly thought you could teach me something…"

"…about being an outcast?"

"...about being alone."

They played the game a third time. Jessica's hand again formed paper. Eugene's fist formed a rock.

"Paper covers rock," said Jessica, placing her gloved hand above his gloved fist. It hovered there, before she placed her hand on his.

"My parents showed me the newspaper articles about you," said Eugene, stepping back, their arms falling to their sides. "It was their way of telling me that someone is worse off than I am, but you're not worse off, are you? You're the bane of the town, but you're not about to die."

"Would you prefer me to die?"

He removed the gloves from his hands and dropped them to the floor. She removed hers and placed them on a table. "I'll become weaker," said Eugene. "This body will become like a corpse awaiting cremation. The problems you think you have are luxuries for people alive."

"I can only deal with problems I've got."

"I disagree with you, about what you said in the newspaper."

Jessica shrugged her shoulders. "Do you hate me?"

"I don't care enough what people think of me to hate you."

"Thank you," smiled Jessica.

"That doesn't mean I like you." He sat down on his sofa bed while she remained standing. "Would you be here now if it weren't for all your problems?"

Her answer shamed her, but she was trying to be truthful. "There's nothing else left for me in Molong," she said.

"I can't give you what you're seeking."

"You already have."

"Where will you go?"

"If I'm not welcome in my country, then I'm not welcome anywhere."

"You're very pretty," said Eugene, leaning to the side along his sofa bed. His eyes never left their train upon her, as he lifted up his legs onto the cushion and placed his head against a pillow. He lay there, in his clothes, pulling a white sheet across him as he would in bed. "I wonder what people would think if they gave themselves a chance. Time is mine to opine about anything I want, dying in the house to which I was born."

"Will you tell your parents I was here?"

"I'll hide your gloves among the rubbish."

He began to smile. That was reason enough for Jessica to smile. "We're partners in isolation, aren't we?" she said.

"No," he answered. "I'm ogling you."

Jessica lowered herself to the floor. She collected her handbag and returned her sunglasses to her eyes and hat to her head. "I should go."

21

THE MOB

Before the sun had set, the bars along Bank Street were already busy. In the Telegraph Hotel, burly Stig Ronson, lanky Neville Hayes, and red-haired Cody Allchin stood where they stood most Saturday nights. More than a year had passed since each of their eighteenth birthdays, when in turn they'd first proudly showed their driving licences to bartenders. For days and weeks thereafter, they'd been keen as patrons much older to be asked to produce their proofs of age. Their frayed bush hats, torn flannelette shirts, and faded denim jeans of labouring days gave way to their newest checked flannelette shirts and dark blue denim jeans on Saturday evenings, when their hair was combed and faces shaven. In their hands were schooner glasses of cold draught beer.

Hannah and her friends wore open-necked blouses and leather skirts even shorter than those they'd worn at school. "We're going to Orange," she told Stig.

"That's boring," replied Stig. "We're fun."

Hannah looked at her friends. Neville had been involved with Hannah's older sister for more than four months, before she moved to Dubbo. Stig had never had a girlfriend, in spite of all the conversations he'd foisted upon Hannah, her friends, and every other woman with whom he'd been at school. Cody just wanted to play.

"We'll see you boys another time," said Hannah, as they left.

"Ohh," groaned Stig.

Neville brought three more glasses of beer to the table, while Stig and Cody looked around the bar for women they knew or wanted to know. The only women there were among men.

"We've struck out," said Cody, "again."

"Not yet," said Stig. "We've got wallets of money, good looks, and women waiting for us."

"You've been drinking too much," said Neville.

"You can't drink *too much*," replied Stig, slapping him on the shoulder.

"We could see what the talent's like at Freemasons," said Cody.

"When we've finished these drinks," said Stig, raising his glass.

Their glasses soon emptied, Stig, Neville, and Cody wandered outside, where the sounds from the bars permeated the street. The three young men swaggered along the footpath to Freemasons Hotel. "Your shout, Codes," Stig told him.

Stig led Neville to three women from the year ahead of them at school, sitting at a table with their legs crossed and short skirts exposing their pale knees. "Great to see you," said Stig, pulling up a chair to join them.

"Hello, Stig," sighed Melinda, her long hair brushed into a life of its own. She looked up at Neville. "Hi, Neville."

Janice turned her shoulder away from Stig, resting her glass of wine on her lap. Cody brought Stig and Neville their next glasses of beer. Erin watched silently.

"Do you mind if we join you?" asked Stig.

"You already have," replied Melinda.

Neville tapped Stig's arm. "Let's sit somewhere else, Stig."

"Why?"

"Come on, Stig."

Stig turned to the women. "We'll all sit at a larger table."

"We have to go," Melinda told him.

"We could have one drink," persisted Stig.

Melinda looked at her friends. They remained silent.

"We'll get another table," said Neville, taking Stig by the arm. Neville turned to the women. "You're welcome to join us if you want to."

"We'll be there," said Stig, pointing his long burly arm at another table, no bigger than the one from which Neville was dragging him away. "Why didn't you want us to stay?" he asked Neville.

"They didn't want us there."

"Yes, they did."

The three men drank their beer, with Stig watching the women they'd left behind. "I think Janice likes you," Stig told Neville.

"We don't want to upset her and her friends."

"Coward!" said Stig, who took a long drink of beer to ignore him. When he looked back again, Melinda and her friends had gone. "What the...?" he cried out, starting to stand. Neville held him down. "Now what do we do?"

"We could go to the RSL," said Cody.

"And get more of the same?" said Neville. "Can we find a party somewhere?"

"We'll walk around listening for music," said Cody.

"We'll drive," said Stig. "We'll get back to the pubs sooner."

Their drinks finished, the three men stumbled back to the footpath. With night settling and street lights shining, Stig's gaze fell between empty shops to the Wing Hang restaurant.

"I hate Chinese food," said Neville.

Stig turned to his friends. "I know who might be home, dateless," he smiled, "the woman in the newspaper."

"Let's watch a movie," said Cody, "or football."

"It'll be hilarious," Stig insisted. "What's her name?"

"What would we do if we found her?" asked Neville.

"Laugh," said Stig. "We can make it up as we go along."

"Are you sure you want to do this?" asked Cody.

"She might breathe fire on us," said Stig, waving his fingers in the air like a warlock, "or bake us in her oven."

"I am curious to know what she's like," said Neville.

"What can we lose?" asked Stig. "Nobody cares what people

say to her. Worst thing happens, we get bored, and then watch a movie or football."

Neville and Cody looked at each other. Neither spoke.

"What's her name?" asked Stig.

"Jessica Rawlins," replied Cody.

"That was it," said Stig. "Who knows where she lives?"

"She mentored my sister," said Cody.

"Codes!" said Stig, hugging him.

"My sister really liked her. She was good to her."

"So?" retorted Stig. "Your sister's not you."

"I don't know if I should tell you where she lives."

Stig persisted, as Stig did. "We'll have some harmless fun."

Cody looked at Neville, who looked silently back at him. "She lives in the old hall," said Cody, "on Edward Street."

"Let's see whitey-whitey," declared Stig in a mock staccato.

Stig led them up Bank Street, Neville and Cody hurrying to keep up. Stig turned into darker Edward Street and quickened his pace still more. A light shone and music played from inside the old Molong Hall, but the gates across the driveway and pedestrian path were closed. Stig pushed at the gates but they held fast. He then thrust his hand through the opening in the smaller gate, released the latch, and threw it open.

Stig strode up to the front door alcove where he thumped on the solid double doors, before spinning around. His spectators, Neville and Cody, stood outside the open gate.

The music inside the house ceased. One door opened a short way, revealing the face from the front page of the newspaper.

"We thought you'd be alone," said Stig. "Nobody wants to see you tonight, huh?"

Neville and Cody giggled, as Jessica started to close the door. Stig threw his hands towards the door to keep it open, but the door closed and bolt caught in its lock before his hands hit the door. "Psycho!" he screamed, "who you going to pick on now?"

"Let's go," Neville called to Stig.

"Who's going to defend *her*?" asked Stig. "Who's going to punish us fighting intolerance?"

"She's not worth it," said Neville.

"She's not worth anything!" screamed Stig. "Come on out

of your Ku Klux Klan country club, you cowardly creep!" He clenched his fist and punched it against the doors. "Let's hear your tough words now, lady!"

Jessica screamed loud through her home, but not so loud to the world. Neville started to laugh.

"Got a speech to make, fascist?" screamed Stig. "The rally is here!" He again faced his friends. "I told you this would be fun."

Stig turned back to the doors. "Hey, little piggy with your swastikas and jackboots," he called, riding with the wind behind him. "It's the big, bad wolf, and I'm going to huff, and puff, and blow your house down!" Stig reached out his arms wanting to push apart the walls of the alcove, his chest up and out. He then spun around and again punched the doors.

The doors shook and Jessica jumped. The rear doors through which she could flee were also those through which the mob could come.

Neville and Cody continued to laugh when suddenly, Stig stopped. "Aw," he moaned, "I'm sorry, Jessica." He ran his hands across the door, caressing it. "Can I have a kiss?"

Stig kicked his boots against the door as violently as he could. "It's you I want to kick, bigot," he screamed. "Where's your love, bitch? Where's your compassion, bitch?"

Jessica screamed for him to stop. Cody clapped at the spectacle. Neville clapped louder.

"Nazi! Nazi! Nazi!" screamed Stig. "Die! Die! Die!"

Jessica screamed and screamed for anyone to help her, but her screams weren't saving her. Nobody was coming.

Stig leapt down from the alcove and towards a front window. He thumped the steel mesh over the glass. Jessica screamed again. "You don't take it as well as you give it, do you, dog?" he screamed.

At a brightly lit window of an adjoining home, a man stood watching. Stig waved at him. The man stepped out of sight, drew his curtains closed, and switched off the light.

Trees obscured the lights of other homes, but Stig saw a man and woman standing outside one house watching the commotion. The woman touched the man, said something, and they hurried back into their home. Thick curtains already covered their windows, but a low corner of one moved enough to reveal a moment or two of light, before what must've been a face obscured it. Stig raised his arm high in the air. The curtain closed again.

Outside Jessica's home, small white stones formed a reckless little path. Neville collected several stones in his hands, and threw them at a window. "Whoa!" he cried out.

Slipped down behind the door into a crumbled heap on the floor, Jessica gasped, awaiting the next assault. The hatred that bore down upon her might've come to hurt or kill her; she couldn't know. She seized her quivering arms and legs, ready to run. Panting for breath, she tried to still her thumping heart to hear what voices, footsteps, or other hints of a looming battering lurked outside, planning something; the silence was no less threatening than noise had been.

Taking advantage of the lull, Jessica scrambled across her wooden floor. She quickly dialled her telephone.

"Emergency," answered a woman.

"Help me," whispered Jessica. "I'm being attacked."

"You're Jessica Rawlins, calling from thirty-three Edward Street, Molong?"

"Yes. Please come quickly."

"I'll alert the police. Do you need an ambulance?"

"They're going to kill me," she begged. "Please, come quickly."

"You may hold the line." Jessica gripped the telephone with both her hands too fiercely to let it go.

Outside the gate, holding more stones in their hands, Stig, Neville, and Cody stood watching three on-comers walking towards them. A middle-aged woman's arms rested through the arms of a taller middle-aged man and taller-still sinewy young man beside her. "Owen Masterton," exclaimed Stig.

"Hello Stig," replied the young man, "Neville, Cody."

"Why aren't you in Sydney at university?"

"I'm home for the weekend."

Owen and his parents stopped walking when they reached Neville, Cody, and Stig. Their arms fell apart.

"What's happening, lads?" asked Owen's father.

"It's the home of the racist," said Stig. "I think she's a bit mad."

Owen's parents resumed their journey. "You come when you're ready, lad," said his father.

"Is she in there?" Owen asked his friends.

"Scared like a rat," said Stig.

"I wish I'd known," said Owen, raising his voice for the racist to hear. "We could've prepared banners like *'Kill the Fascists'*."

Neville laughed. Stig and then the others showed Owen the stones in their hands.

"We can do better than that," said Owen, looking around. He found two large rocks he picked up. "Jeez, I hate white people."

His strong hand ready to throw, Owen stepped through the open gate towards the house, quickening his pace. Veering towards the brighter window, he hurled the rock. It struck the mesh across the glass and bounced away.

Again, Jessica screamed. Gathered at the open gate, Stig, Neville, and Cody laughed.

Owen took his second rock in his strong hand and surveyed the house. The only window not covered by mesh was a half-circle above the front door. He stepped back for space, then ran up and, more carefully than he'd aimed the first time, threw the missile rock towards it.

The window smashed apart in a glass explosion, jettisoning jagged knives. Jessica screamed hysterically, the open air making her all the more audible outside, as cut glass sprayed over her. The rock thumped on the small floor too close to her, bouncing a few times before settling by the skirting. "Please," she wept.

Stig, Neville, and Cody cheered. In answer to their applause, Owen turned and bowed. "This is great!"

Stig, Neville, and Cody threw their handfuls of white bullet stones towards the broken glass and window, with enough of them passing through the hole to spray shrapnel over her. She screamed again, a tiny beaten scream not expecting anything to come of it, while the boys as men laughed.

"We need boulders," said Cody.

The four men rushed back to the roadside, where they

collected the largest rocks they could hold, until the bright headlights of a police car with its flashing blue light shone upon them. Dropping the rocks to the ground, they slowly stood upright.

The police car stopped in front of them. Sergeant Vaughan stepped out. "What's she said now?"

"We're defending diversity," said Owen. "Stig told me she's a racist."

"Did you see the *Molong Express*?" asked the sergeant.

"I don't read newspapers."

The others remained silent, until the sergeant targeted his eyes upon them. "Stig did try to talk to her," said Neville.

"We all tried to talk to her," said Owen.

The sergeant focused his eyes upon Cody. "How do you reason with someone like that?" asked Cody.

"Wait here, boys," the sergeant told them. He baulked a little to see the broken window above the front door, before proceeding towards the house. "Ms Rawlins," he said loudly, before knocking on the door. "Sergeant Vaughan."

The door remained closed.

"Ms Rawlins," he called again.

The door slowly opened. Jessica appeared, shaking. Falling forward, she collapsed crying uncontrollably into the sergeant's broad blue bulbous chest.

His duty was to stand there while she leant upon him. The sergeant did his duty.

"Why?" she strained to ask.

"You're a fascist," yelled Owen.

"Not so loud," the sergeant told him, turning as best he could with Jessica leaning against his chest, not letting her fall. "Go home, boys."

"Go home?" said Jessica, lifting herself from the sergeant's chest. "They could've killed me."

"I didn't arrest you when people wanted me to. You should feel fortunate about that."

"Fortunate?" said Jessica, stepping away from him. "I don't feel fortunate about anything."

"If I charge them, then I'll have to charge you. You did provoke them."

Jessica turned towards the faces of the four, before stumbling back inside. The soles of her shoes collected slivers she couldn't see as she stepped around the stones and largest pieces of glass and fell into the sofa, shielded from the eyes of giants coming close and looking through the gaping hole and broken window.

She lay huddled there, gazing into the haze where her home had been, away from sight and harm. Her legs folded close to her chest, her face pressed against a cushion and her slacks-covered knees. She'd become weary of weeping, but still quivered, becoming cold. The street people who would've killed her were her neighbours in the town, young enough to have been students at school with her.

The sergeant followed her into the room, leaving the door open behind him. He picked up the telephone handset and replaced it on the receiver. Collecting the rock and some stones from the floor, he returned outside.

Through the open gate to the street, the four remained. "You shouldn't have done what you did tonight, boys," he told them.

"If the police aren't going to deal with fascists," replied Owen, "what else can we do?"

"Do you know what a fascist is?" asked the sergeant.

The boys were silent, before Stig ventured a guess. "A person who judges people by their faces?"

"If I'd arrested her," asked the sergeant, "would you have come?"

"You could've come with us," retorted Owen. "You could've thrown the biggest rock."

"Please, all of you," said the sergeant. "Do you want me to tell your parents what you've done?"

"I'm telling my parents," said Owen. "I can't wait."

"I can keep her from pressing charges..."

"We're the ones who should press charges," insisted Owen, "for all the offence she caused."

"She's a Nazi," said Neville.

"Do you know what a Nazi was?" asked the sergeant.

Neville fell silent, before cautiously answering. "It's like nasty?"

"Do any of you know what a racist is?"

"Someone who doesn't want immigration," said Stig.

"Run along, boys," the sergeant told them.

The young men looked between themselves. Neville nodded. Cody nodded. Owen sulked, but finally nodded. "Do you want a beer at the pub?" asked Stig.

"Don't drink too much, any of you," the sergeant told them. He dropped the rock and stones from his hands at the edge of the road, among the other rocks and stones. He then walked back through the gate and up into the house.

Jessica lay huddled in the sofa. "Who were they?" she asked him.

"They won't come back. I spoke to them."

"That was all you did?"

"Did you want me to give them official cautions?"

"This wasn't an argument you missed tonight. It was assault."

The sergeant looked around the room. "If you have a dustpan and broom, I can tidy the floor."

"You know, they'll soon be in a bar boasting of my broken window as a trophy. People constrained from all other hatreds are free to hate and harm me."

She gave him time to answer. He didn't.

"Will you be making a report about tonight?"

"Your call to emergency services was logged."

"A small record in remembrance of me?" she muttered. "I should thank you for saving my life, but will you protect me tomorrow night?"

"You could help yourself."

Jessica looked up at him; weary of the fault he laid upon her. "My life would be easier if I was like the people hating me," she said, "but I could never be like them. Hating people for what they do I can understand, but not for what we think or feel. Only people unable to recourse with words resort to weapons. The responses to weaponry might need to be weaponry, but the responses to words should always be words, no matter how right or wrong, inspirational or insidious, noble or malicious.

The fighter acknowledges that words have no answer when he resorts to his sword.

"If I start to believe what people say, then I'll think their opinions about me matter. My opinions don't matter, except to me, because someone thinks they matter. What strangers think of me is none of my concern, only what they do. I would rather a hundred men hate me without touching me than one man try to hurt me, whatever he thinks of me. Judgements matter when people act upon them."

"Apologise for what you said, Jessica. Say you didn't mean it. Say you were wrong."

"Do you know what I said, Sergeant?"

"You offended a great many people."

She laughed, just a little. "That, I seem to have done, and for that, I could be dead."

The ensuing silence conceded that neither Jessica nor the sergeant could make the other understand. If she couldn't save him from his ignorance, then neither could he save her from hers.

Jessica stretched her legs and forced her feet from the sofa to the floor, where speckles of shattered glass lay like drops of silver sweat among the sprinkled gravel. Holding her arms across her chest, she stood up.

Floorboards creaked as she moved meekly past the sergeant to the open door, waiting for the sergeant to depart. The man doing his duty at the far end of a conversation could only read the lesson to her eulogy. He couldn't bring her back from the dead.

Sergeant Vaughan stepped forward and into the open door about to leave, when he paused and turned towards her. "Will you at least *consider* apologising, Ms Rawlins?"

She didn't face him. "Will you at least consider how trivial my remark in conservation was?"

22

THE PARIAH IN A BROKEN GOLDFISH BOWL

After Sergeant Vaughan departed, Jessica closed and deadlocked the door as small protection. Floorboards again creaked as she stepped cautiously towards a lounge room window.

Through the mesh, beyond the light and dark, more people might be standing in the street. She could try to see them, but her trepidation might inspire them to come again to hurt her. They could take all her money if they wouldn't touch her.

In her last fight for life, she could face her enemy more easily if it had a face but it had a thousand faces. It had no face at all.

Jessica closed the brittle blinds and fastened shut all the remaining windows of the house. She couldn't close the battered glass above the door.

She then huddled in her armchair, grappling for a thought where there was none. Street lights cast what looked like horizontal prison bars through the gaps between the blinds.

The broken window was a pattern she couldn't quite discern above the door, through which small sounds trickled from the town that didn't want her. The jagged glass might cut and fend intruders away. It might not.

People could be outside waiting for her. She pulled her feet up onto the cushion close to her, leant her head against her knees, and was alone.

The long night was slow to pass. The lights still shining made it slower. They shone on broken glass, scattered on her once precious coffee table and floor around it. She might be sitting on some more.

The town became quiet since last she noticed it, but for the sound of her slow breathing. The silence was nearer to being tolerable than any noise had been.

Jessica kept herself awake with nightmares she couldn't separate from fears and thoughts of fears: barking wolves tearing at the walls. Her mind stumbled over images of people clamouring to kill her. The images stumbled back again.

Sometime she must've slept a little, but if she did she woke again uncertain that she had. If hers were dreams, they were those of a little piglet running from the wolves, in the nightmare of her nights.

The light of Sunday morning was small security; the sun through later summer rose a little lower every morning. The air was warm without being hot, as outside was. Days would cool when autumn came; autumns the world over could make towns without seasons seem neither one season nor the other.

Still wearing her crumpled clothes of yesterday, her blonde hair ragged on her head, Jessica sat there much too early and too late. Moving slowly in the motion of a wake, she rose, and extinguished electric light.

The broken glass and gravel strewn across the floor reflected the terror of the night; the sergeant had removed only the worst of it. Jessica opened the cupboard in the laundry and pulled out a small hand broom and dustpan, her slow chore distracting her fraying nerves from everything inside her mind.

The *Molong Express* newspaper from the week before last lay beneath the laundry sink where she'd left it. Jessica laid it on the lounge room floor and knelt beside it. The largest cuts of glass she carefully picked up and lay on it: that first picture and article about her. Smaller pieces and gravel, she brushed into the pan, which she tipped onto the picture of her stupid smiling face.

Slivers of glass, reflecting daylight from above the door and through window blinds, threatened to remain. Tentatively she crawled around the polished floor, stopping at each reflection, carefully collecting it on her fingertip and leaving it on the newspaper. She rested her slack-covered knee against a patch of floor she knew was clean, while she persevered.

Striving to remove every trace of anything that hurt her, Jessica checked the floor again and found another sliver. She cleaned the coffee table. She found some slivers in the sofa. Gingerly, she folded the newspaper into a package, burying the rubble in the image of her silly face inside it.

She'd leave the myriad of pointed shapes of broken glass above the door to a glazier she'd find on Monday morning: another chore to undertake and expense she could ill afford. Among the stationery she'd brought home from university was a roll of adhesive plastic tape, plastic sleeves for holding sheets of paper, and pair of sharp metal scissors. Joining the plastic sleeves to the remaining glass and pane, Jessica completely covered the hole. Using the scissors as a small hammer, she struck tacks through the tape and plastic sleeve into the wood, keeping out the weather as best she could.

The telephone rang. Jessica looked timidly at it, lying noisily on the floor. The person dialling might've meant to dial a different number. The caller might be Bede. The call might bring her bad news, although she couldn't see what bad news remained.

Jessica picked up the handset. The caller had gone.

She dialled the number of Bede's home in Orange. The telephone answered and Jessica started to speak, but Bede's recorded voice spoke through her earpiece first. "G'day, everyone," he said, in cheerful ignorance. "Bede, Gemma, and the little person are away from the telephone at the moment, but we really want to speak with you, so please leave us a message after the tone. Bye, for now." Bede and his wife always left their telephone answering machine activated, and listened to the voice of the person telephoning before deciding whether to pick up the handset.

The tone sounded. "It's I, Jess," she whimpered.

She waited. Bede didn't pick up the telephone.

"I hope everything is fine for both of you. I'm sure it is. Things go well for you, but I had some trouble with the mayor and worse trouble since then. I love you both, all three of you."

She dialled the number of his mobile telephone. Her call diverted to his home. "G'day, everyone," her brother's happy voice said again. Jessica ended the connection.

Beside her silent telephone, Jessica's diary lay fruitlessly. Her friends from university had returned to their hometowns. Had they eaten with her at the Pickled Pepper Café, they might've argued with her, or asked her to explain, but Jessica could no longer presume their friendships would survive disagreements. She wouldn't test her final friends by calling them.

The room light became more muted. Staying out of sight from anybody watching, Jessica pinched a strip of blind with each of her hands. Ever so carefully, she opened them just enough to peer outside, where high white clouds and low dark storm clouds tussled for possession of the sky. Jessica wondered which clouds would prevail, above the town of twilight and a cloudy day.

Few cars drove along Edward Street so early Sunday morning. Nobody tall enough appeared above the fence. The gates were closed, without padlocks.

Carrying the newspaper bundle of broken refuse to her garbage bin, the air outside was colder and damper than inside, but more tranquil than her home had become. Watching her was a neighbour at whom Jessica almost smiled, but there wasn't any point. He stood motionless, as her fingers struggled to grip the garbage bin lid while her arms held her bundle. He watched her place the bundle on the ground, open the lid, place the bundle in the bin, close the lid, and walk back to her house, where she closed and locked the door.

Eating sparingly, Jessica felt a little better for the sweet stewed apricots inside her. A knock came through the doors.

"Jessica," spoke a voice, not too loud, "Charlie Quinn."

She remained completely still. Any comment she made to him would be the next stupid thing she said.

"The boys told me what happened last night," said Charlie. "They say they tried to discuss your points of view, but you screamed at them and slammed the door at them. They said they broke the window trying to make you understand the need for tolerance." With his every word, Jessica sunk further in her skin. "I want to hear your perspective." It was all perspective.

The doors were silent for a minute, before she heard the sound of footsteps leaving. At the window, she again carefully pulled apart the blinds just far enough to peek. Charlie stood at the open gate, with his camera lens pointed up at the broken window.

Beyond the open gate, an elderly passer-by stopped. Wearing a black hat, he stood staring at the setting of her terror; it wasn't broken yesterday. Two black Scottish terrier dogs on their leashes scurried about him, rubbing their noses at the stones on the ground.

Charlie closed the gate when he departed. The man opened it again.

He didn't seem to see Jessica watching him. He mightn't have cared if he had, or might've thrown more rocks. Again, she'd be the target in a sideshow game walking back and forth across the room. In that place to hide where everyone could see her, Jessica wouldn't step outside again that darkening day.

More voyeurs came to gaze through the open gate, some apparently by chance and others for the purpose. Lovers holding hands paused to see. Four men and women set chairs and a wooden table by the footpath, from which they ate sandwiches. One caught a glimpse of Jessica at the window and pointed her out to her friends. None of them approached Jessica's door.

She tried to think of places she could go where nobody would notice her: places without people, or with people disregarding her, not touching her. She often checked the time. Too little of the day and too much of another night remained.

Watching the blinds darken, Jessica waited for the rain. Thunder resounded from black clouds exploding in a summer storm, louder than any storm she'd previously experienced. Rain outside once made Jessica feel cosy in a home, but every gust of wind blew more broken window water against her flimsy cover, patting the floor inside the door. Her broken home became cold and damp, inside her tiny chair.

Pushed under the front door appeared a long white envelope;

surely nobody hated anyone enough to brave such a storm to venture out and kill her. Jessica picked it up and opened it, in the bad light of a dark day. She removed from it a letter signed by Derek, on behalf of Mister and Mrs Cadwallader, formally demanding she leave the house within a week.

Jessica pulled open the door, where the storm roared louder than it had inside. Derek under his black umbrella was about to close the gate when he saw her. He stepped back up to the alcove and stood before her, out of the worst of the pouring rain. "I'm sorry, Jess," he yelled, above the screaming storm behind him, "but they're the instructions the Cadwalladers gave me. I can't give you any reasons, and I can't do anything about it."

"The Cadwalladers can fix their own stupid window," yelled Jessica, before slamming the door shut. The Cadwalladers would withhold the costs of repairing the window from the bond that Jessica deposited when she signed the lease.

Jessica slid downwards, soon lying on the floor. That squalid, darkening space was her shelter from the storm, but those fragile walls would soon dissolve in the encroaching rain. The Cadwalladers had no faces to keep Jessica from hating them, except that names on a notice to evict were difficult to hate. Her final eviction was in written form: confirmation of her execution of which she'd already heard. She'd already felt too much to feel much more.

She should try to get a job, but nobody would employ her. She should try to find a home, but nobody would accommodate her. Owners of other homes to rent would care or know somebody who cared about their reputation. They would refuse the wicked woman's application to live there, without giving any reason why they did.

Jessica was most vulnerable where everyone could find her. Lying there was wasting time she could spend running away. Her head dipped low, hiding from anybody watching through the walls, she crept upstairs.

She closed and locked her bathroom door, not much longer her home, but hesitated before removing her sweated blouse and slacks. A crack in the wall, a tiny hole, would allow anyone to watch her. Nobody could hide there, not even her.

Jessica set a warm, hard running shower, not too hot, before she pulled away her clothes. Naked, she looked around, before stepping into the shower spray. Her eyes remained upon the doorknob. If it turned, she knew to scream for help that wouldn't come.

Taking a bar of soothing soap, she washed her face and hands so soiled from crying. She rubbed her ugly body with a sponge, trying to force away every stain of tears inside her skin. Falling on her flesh, the shower water helped her hope each next minute would be better than the last. Her life – that awful life – drowned in the water, the remnants of recent days spiralling through the plug hole to where she'd never again see it.

Steam covered the closed window. Water dripped from the walls around her. Jessica peered through the mist to see the bathroom door still closed. Steam covered the mirror above the washbasin.

Dirt lingered somewhere on her. Taking a brush, she mercilessly scrubbed her tawdry flesh again. Falling water rinsed everything and more from the bristles of her brush, until only bubbles ran. Jessica couldn't change a thing; she couldn't stop being dirty. She could never again make her life what it had been.

Weighed down by thoughts, her hand lent against the smooth ceramic wall tiles supporting her arm and her, until her hand and arm soon buckled. Her brush dropped, her shoulder lent against the sodden tiles, down which the water rolled.

Unable to hold herself under her wretched waterfall, she slid slowly down the tiles until she rested on the shower floor, her face against the claustrophobic wall. In her chance to feel the pain, she wept in her wet prism. Water splashed over her wailing head and shoulders, her legs covering the plug hole, blocking the water and her tears from spiralling away.

The whirlpool of all water swirled around her. Drowning in damnation, gasping for her breath, Jessica's tears mixed into a single torrent with the water falling through her. She could pound her head into the blackness, but still not make it numb. Strangers, who wouldn't break another law and who gave money to a dying-man charity, would choke her naked neck in their bare hands to death.

Sometime, the falling water cooled, as the hot water tank exhausted. Jessica reached upwards to the taps, moving her legs enough to allow water to the drain. She turned off the cold and then the hot water taps, although she could no longer distinguish the waters flowing from them.

The shower noise had ceased, leaving only the screeching of whirling water draining downwards. Jessica remained in her wet bath cubicle, numbed to the enamel at her skin. The last water whistled away, the bathroom was again silent, but for her intermittent breaths against the tiles.

Jessica slowly rose. The bathroom floor and bathmat were wet. Hanging neatly from the rack, she took her yellow towel and rubbed water from her wettest hair. She wrapped the towel around her, dipped her head, and cautiously unlocked the bathroom door.

The door open, mist released from the bathroom flowed past her to the ceiling. She scurried to her bedroom.

She closed her bedroom door, not high enough above the ground. The twilight of another night approached to harm her, but she didn't switch on lights that could attract attention. Nobody should know that she was there.

Her towel remained around her, as she lay on her old bed. Turned on her side, she pulled up her legs and closed her eyes, lying inside her towel like the little girl she would gladly be again. Her towel and moisture comforted her, as no person would again.

Her anguish should've warmed her, but her arms and legs shivered in the cool. She lay better in her bed, under sheets and thinning blankets to protect her. She wrapped them close around her, almost buried among them against her face, but she was destitute.

23

PAIN RELIEF

Sometime through the night, when there was no reason to believe the dawn would come, Jessica tired of being so tired without sleeping. She turned on the electric light beside her bed, climbed out, and dressed into her long and lonely nightdress. She stepped senselessly into her satin slippers and wrapped herself in her long pink dressing gown, tying the cord around her waist.

Lying on her white dressing table was the unopened box of paracetamol tablets she'd bought some days earlier: so long ago, but not nearly long enough. The more she looked at it, the more her body ached. Feeling every nerve and muscle while trying not to feel it, mere time had proven no relief.

Near it lay her watch. She didn't check the hour, for fear of what she'd learn. Sunday night can't have become Monday morning if she'd never been to sleep.

Jessica sat on her blue velvet cushioned stool. The dressing table had been hers all her remembered life, in the bedrooms of her homes, reminding her of where she could no longer be.

The round mirror on a rusting metal stand had reflected her face through growing years. In the silver glass that night, she was hideous to see. Despair had drained her eyes, weary of the war she'd only lost thus far. Anyone would be ugly to be her.

"How strong are you?" she asked her reflection, little and lost. "How strong are you, now?"

Tears filled her eyes as she considered her reply. "Not very," she whispered, comprehensively beaten, "not strong at all." Denied her last refuge from the streets, Jessica didn't know where little girls went when hell expelled them.

If the earth wouldn't open up and swallow everything, then it could at least open up and swallow her: absolving her from the anguish that was all she had become. Her regrets were too great a burden for one stupid wonderer to bear; Jessica wished she'd known two weeks earlier what she'd learnt since then. Her words at the café had been too few, too trite, to warrant anything, but they'd swept away her life in twelve days of unrelenting slaughter. If the country of her birth was crazy, then so was she.

Her remark was unimportant, her feelings almost as much. She slipped the tablet box into the pocket of her gown.

Downstairs was dark, but for the glare of street lights again casting horizontal prison bars through the Venetian blinds. They reminded her how close the outside world could be.

Facing away from it, Jessica wrapped her dressing gown cord more tightly around her narrow waist and tied it faster still, before she set the lounge room light shining. The world wet from the rain was almost dry. A rainwater pool on the wooden floor leaked too slowly through any cracks between the boards. Her tear-stained passing home wasn't hers to keep; nothing left was hers to lose. She'd become the broken window.

Removing the tablet packet from her pocket, Jessica sat exhausted in her single old armchair. She struggled with the flaps across both ends, where small notices warned her not to use the tablets if anyone had tampered with the adhesive stickers; her tiredness made instructions difficult to read. She finally removed one sticker, and opened that flap and end.

Ten aluminium foil sheets of ten tablets each in plastic bubbles slid from the packet onto her coffee table. A foil sheet scratched her fingers, but her fingernails cut the foil spilling out a round white tablet. No longer could she shy away from the weakling she'd always been. She might leave the packet in the house when she departed but, for then, she broke another bubble. A second tablet fell.

From the kitchen, Jessica took a glass from the draining tray beside the sink and poured rough water from the tap. She braced herself, planning the motions she would undertake to ease the pain. She placed the two tablets onto her tongue, and washed them down her throat.

The refrigerator was becoming bare, but for the last bottles of cider and wine she'd bought for Derek. They'd be a burden to take with her, wherever she went.

Jessica opened a bottle of chardonnay and took a wineglass from a cupboard. She poured herself a serving, which she held close to her face: the fragrance from distant vineyards fresh and full. Her first sip of wine whisked away the taste of tablets. Wine was a better medicine.

The next sip might still her heart, as her thoughts and fears of every day mumbled in her brain. She'd wanted to be good, wanted just to think. She'd expected loyalty like the loyalty that she had always shown. She wanted to know truths and how to use them. She wanted to make a life that made everybody better. She wanted to be somebody that she had never been. She'd wanted freedom to feel, but felt too much.

Jessica mulled around the hollow of the house, drinking from her glass. In the spare bedroom were textbooks, lecture notes, and essays from her university studies in boxes on the floor. She shut the door on them.

No guests would share her wine with her. Jessica would need to finish that bottle or waste it. Her second serving so filled the glass as to reach the rim. She bent her head down near the kitchen bench and sipped from the yellow, until she could carry it without spillage.

Jessica grappled for any thought to make of anything to do, but she was very tired. Too much was happening: her mind not hers alone, too little heart remaining. Too many of her motions had come from directions not her own, her choices much too few.

Two paracetamol tablets hadn't cured her of her pain. Jessica took a third from the sachet.

She was pitiful she knew, but she was the only person pitying her. She was tiring of the will.

Sitting back in her armchair, Jessica rested her heavy head against her elbow and folded arm. She wanted to think to wonder, about more than life and work. If the cure from her demise was silence in the wasteland of her mind, then she couldn't take the cure. The chalice would chafe her lips.

Jessica raised her glass in toast to people who despised her. They might've been correct; eternity would be more restful if she never had been born.

Nobody cared but her that she could die at the hands of strangers hating her; maybe she shouldn't care so much. Who would know if she had died? No one would feel regret for anything said or done to her.

Her death would be the town's relief, when everything could return to what it was. If she truly was as good as she once presumed she was, perhaps she should make that sacrifice. The silence in her head might never come.

The wine clouded her thoughts, but clouded thoughts might harm her less than clearer thoughts had done. The wine obstructed reason, but reason hadn't served her well. Wine made her a more pleasant mode of crazy than her country made her. It freed her mind from thinking clearly. She wasn't good at thinking. Her thoughts made thinking difficult.

She was the heroine and culprit, the martyr and the clown. If she'd been a little cleverer then she would've known she was a fool. She should've been circumspect, and never said a word. She should've stayed alone, saying even less.

Jessica couldn't change her life. Her cause was lost, and might've been lost before she spoke her little words. Were it not for one remark, she would've uttered another indiscretion to other friends of friends. She could only be as she was and always had been, making her fate inevitable. If wiser minds had warned her two weeks earlier not to think aloud then she would've fobbed away those warnings of the fortnight that she died.

She rose uneasily from her chair. Jessica poured herself a third, or perhaps fourth, glass of something wine. The last wine in the bottle shouldn't waste, and she left the bottle on the coffee table where she would not forget it.

The air was becoming colder in that cold house. Windows were the coldest bits of all, none more so than one broken. She extinguished the upstairs lights so passers-by might forget that she was there. She closed the inside doors.

Darkness was safer than the light. Jessica extinguished each last light but a small floor lamp by the lounge room wall. Under a high ceiling, the room was a dirty shade of night.

"Dear God," the fallen woman prayed, sealed in her ghosted solitude, "might only you and Bede know that I am here."

Her brother would not abandon her, but she'd once known her aunt and uncle would not abandon her. They might've spoken with him since last they saw her and told him he too should ostracise her. Without a car, she couldn't reach his home and wait for him, but she preferred him never to call her than to abandon her to her face. He was too far away to harm or save her.

The only sounds she heard were wine seeping through her mind. She couldn't blame her brother for not wasting time with her. She'd try for one last act of kindness by not asking him again. He deserved better than her being his sister.

She would fly away somewhere, if only somebody could carry her. She might fare less badly somewhere else.

Still lying on her coffee table was the last of her wine bottle. Jessica rested her glass beside it, so she wouldn't slip and spill it. She tried to sit on the timber floor, but became tangled in her dressing gown. She loosened the cord around her waist and let it slip onto the floor. Her gown fell freely around her. She pushed her sweated slippers from each of her feet with the toes of her other foot.

Nestled on the floor, her legs folded beside her, Jessica filled her glass another time. The wine might've affected her and she would sleep long, until her head no longer hurt.

Also on the table were her tablet sachets: her panacea. Five tablets were missing from one sachet and Jessica looked inside the packet for them. She looked around the floor, but couldn't find them.

She began to play with what remained: cutting foil, breaking open the sachets, pressing plastic bubbles, and spilling round white tablets to the table. She took two in her left hand and the glass of wine in her right. She slipped the tablets into her mouth and the wine swept them to her throat.

Jessica's half-empty glass stood peacefully on the table. It was more tranquil than anything else had been or might ever be.

Five, or six, tablets hadn't soothed her pain. The remaining sachets were her sustenance and nourishment. Her arms moving uneasily in a breeze that wasn't there, Jessica ruptured more bubbles, spilling more tablets to the table; Jessica had enjoyed too little fun through recent days. That night would be her last bad night; she wouldn't take tablets after it.

She broke more bubbles, watching those novelties in white and round fall to the table. One tiny plaything rolled away, falling to the floor. Jessica reached down, almost slipping, to pick it up and place it with the others.

The table supporting her, sitting on the floor, Jessica opened another sheet of foil and bubbles, and another. She would soon need to leave that little house, through which the rain would come again. The powder pills could relieve her aching head, and leave her lying there forever. Her traumas might never end without them. Pills she did not consume would be wasted. The last plastic bubble in the last foil sheet pressed, almost a hundred round white tablets lay on the table.

Jessica took another tablet in her left hand and wine glass in her right. One tablet wouldn't help her, and she picked up another, another, and another. Each tablet didn't taste of anything material, but it might taste of something good or bad if she took enough of them. She placed them in her mouth, but the sense of them was brief before she washed them down with one gulping swill of overbearing wine.

Her head remained sore, but not as sore as it had been. The tablets were her last chance to find serenity that night. Sleep would be calm relief in pleasant solitude, if she ever reached so far. Any coming sleep would be better than any recent sleep had been. The air was very cold.

She pushed more tablets to her mouth, washing them with

wine, her mind slowing. Becoming faint made Jessica a little less confused. The wine was almost finished, but scores of wasting tablets remained on the table. She leaned towards them, closer to them, feeling for their aroma.

Her left hand turned until she saw her palm. She drew her thumb and fingers together, bending her hand into a cup of brittle flesh, into which her right hand dropped a tablet from the table. Her right hand collected more tablets, until her left couldn't hold any more. Slowly she raised her hand and lowered her face until the tablets were close to her nose and mouth. They exuded no aroma. They said nothing. They didn't move, but for the trembling of her hand.

Into the room, a hint of orange glow began to light the blinds, obscuring the stains of broken glass. The colour new to her made her imagine a place away from there. She liked being in that place, as she'd not liked being anywhere since her infernal conversation at an infernal town café. She could never again be where she'd been before that twelve-day conversation, on what stupid people called a lovely day.

It could've been her time to learn what life could be, but for her ill-famed dumb remark over lunch she never ate. She'd lost her place to live and stepping board into a future. She'd come home to find herself a life, but she might never find it. She should never have come home. She should never have been born there. She was a silly, little orphan girl: a child of the damned.

The eternity she would suffer without change was more daunting than finality. Her cup of flesh and powder, the change for which she was so desperate, edged closer to her hungry lips. Her cautious, tempted mouth opened too slowly, before the tablets tumbled to her tongue. She tasted powder, but the unwieldy rocks were difficult to hold inside her mouth or swallow. She couldn't grip them between her teeth to bite them.

Her shaking hand picked up the glass and poured the last small pool of wine into her mouth; she wouldn't open another bottle she couldn't finish. The coarse ground stones slid to her belly, choking her, but every rock inside her belly made the pebbles remaining in her mouth easier to manage. She swallowed more, until her mouth was empty. She'd suffered too much pain to fear the pain of her relief.

What had been prison bars across the blinds became gentle, rippling waves. The lights of daytime might be coming to her place she'd never before been, without knowing where or when it was or how she came to be there.

Jessica started to stand, wanting to go to bed and fall silently to sleep long enough for everyone alive to forget, but she stumbled and fell. Something curdled in her stomach, seizing her. Lying on the floor, she closed her eyes and pulled her folded legs into her chest, as she'd been before her birth. If she tried to move she'd feel too weak. With the last breaths she could muster, her mind abated, as did the pain.

24

THE ORPHAN'S MOTHER'S SON

Eight o'clock Monday morning wasn't too early, thought Bede, to telephone his sister; he and Gemma had returned to Orange too late the previous night to call her then. Dressed in his white business shirt and sharp, silver-grey trousers, with his blond hair neatly brushed and the aroma of shaving cream fresh in his skin, Bede telephoned. Jessica didn't answer. "Do you think she's all right?" he asked Gemma.

"She might've started a new job."

Bede collected his silver-grey jacket, before kissing his wife on the lips as he did every morning setting off to work. This morning, he hesitated before leaving. "What's the point in being a manager first to arrive every day," he asked, "if I can't be a little late, once in a while?"

Clouds obscured the sky, as Bede drove his car onto the Mitchell Highway towards Molong. Checking his speed, he drove as fast as he dare. He could comfort Jessica better sitting with her, holding her hand, while she talked about whatever the mayor had done, or whatever more the newspaper had done, than he could by one-dimensional words through a telephone connection. Whatever distressed her distressed him.

Bede left the Mitchell Highway at Wellington Street, turning into Peabody Road and his aunt and uncle's home. Parked outside the house was the old car his aunt had lent Jessica. Opening the car door, the outside air was cool. "Is Jess with you?" he asked his aunt at her front door.

"She most certainly is not!"

"That's her car," said Bede.

"*My* car," his aunt corrected him.

"She's not answering her 'phone, and the message she left me yesterday sounded distressed."

"We're all distressed, Bede. Why don't you come in? I can make you scrambled eggs."

"I need to talk with her."

"Don't let people know."

"She's my sister."

"I am your aunt."

Bede sighed. "I'll talk to you, later."

The rising wind blew the leaves along Edward Street, where Bede parked his car outside the old hall at number thirty-three. The gates in front of Jessica's home were closed. Wearing his silver-grey suit and jacket to be warm, Bede reached his hand through the small space in the pedestrian gate to the handle. He pushed open the gate.

There'd been a time Bede would've supposed a broken window was the result of an errant cricket ball he'd struck; perhaps boys on the street had struck a ball so far. The alcove around the broken glass was scant protection from another coming storm. Bede knocked on the wooden doors.

Jessica didn't answer. She might've been asleep.

The time was not yet nine. She might be resting. Bede knocked again, loud enough for her to hear if she was awake inside the house but not so loud as to disturb her if she was asleep.

He waited long enough for Jessica to come to the door from anywhere in the house. Nothing stirred. "Jess," he said, without shouting. "Are you home?"

Footsteps came from behind him. Bede turned around to see an old man, dressed in his almost familiar clerical white collar and dark grey shirt and trousers. "Reverend Underly?" asked Bede.

The reverend stopped. He looked up, studying the broken window.

"Do you know about that?" asked Bede.

"Some boys did it deliberately, I'm told. The newspaper asked me to comment."

"Is Jess all right?"

"I'm told she is."

Bede placed his right hand on the doorknob, turned it, and tried to push open the door. The door was locked. He knocked again, as loudly as he could. "Jess!" he shouted. "Are you there?"

"She might've walked somewhere," said the reverend.

"Where would she go?" Bede shook his head, trying to think, before turning back to the reverend. "What comment did you give the newspaper?"

"I said I would speak with Jessica before saying anything. Charlie Quinn gave me her address."

Bede left the alcove to stand before a mesh-covered window. He tried to peer between the blind slats to see into the lounge room, but couldn't. Nor could he see anything through the fine gaps around the edges.

The reverend stood at the other window, also trying to see into the house. When he'd finished, he turned to Bede and shook his head.

Bede hurried around the house to the rear door. It was locked. He looked through windows low and high, but couldn't see a person. He couldn't see a movement.

He returned to the front of the house. "I should've come sooner. I should've come last night, but I presumed she was asleep."

"I can wait until Jessica comes home," said the reverend.

Bede returned to the front door, where he stood up on his toes as tall as he could make himself, but still couldn't see through the broken window. He reached his arms and hands up to the broken windowpane and pulled himself up, resting his weight against the alcove and balancing his foot on the doorknob. The reverend stood with him, his hands against Bede's back to keep him from falling, as Bede pulled himself high enough to look through the glass. On the floor of the shaded lounge room, lay Jessica in her crumbled pink dressing gown and nightdress.

"Jess!" he cried out. She didn't move. Bede reached his hand against the jagged glass. "Ah," he cried, cutting his hand, pulling it back, losing his balance, and almost falling. The reverend kept him against the door as he slid downwards.

Holding his cut hand with his other, Bede turned his side to the door as the reverend pulled away. Bede pounded his shoulder against the right door: the door that normally opened. It shook and his shoulder hurt, as did his hand.

"Jess!" he screamed. His shoulder pounded the door again and it shook again; the lock and hinges might've been becoming loose. Bede pounded it again, forcing it further each time he did, until it flew open.

"Jess!" he cried out, as he rushed into the house. "Wake up!" He stumbled as he reached down to the floor to take his sister in his arms. "Wake up!" He shook her body trying to ignite a life in her he didn't know was there. "Jess!" he screamed, but she hung limply in his arms.

The reverend had quickly followed him inside. Looking around, he soon saw the telephone on the floor, picked it up, and dialled. "I need an ambulance immediately at thirty-three Edward Street, Molong," he said. "A woman is unconscious."

On the table was an empty wine bottle and glass, along within a little paper box, sheets of ruptured foil and plastic, and dozens of tablets. Bede picked up the empty box. It once contained headache tablets.

"The patient might've swallowed pills and alcohol," the reverend said into the telephone. He dropped the handset to the floor and rushed quicker than an old man should into the kitchen, where he poured a full glass of tap water he rushed to Bede, spilling just a little.

Holding Jessica's head and neck upright, Bede clasped her cheeks trying to open her mouth. Crouched over them, the reverend put the glass against her lips and tried to pour a little water into her.

The water spilled from her unconscious lips onto her chest, while Bede lifted her chin to let water in her mouth drop to her throat. "Drink this," said Bede, without knowing if she could hear him.

"Our Father," prayed the reverend, "bring back life to your child, if it be Thy will." He placed the glass on the table too quickly to keep it from tumbling over, spilling water around the tablets there. "Help her up," he told Bede.

Bede lifted her to the armchair, trying to shake her sensible so anything else fell out. "I should've brought you to my home a week ago," he told her, his sister in his arms, as he started to cry. "I should've protected you."

Their lives together watched them from the corners of his mind. Their parents told him a new baby would be born; he'd been so happy. She was a little girl, a beautiful sweet girl, who'd played. She learned from him, and trusted him. He'd tried to teach her from his experience of years not many more than hers, but hadn't taught her well.

"Please Jess," he wept, while his brain burned with agony. "Not yet."

The sound of a siren brought him small relief. Bede turned to face the door, willing the paramedics closer to them and ready to call out to them. The reverend stood at the open door. The siren stopped, as Bede saw the shine from oscillating lights.

"Here she is," called out the reverend, stepping back and pointing towards Jessica.

Soon bounding into the room were two ambulance men in long blue uniforms, one carrying a box of medicines and implements. Bede held his sister out for them to take her.

Bede stepped back while they tended to her, trying not to obstruct them. One ambulance man picked up the empty packet of headache tablets and saw the sheets of broken foil and plastic. "Do you know how many she swallowed?"

"No," replied Bede. "She never normally takes medicines, any medicines."

"We'll take her in," said the taller of the men, as he lifted Jessica in his arms. His colleague rushed ahead of him, as he carried Jessica out of the house.

"I'll come with you," said Bede, following them outside.

"No, you won't," said the man carrying Jessica.

The other ambulance man had opened the doors at the rear of their white ambulance with blood red markings, and dragged out a collapsible gurney. The man carrying Jessica lowered her onto the gurney, pushed it into the back of ambulance, and climbed into the vehicle beside her.

"Will she be all right?" asked Bede, as the other man closed the rear door and went to the driver's seat. The siren again blared and throbbing lights swirled around as the parting ambulance sped away, swinging around the corner.

At the side of the street, terrified that she might already be dead, Bede remained. The siren faded, until the only sound remaining was anger rising in him.

A hand rested on his shoulder. "I found these," said the reverend.

Bede turned towards him, causing the reverend's hand to fall from his shoulder. In the reverend's other hand was a packet of adhesive bandages.

"Your hand," the reverend explained.

Bede looked down at his right fist, seeing that it was clenched. He opened his fingers, peeling back the trail of drying blood where he'd cut his skin on the broken window.

He closed his fist; the reverend couldn't comprehend. Jessica had been part of his life for as long as he recalled. He'd been with her becoming a child, a young woman, but the world reduced her to being baggage in the back of a screeching ambulance. Vulnerable, small Jess would've saved them all if she could do so, but they tormented her to anguish so great she might've ended her short life. She destroyed herself for them, and he hated them as she'd never hated them.

His pain was immeasurable, more virulent and violent than any other he had known. Love and fear clenched his arms and body in a temper to fight anyone for her, as he should've fought much sooner. He spun around, wanting to punch and kick anything. Only the reverend was there, looking kindly and inanely before him.

Peering at him from behind their curtains, Bede sensed the grubby eyes of little people no doubt laughing among themselves. None appeared for him to strike.

If a car came across him then Bede would joust it to the death. None was willing to defy him.

Bank Street, the town centre, taunted him to come. Bede began to move towards it.

"Wait," the reverend told him.

His blond hair waving from his head, his silver-grey suit like armour he didn't need, Bede's feet pounded the street side as he stomped, strode, and soon was running towards the jury that had sentenced Jessica to death. Damning for all time the killer cowards who'd wronged her would be vengeance for the sweet poor girl they'd massacred.

25

THOUGHTS, WORDS, AND OTHER FELONIES

Heavy glass doors sealed the lobby to the Cabonne Council offices, uncommonly busy even for a council meeting day. The chamber was a large rectangular room, with a seductive glow from fluorescent ceiling lights. Neither too light nor too dark, they made the formal chamber almost restful. Three flagstaffs stood at each side of the presidium, six flags in all hanging like curtains in no obvious order. The council flag and ubiquitous emblem declared Cabonne Country to be Australia's food bowl.

Affixed to the left-side wall was a series of tall timber boards, listing the names, titles, and tenures of mayors not just of Cabonne but of four shire councils that had progressively amalgamated through the latter years of the twentieth century to become Cabonne. Hector Xiedergrain's name wasn't yet on a board, so certain he was that it didn't need to be. Everybody knew him, and his tenure would continue for a long time to come.

The boards normally dwarfed the few people quietly occupying their scattered chosen chairs in the public gallery, watching proceedings. A handful attended particular meetings because agenda items interested them, such as anything related to reviving the old mine. They sat in chairs at the back of the gallery and, after the councillors had dealt with those items, they quietly stood up, sometimes bowed, and walked quietly out of the chamber.

Each meeting at her dedicated desk, a council secretary carefully transcribed people's public words. An audio cassette machine recorded the meeting to supplement her transcription. Whatever she thought she heard or the machine thought it recorded, the meeting minutes would record what the mayor and councillors, upon reflection afterwards, heard and meant to say.

Charlie Quinn normally sat slumped at a swivel chair and table reserved for him at one side of the chamber. The table against the wall could accommodate more journalists but only Charlie came, easily observing all parts of the chamber and discreetly entering and leaving at any time; he never bowed. Charlie scribbled notes with a pen on paper and, when the proceedings slowed, composed newspaper articles in his small portable computer. He reviewed and polished his words and phrases, typing letters and moving paragraphs.

Not so that Monday morning, when Charlie sat upright and alert. A hundred or more people filled the gallery to witness the mayor and councillors' response to the infamous Jessica Rawlins. They nibbled peanuts from their bags and chocolates from their pockets. In their laps, they browsed through magazines, waiting for the spectacle.

At nine thirty, when Cabonne Council meetings normally began, Mildred Thompkins slipped into the chamber, close to Charlie. "Agnes Plavin called for you," she whispered. "Jessica Rawlins' brother Bede has been there, raving and ranting. There's blood dripping from his hands."

"You better tell the mayor."

"I have. We've called Sergeant Vaughan."

A door at the side of the chamber, near the front wall, opened, as Mildred slipped away. The public gallery rose to its feet. Charlie stood more slowly than other people stood.

The mayor slowly proceeded into the chamber regaled in his new long red council robe lined with black velvet, mock sable fur, and lace frill. It made all other clothes in the chamber uninteresting, but Charlie was no less comfortable in his baggy suit. Adorning the mayor's thick mane of hair was his new black mayoral hat. Around his neck hung the bright new gold-plated sterling silver chain of office, comprising forty-eight shields on wreaths set in two rows. Smaller gold plated pendants represented each of the councils that long ago amalgamated to form Cabonne Council. Larger than them was the ornately enamelled Cabonne Council seal. Mildred Thompkins had already sent Charlie a detailed description of the new garb to include in his newspaper.

The mayor headed a procession of eight other councillors, the general manager, and council heads of staff, all stepping in slow time with him. On a raised platform at the head of the chamber, the mayor stood at his tall-backed chair, behind his long bench. The general manager and other senior staff stood at their chairs at each side of him, slightly lower than the mayoral chair. The councillors stood at their chairs behind the arc of desks in front of him. Behind the councillors, people stood in the gallery. The mayor sat down, allowing every other person in the chamber to sit in staggered unison.

Basking in their expectation, Hector Xiedergrain sat taller than usual before the chamber that morning, with a gavel close to his right hand. "My good and fellow citizens," he said, speaking to the occasion, "I regret our first and most important order of business must be to remove a stain on our beautiful shire. I speak of that most heinous and vile act, which occurred at the Pickled Pepper Café."

Councillors shook their heads. Heads of staff waited their cue.

The mayor continued. "The cruel, cowardly, and evil vilification wrought by an obviously troubled young woman is an anathema to the tolerance that I, and everyone in this country, values so dearly. We won't tolerate the intolerance of those who would judge our fellow human beings. I am thus moving today a new ordinance: the Diversity Ordinance." The mayor picked up the uppermost sheet of paper from those on the bench before him and read from it. "The council and people of Cabonne affirm our right to diversity, and prohibit anyone from any expression of a divisive and offensive nature. The penalty for a breach of this ordinance shall be a maximum of twenty thousand dollars and three months imprisonment."

The councillors sat silently. The public gallery watched the mayor.

"Would any councillor care to speak to the motion?" asked the mayor. One councillor nodded his head. "Councillor Batley."

Councillor Batley, a stocky middle-aged man, rose to his feet. "Mister Mayor," he said. "You have spoken today on behalf of all of us who cherish our freedom and way of life." He spoke as a statesman, his oratory rising, commanding his element, as Charlie had never before heard him. "The Diversity Ordinance allows us, as a shire, to atone for what happened. It will ensure that we never again suffer such indiscretion. I, and all our fellow councillors and residents, support this motion."

"Hear, hear," said Councillor Sewell. Other councillors nodded their concurrence.

"Would any councillor care to speak against the motion?" asked the mayor, in accordance with usual procedure. Nobody answered. "Then I'll put it to the vote. Would those in favour say 'aye'?"

The councillors before him clearly said "aye." Some said it twice or three times, looking around so Charlie and other people knew they'd said it.

"Would those against the motion say 'no'?"

Nobody spoke. Nobody flinched.

"I declare the motion carried."

The mayor's head slowly turning, his eyes paraded around the chamber. A man in the audience raised his hands and tentatively clapped. Briony Keyte began clapping, encouraging the man to become louder. Lester Cullen clapped with her. Soon, the hundred or more people in the gallery, along with the councillors and staff applauded like ten times their number: the thunderous, rapturous applause Charlie had predicted in the last edition of his newspaper. (He'd use that phrase again, that thunderous, rapturous applause, in the next edition, knowing nobody but Agnes would recognise the repetition.)

The mayor nodded his acknowledgement. Not so crass as to clap themselves, only he and Charlie didn't clap, along with the secretary recording notes. The mayor's eyes lingered more upon Charlie than upon anyone else. If he contemplated another conversation between them afterwards, there was no need.

The gallery, councillors, and staff continued clapping and cheering for more than a minute, too fearful of being the first to stop, before the oldest hands in the gallery began tiring. The clapping started to wane, when the mayor gently raised his hand asking them to finish. He asserted control as much in silence as applause, but the energy of those accolades remained.

"I fear," the mayor resumed, "we can do more to safeguard the unity and diversity of our society, from the evil actions of one nasty, disturbed person."

People in the gallery nodded. Mildred Thompkins walked around the desks at which the councillors sat, distributing sheets of paper; councillors whispered to each other. She distributed sheets to the general manager and other council staff, before proceeding to the rows of chairs in which the public sat, passing out sheets of paper. People took one sheet and passed the rest to the next along their row. Finally, she gave a sheet to Charlie.

On the sheet were twenty or more different motifs referring to diversity, defining the shire by it. Charlie turned over the sheet expecting to see more. There were no more.

"I move," proclaimed the mayor, "that council express the will of the people by expending a hundred thousand dollars to promote diversity throughout the shire. Is there any discussion?" One councillor raised his hand. "Councillor Hagarty."

Councillor Hagarty stood up. "Your worship," he said. "We all wholeheartedly support the principle behind your proposal, but having refused other proposals for lack of council funds, does the council budget make provision for such expenditure?"

"Are you opposing diversity, Councillor?" replied the mayor, drawing upon his deepest, most bellowing and commanding voice.

"No, your worship."

"Then you support the motion."

Councillor Hagarty sat down. He adjusted himself in his chair.

"Is there any other discussion on the motion?" asked the mayor.

The chamber was silent. People appeared not even to breathe, for fear their moving chest might be construed as dissent.

"Good," said the mayor. "Those in favour say 'aye'."

"Aye," said eight councillors in unison.

"Anyone against the motion say 'no'." The mayor stared at Councillor Hagarty.

The councillors didn't move. The chamber was silent.

"I declare the motion carried," said the mayor, his voice rising and him rising with it. "Every existing council sign and many more new signs throughout the shire will laud diversity: every road, park, and public building." He stood in full flight, with his red mayoral robes and black hat full length before his audience. "Some ideas for our new slogan, logo, and flag are in front of you. They'll be our new council letterhead and on every council notice and publication. We can commission a book, *Our Great Diversity*, with the title in large gold letters on the cover and a foreword by me, dominating the shelves in every bookstore, newsagency, and library." He stretched out his arms encompassing his people. "We could compose a melody and lyric for the children to sing. We'll win awards I'll be pleased to accept on your behalf."

The mayor finished, standing still. Lester Cullen began clapping, commanding Briony Keyte and other people to clap too. Councillors and council staff clapped with them; Councillor Hagarty clapped particularly keenly. People pounded their hands together, inspiring each other to pound them still harder into a crescendo. Briony and Lester stood at their chairs in ovation. Others quickly rose to stand with them. The elderly widow Mrs Kincaid struggled to take hold of the chair in front of her, but she rose to her feet and held her balance long enough to clap.

The councillors all rose from their seats with their ovation. The council general manager and staff rose after them. The secretary stopped transcribing the proceedings of the meeting and rose to her feet clapping. Charlie Quinn clapped with them, although he alone remained in his chair. Realising he ought to appear impartial, Charlie stopped.

His grin broad, the mayor revelled in the audience's resonance with him. Every accolade affirmed him as the hero he knew unwaveringly he was.

When the eldest people in the chamber became weary and resumed their seats, the mayor also sat down. The rest of the people sat.

The door at the rear of the chamber burst open. "Ah," cried the seated man against whom the door thumped.

People turned around in their chairs to see a blond young man Charlie didn't recognise. Wearing a silver suit, he strode along the aisle beside the gallery, creating a wake of people leaning away. The stark intruder headed towards the mayor, sitting high behind his long wooden bench. "You're presiding over hell from a toy box," he roared.

The mayor thumped his gavel on his bench. "You're out of order," he scolded him.

"You're out of order!" The man strode between Charlie and the councillors, the councillors leaning back in their chairs away from him, as the man reached the floor space between them and the mayor. "You pompous fool in your red robes, fat hat, and golden dog collar!"

"You're Jessica Rawlins' brother, aren't you?" said the mayor.

Somebody screamed. Other people huffed and murmured in disgust. The council secretary sat motionless.

The mayor's presidium and semicircle of councillors' desks almost surrounded him, as Bede turned around to address everybody there. "You know Jess," he told them. "She's the one you tried to murder. You might've succeeded."

"Leave this chamber now, Mister Rawlins," said the mayor. "This is a public meeting."

"This is a pit!"

"Where is Sergeant Vaughan?" asked the mayor. Some people gasped. "We have a madman at the council."

"Don't we?" Bede retorted.

Their heads bowed low, several people fled from the gallery

out the rear door. Charlie sat bolt rigid in his seat, ready to run or scramble to the floor.

Only the mayor in his dominion sat defiantly behind his podium. The thump of his gavel at the bench bolted through the chamber. "Take him away."

No council officer stepped forward. Nobody moved.

"Aren't any of you brave enough to subdue him?" asked the mayor.

"Jessica might've killed herself," screamed Bede, throwing out his arm and pointing his finger at the mayor, "because of what you did to her."

"She brought everything upon herself, Mister Rawlins."

"She thought about things, hazarding beliefs greater than yours. She felt things you're too dumb to feel. She disagreed." Bede swung around again, confronting the councillors and gallery and letting them confront him. "Don't any of you automatons think for yourselves?" he begged of them, his pointed arm roaming around to point at each of them. "You let others tell you your beliefs. My sister wasn't trying to persuade you to her point of view. She was trying to persuade you to yours!"

"This is not a place to proselytise," declared the mayor.

"This is not a place to think, feel, or love," said Bede in his arena. "All of you who tormented her, you killed her!"

Sergeant Vaughan appeared at the rear of the gallery. The sergeant unfastened the flap in his gun holster. He held his hand above his gun.

"Sergeant Vaughan," the mayor commanded. The councillors and gallery turned towards the sergeant behind them. "Take this lunatic away,"

"Stay where you are," Bede raised his open hand at the sergeant, countermanding the mayor's order, holding the sergeant at bay. "You're someone else who drove her to her death."

"This is the brother of that Rawlins woman," explained the mayor.

"Why you..." said Bede, turning back to the mayor and moving towards him.

The sergeant drew his gun from the holster and raised it high. Several people gasped. People clamoured away from any line of fire.

Holding it with both his hands at the end of his outstretched arms, the sergeant pointed his gun at Bede. "Don't do it," he told Bede.

Bede turned back to the sergeant and the barrel of a gun aimed at him. "This is freedom?" Bede cried out.

"Sergeant," said the mayor, "arrest this criminal, this brother of a criminal."

Bede spun back towards the mayor. "Damn you," he screamed, as he stepped towards the podium, leading with his open arms and hands up high.

"There's blood on his hands!" a woman screamed.

"Shoot him," demanded the mayor. "Sergeant, I order you to shoot him."

"Stop," screamed the sergeant, as Bede lunged towards the mayor. "I will shoot."

Bede crashed into the wood-walled podium, blasting thunder throughout the chamber. Council staff jolted back in their chairs, the mayor didn't flinch, but the sergeant's fingers squeezed the trigger of his pointed gun. Men and women screamed, as the bullet struck the silver-suited Bede through his back. His exploded body stopped moving, pressed hard against the wooden panels of the mayoral bench; his wide eyes shocked at the new agony within him. The mayor glared down at him from his high mayoral chair, while Bede's arms reached up towards him, staggering slowly. Slowly he slipped down the wooden wall, towards the hell-fired floor.

The sergeant's gun high in his outstretched hands and arms remained trained on Bede as he walked forward, as if Bede were about to twitch before his eyes and rise again. People wept. Lester Cullen embraced Briony Keyte, as others embraced each other.

The mayor collected his composure. "Would you please call an ambulance?" he asked the general manager. She hurried away.

The sergeant and his pointing gun edged forwards, towards the figure crumpled on the floor, so well dressed to have been insane. Everybody close enough to see watched Sergeant Vaughan, his right hand still pointing his gun towards the body on the floor, kneel down and press two fingers of his left hand against Bede's neck. Looking up at the mayor, the sergeant slowly shook his head.

The sergeant examined the dead man's empty hands; the dried blood seemed very little, from where Charlie sat. He returned his gun into its holster. He dipped his head into his hands.

The mayor faced the councillors, staff, and what remained of the public gallery. "We won't follow usual protocol today," he told them. "Would all members of the public please leave your name with a member of council staff before departing? This will assist Sergeant Vaughan if he wants a statement from you. A notice with details of any supplementary council meeting dealing with the rest of the agenda items will appear in the *Molong Express* on Thursday. This meeting is now adjourned. Thank you, and good day."

26

ERASURE

Charlie Quinn remained at the table at the side of the chamber, watching and listening, closer to the story than he should be. The council secretary stopped the recording machine.

Hector Xiedergrain remained in the dressage of his office, his red robes like Pilate before and after death. "Find out where he lived," he told council staff, directing events with his usual demeanour. "Find out what happened to Jessica Rawlins."

Sitting in a chair near him sobbed Mildred Thompkins, holding her small handkerchief in her hands. The mayor left his presidium to stand by her, resting his hand on her shoulder. "Now, Mildred," he said. "Don't be like that."

"It's not fair."

"Did you know him?"

Constable Tarrant photographed the body in a silver-grey suit. He marked its position on the floor with a clumsy outline. More police came from Orange to speak to Sergeant Vaughan and the mayor.

Ambulances didn't speed to the dead as they did to the living. "We've already met," said an ambulance man of the figure on the floor. "What happened?"

"He ran amok," replied Constable Tarrant.

"He didn't seem the type."

"You never can tell."

The ambulance men told the police, mayor, and Charlie Quinn they'd taken Jessica unconscious to the Molong District Hospital, after she'd overdosed on headache tablets. Securely sealed in a black vinyl body bag, the ambulance gurney carted Bede's body away.

Shocked councillors, staff, and citizens gave the police their testimonies of what happened, which police recorded in their notepads. They'd never before seen anybody shot. They'd never before seen anybody dead.

Men wearing suits weren't normally dangerous, someone remarked. The dead man had attacked the mayor. Another witness wondered what made Bede Rawlins crazy, although he had been unruly at school. He, another boy, and his girlfriend infamously assaulted two girls in their year, tying their hair together.

More than an hour after the shooting, only Charlie remained in the chamber. The only corruption from the calmness was the outline on the floor, marking where Bede's body fell. Standing there seemed disrespectful, until not standing there seemed even more so.

The longer Charlie stood with that ghost silhouette, the more the meeting place became again the bland room of furniture, flags, and boards it must have always been. The chairs stood disorderly but empty, without panicky people running away or wishing they could run. There was no angry man with a gun pointed at him, that man with a gun no less frightened. There was no mayor, willing him powerlessly to fall, the threat that never was.

The mayor, dressed out of his new mayoral clothes and again wearing another of his open-necked pale cotton shirts and long business trousers, returned to the chamber. He closed the doors from the corridor outside. On the table where he'd sat through the meeting remained a jug of lukewarm water, from which the mayor poured two glasses.

Charlie placed his glass on a table without drinking from it. "Do you have any messages for the dead man's family?" he asked.

"Did he have a family, Charlie," asked the mayor, "apart from the Rawlins woman?"

"Jessica," said Charlie. "Her name was Jessica. Their aunt and uncle live on a farm on Peabody Road."

"They have my sincerest condolences."

Charlie pointedly stepped back to the table on which his notepad lay. He sat down and wrote those words.

"No, make that just my condolences. The police will determine whether his family was partly responsible."

Charlie struck a line through the word the mayor had deleted, before standing up again. "Bede Rawlins wasn't armed."

"Nothing like this has happened here before," said the mayor, "but sadly, it can happen anywhere. Everyone is dismayed, but we will recover."

"It wasn't supposed to be like this," replied Charlie, wandering away from the mayor, past the rows of empty chairs in the public gallery. "Nobody should've been hurt. Nobody should've died."

"You were here," said the mayor. "Vaughan did what he needed to do."

Charlie reached the rear door where Bede Rawlins first appeared. Several chairs in the rear rows lay on their sides and backs, where people rushing out had pushed them over. "I was thinking about you," said Charlie, "ordering the sergeant to shoot him."

"I didn't order Vaughan to kill him, Charlie, but I needed to do something. The risk to the public might've been minimal, but we can take no chance with public safety, no chance at all."

"Was that public safety, or your safety?" asked Charlie, bending down to pick up a chair knocked over. He stood the chair upright.

"My safety is public safety, Charlie. Anybody who would harm me could harm you or anyone else. What I did today, I did for all of us."

Charlie looked disparagingly at him, still in that space at the front of the chamber where Bede Rawlins died; the mayor's eyes never left him. Charlie picked up more chairs, setting them upright. "Doesn't seeing a good man die change anything?"

"I don't like this business either, Charlie, but the task now is to explain our position to the people. The council will consider if we need to do anything more to secure the safety of the shire, but no town anywhere can do everything to protect itself from mentally unstable people. That man today, Bede Rawlins, didn't live in the shire. He was an outsider. His sister was a troublemaker."

"Was it trouble somebody needed to make?" asked Charlie.

"The family has a history of antisocial behaviour," said the mayor. "It's the only such family, I might add, here. This has always been a peaceful place and is now one again."

"I'll tell the truth," Charlie said calmly, setting the last chair upright. "That's all I'll do, but don't expect me to decide too readily what the truth is."

"I can tell you the truth, Charlie. You don't need to ask."

Charlie walked along the aisle at the far side of the chairs and councillors' tables, under the timber boards of past mayors affixed to the wall. "How many people applaud you rather than risk being seen not to applaud?"

"I'm working on a new ordinance, Charlie, the Free Thought Ordinance. We'll ratify the right of citizens to proper mores in a cohesive and integrated society. Jessica Rawlins' improper thoughts won't impinge upon the proper thoughts of every other person in the shire. We'll prohibit people from harbouring any thought incompatible with our right to diversity."

Charlie returned to the mayor and the outline of a corpse on the floor. "What would you have me write about the death of Bede Rawlins?"

"The same as I wanted you to write about the words of Jessica Rawlins: nothing. Write about the price of eggs rising by two cents a dozen or a pot falling off a windowsill, but don't write about race or anything like it."

"You're about to spend a hundred thousand dollars promoting diversity."

"We won't talk about race, but about racism. We won't mention any of the things about which we're promoting diversity. We'll just talk of diversity."

Charlie leant back against the councillors' tables, pushing

away a small timber mount marked with a councillor's name. "People are already telling each other what happened today?"

"It's such a misfit for what they believe about everything, Charlie, they'll soon stop talking about it. They'll put a black box around it in their brains and as good as forget about it before the end of the week."

"We build their black boxes," said Charlie.

"We keep everything straightforward, so that's all their simple minds comprehend. They'll dwell upon what makes them feel clever and good, what they think they understand. They don't want to think about things that debunk their beliefs, when all they need are thumbnail perceptions."

The door near them opened. Sergeant Vaughan stepped slowly towards the place Bede Rawlins' body fell until he stood beside it, staring at the lines on the floor.

"Any comment, Sergeant?" asked Charlie, hurrying back to his table. He held his hands above the keyboard, expecting it to intimidate the sergeant.

"The Police Association advised me not to speak to the media."

Charlie swung around in his swivel chair. The sergeant still stared down at the lines of a corpse.

"You're a hero, Sergeant Vaughan," the mayor told him, "a real hero." He poured the sergeant a glass of water, but the sergeant declined. "You're very modest, very humble, I know that, but we should do something for you: give you freedom of the shire, have a parade for you through the streets."

"You could be Volunteer of the Month," quipped Charlie.

"There'll be an inquest," said the sergeant. "The State Coroner will come."

"We'll obviously co-operate with any investigation about the tragic events this morning," said the mayor, sounding all very official, "but I hope they can wrap up their investigations quickly so we can move onwards. Nobody cares when police kill white people."

"Do we forget what happened today?" asked the sergeant, crouching low to where he'd felt Bede's lack of a pulse. "If I've kept the peace, then this is peace to suffer."

"Don't dwell on the past, Sergeant, except to remember your bravery. Look to the future."

"Internal Affairs will conduct its customary inquiries and processes," said the sergeant, standing up again, "as it does after any police shooting."

"The Police Association will arrange legal representation for you," said the mayor.

"I don't want it, but I'll take the Department's offer of counselling. Everyone gets counselling. I'll tell the truth to the best of my recollection, to be judged according to facts. Others can try me for what I've done today. I won't contest any findings, I'm not sure I was right, but if I'm ever again a serving policeman, I'll charge four men for assaulting Jessica Rawlins last Saturday night."

"Don't blame yourself," said the mayor.

The sergeant laughed. "You think you have authority to order everyone what to do, but you have no authority over me." He ambled back to the open door. "I only thought you did."

The sergeant departed. The mayor closed the door after him.

"How can this have happened?" asked Charlie, standing up again.

"Don't make more of this than needs to be made."

Meandering around the tables at the front of the chamber, Charlie stopped beside the mayor's high chair. "A woman almost died today, because of you and me." Charlie sat in the mayor's seat. "Her brother is dead, a better man than you or me. What else do we make of it?"

"You could've ignored her, Charlie, but you made her a celebrity."

"You made her a martyr. Jessica smouldered and Bede burned at the stake."

"You saw him threaten us."

Sitting in the mayor's chair in a meeting for two was Charlie's chance to define. "Wouldn't you rather loyalty than laws, standing with people with whom we disagree, supporting words we don't believe because we support the people who do?"

The mayor remained standing where Bede fell and died.

"You're not suggesting we let people say whatever they want to say?"

"We could wonder who our people are. For Bede, his people began with his family."

"You better decide who your people are, Charlie."

"In whom do you believe, Hector?"

"Me, everyone."

Charlie laughed. "Bede and Jessica Rawlins believed in much more. They believed in each other."

"We don't like martyrs, Charlie."

"We just create them."

"Don't create any more."

Charlie stood slowly from the mayor's chair. "I wish I had somebody willing to stand beside me the way he stood beside her," he lamented, drifting back towards his swivel chair. "I wish somebody would fight for me as the rare and admirable Bede Rawlins fought for her."

"I assume, Charlie, this incident has traumatised you."

Charlie had no heart or stomach to answer him. He sat back at his computer and deleted the words he'd typed that morning. He tore out the pages of his notepad on which he'd written and screwed them into wads he threw into the air.

They fell to the floor, where the tall mayor crouched down to collect them. He collected them all before standing again, squeezing them into a bundle his big hands concealed completely.

"We'll devote a full-page cover special to McKenzie's collection of fifty restored antique tractors," Charlie told him. "We'll lose everything about Jessica in the past two editions from our archives, and Ms MacNee won't have kept them in the library. What could've been the pre-eminent news story throughout the country, the like of which nobody had previously seen, won't be reported at all. There'll be no more stories about Jessica, even if she raises her brother from the dead."

"We never need mention this morning again, Charlie," said the mayor, "not even you sitting in my chair."

"If a tree falls in the forest and nobody mentions it, Hector, did the tree fall? If something's not in the newspapers, it never happened."

"It will be as if Bede Rawlins never was," smiled the mayor. "As for his sister, Fergus Millane might be glad for her company out there on his farm."

27

FREE FALL IN EXILE

The small, single-storey Molong District Hospital on King Street became smaller every time the Greater Western Area Health Services reviewed its operations. No longer were there maternity services or operating theatres. Emergency services often depended on the Orange Base Hospital and the Rural Remote Medical Consultation Services in Bathurst.

Reverend Athol Underly often visited his sick and dying parishioners there. Dressed in his clerical collar and commonplace shirt and trousers, carrying a green calico bag, he came there Tuesday morning hoping to be there when Jessica woke. "What more can you tell me about Jessica Rawlins?" he asked a young nurse, of around about Jessica's age.

The nurse clasped her fair hair above her head and wore a minimum of make-up. "She's slipped back to sleep."

The reverend turned to the grey seats in the waiting room, where magazines stood neatly in a pile on a table and a television set stood deactivated. Behind the glass doors of the cupboard were several knitted and other craftwork items for sale; his late wife made one or two still there.

Waiting in the grey seats was a woman not quite as old as he was, wearing a long dark dress, sensible flat shoes, and a grey woollen cardigan. In her hands was a book, but she was looking up at him.

"Ms Ollerenshaw," he smiled.

"Reverend Underly."

The reverend sat beside her, his calico bag on his lap. "I haven't seen you since...," he started to say, before finishing the sentence seemed rude.

She closed her book. "You haven't seen me since I asked you to cease teaching Scripture at school," she told him, with the knowingness of appreciating the reverend had been trying to be polite.

"A parent had complained," recalled the reverend.

"No parent complained. I worried one would."

"Would you have cancelled any other class because you thought a parent might complain?"

"We stopped teaching," she admitted, before holding up the cover of her book: a weary old cloth-bound edition of Martin Heidegger's *On the Essence of Truth*. "I thought I might lend this to Jessica Rawlins."

"Do you visit all your past students in hospital?"

Ms Ollerenshaw shook her head. "Nothing in my work could keep my mind away from Jessica and Bede. Nothing should."

"She doesn't know what happened to her brother," the reverend explained. "Her aunt's not up to telling her. She wants me to do so."

"People don't like imparting bad news," mused Ms Ollerenshaw, "associating them with anything distressful."

"Hospitals are venues for bad news. The doctors don't know whether Jessica's excessive consumption of headache tablets and alcohol was accidental or intentional."

"It was accidental," insisted Ms Ollerenshaw. "I'm certain of it."

"Is that the essence of truth, or what we'd like truth to be?"

Her eyes were slow to respond, but respond they did. "Mister Heidegger never faced the problems we face," she sighed, holding her book to her chest, "but would've fared better than I've fared dealing with them. I never doubted the conduct of my life before Jessica suggested I should."

The reverend sat close enough for him to put his arms around her, if he'd put his arms around any woman since his wife died. "You have always done what you believed to be right."

"And when I doubted I was right? When did I reach the point at which I would always remain? When did I die?"

He'd been no better than she'd been. "We must all keep learning, even if it means acknowledging we were wrong. Learning ends when the teachers cease learning."

Ms Ollerenshaw continued watching him. "We teach our children to work more than we teach them to think. They know more of what to do with their hands than their minds. Our school is not teaching but reinforcing, and we don't need any more reinforcing. What could've been venues for thought are wastelands, where tutors say the same things and frighten each other from questioning, from thinking anything new.

The reverend looked to the green calico bag, sitting uneasily in his lap. "My life that once enthused me has become just praying at my parishioners' deathbeds. Whether Jessica is a curse, soothsayer, or messenger, she troubles me, too."

"Why must some people destroy ideas with which they disagree? Ought not debate be cherished as a means towards learning, in a discipline called philosophy, instead of being feared?" The book in her hand was never more obviously old. "Can't good people wonder, or must righteousness depend upon ignorance? The worst of ideas are those that prevent new ones evolving. In this country, there are no new ideas."

"There aren't even old ones."

Ms Ollerenshaw rested her hand on his arm. "You come back to the school with your Scripture classes, Reverend. They'll debate you the way they fear they can't debate anyone else."

"Books I've neglected too many years were books of heroes," he told her, "who saved ladies from distress without regard for differences in opinions."

Interrupting them was the nurse with whom the reverend had already spoken. "Ms Rawlins is awake and well enough to take visitors," she told them, "ward three, bed eight."

The reverend stood up, while Ms Ollerenshaw remained sitting. "Thank you for listening, Reverend Underly."

SIMON LENNON

"Thank you for talking, Ms Ollerenshaw."

"Miss Ollerenshaw," she corrected him. "Do you know what it's like being unable to say what you feel?"

He took several moments to ponder. "Do you know what it's like being unable to feel what you say?"

She nodded. "Perhaps later, we can talk about your books."

"Perhaps we can," he smiled, a little anxiously for the intimacy she'd implied. If anyone called her anything but Ms Ollerenshaw, the reverend didn't know who.

Miss Ollerenshaw continued to sit. "You see Jessica without me."

Carrying his green calico bag, the reverend followed the nurse past the nurses' station and along the short corridor to a closed door. "When I'm finished checking her," the nurse whispered to the reverend, "I can wait outside while you speak to her." The nurse knocked on the door.

"Come in," came a voice, just loud enough to be heard.

The nurse and reverend entered. The bed to the left of them was empty, but to the right of them in a second bed lay the girl who might've tried to die. Wearing a white hospital gown, lying among thick white sheets and with pillows under her head, it was hard to comprehend Jessica could've so rattled so many people. Standing beside her bed was a tall metal stand, from which hung a clear bag dripping liquid nourishment through a tube and needle affixed with plastic tape into her arm and veins. A chest of drawers stood beside her bed, on the top of which were a jug and cup of water.

Along the wall away from them were several large windows around which the curtains were open. Beyond them were more buildings of the hospital and covered walkways, but no one outside looking in. Hers was a little space segregated from other people, shielding her. They didn't need to know that she had woken.

"Do you like my new home, Reverend?" asked Jessica.

The reverend thought of many things to say. He said none of them.

The nurse placed a thermometer under Jessica's tongue and wrapped a black vinyl band around her arm. She recorded

Jessica's temperature and blood pressure on a graph, clipped to a plastic board that she hung from the end of her bed.

"If I'm obedient," Jessica told the reverend, "they might let me stay."

Dressed in her grey uniform, an elderly volunteer from the Hospital Auxiliary pushed a metal trolley into the room, offering newspapers and magazines for sale. Jessica declined.

"You should drink plenty of water," the nurse told Jessica, glancing in the top of the jug. The volunteer replenished the jug, left Jessica a clean cup, and departed.

The nurse took a grey rubber handle at the end of a cord hanging over Jessica's head and rested it on the blanket that covered her. She then left the room, closing the door. The reverend remained.

Jessica pointed to the small red button on the grey rubber handle. "I'm not pressing that," she told the reverend. "I'm not summoning people for me to ask them more questions and hear them tell me more lies, or hear them tell me the truth."

The reverend held up his green calico bag. "I brought you your handbag, some clothes, and a pair of shoes from your home."

"Does this mean I should visit you sometime, for your sake not mine?"

The reverend rested his bag on the floor by the door. "Your home is advertised for lease in the window of your former boyfriend's real estate agency."

Her eyes looked around the walls and window. "Isn't my new home nice?" she asked, as if presenting it for his approval.

"My sister has been telling me she needs to do something with her spare bedroom."

Jessica's eyes turned back to him. "Does your sister like broken windows?" Her hands rested on the blankets lying over her. "Is she emotionally destitute?"

"May I sit down, Jessica?"

"It's your hospital," she said, turning to her side away from him. "If I'm hiding, I'll hide here forever. If I'm a prisoner, I don't want my freedom. I want to lie quietly alone, unnoticed by anyone, and wonder whether to be glad I'm alive."

The reverend pulled a chair under the window close to her bed and sat behind her. "We can talk about anything about which you'd like to talk, Jessica."

"Talking brings me too much trouble."

"I won't judge you and won't repeat anything you say. The future need not mirror the past."

"Only a fool wouldn't try to learn something from my past."

"I would like to speak with you."

"What day is this?"

"Tuesday."

"I drank too much wine and took too many tablets for my headache, but the doctors and nurses sucked them out of me."

If she wasn't resigned to him being with her, then she should be. "How is the food here?"

"You've visited enough patients to know."

"Ms Ollerenshaw brought you a book to read."

"I'm busy."

"An old man can't protect you. I can only care about you."

She remained silent, facing that wall, before finally speaking. "That's more than most people do."

"I know you have a brother."

Jessica turned to face him, sitting up in her bed. "What about my brother?" she asked him, before her eyes slowly turned towards the bag the reverend had left on the floor. "Who gave you my handbag, clothes, and shoes?"

The reverend saw her brother in the darkness of her eyes. "I was with Bede when he found you unconscious."

"He knows I'm here?"

"He loved you very much."

Tears mounted in her eyes. "What do you mean?"

"He was extremely upset after the ambulance brought you here. He went to the offices of the *Molong Express* and then the council chamber, where something terrible happened."

"Where is he now?" cried Jessica.

"I'm afraid, he was killed."

"No!" she gasped.

The reverend reached out his arms to try to hug her, but Jessica pulled herself away and threw her head and face into the darkness of a pillow. Her arm almost became tangled in her intravenous drip, but the reverend quickly stood, reached across, and adjusted the height of the saline bag so the cord was again loose. "Sergeant Vaughan made a tragic mistake," he told her, stepping back. She was so very small. "He thought Bede was attacking the mayor."

The pillow muffled her voice, but the reverend heard her beg, "What have I done?"

"It wasn't your fault, my child. It wasn't anyone's fault."

Jessica wailed into her pillow, before suddenly she turned back to the reverend, looking up at him standing over her. "Bede never threatened anybody," she cried. Her brother's face reflected in the tears gushing from her eyes. "He wanted to protect me." Jessica fell back into the pillow. "He always did."

The reverend sat back into his chair while Jessica continued to cry, without reason to stop crying. Any words he uttered then would dissipate through the blackness only she could see. He would allay any doubt upon which she might try to latch herself, doubt would distract her from grief, but she asked him no more questions. There was time and other people for that, including the police. She would try to understand, even if she never did. The reverend poured a serving of water from the jug into a glass.

Pulling her head from her pillow, Jessica again faced the reverend, dressed in his softest caring smile and looking back into Jessica's crowded eyes. Jessica fell back into her pillow, holding it in her arm close to her head.

The reverend searched for any cue to words to speak or things to do to comfort the young woman in his momentary care. "There aren't always reasons," he said.

"There are always reasons," said Jessica, lying huddled in her pillow. "It was I and what I said. It was this time and country."

"I envy your brother's loyalty to you."

"You're better without it."

The reverend wouldn't argue with her. He wasn't very good at arguing.

"I want to be alone," she told him.

The reverend slowly stood up. "Ms Ollerenshaw wants to visit you whenever you're ready. If you want to speak with a hospital counsellor, we can arrange it. If you want to talk with me, or listen to me talking, then the nurse has my number."

"We will both be safer if we keep our thoughts and feelings to ourselves."

"The police from Sydney, not Sergeant Vaughan, want to speak with you when you're up to it. They've spoken with me."

"I'll tell them Bede was kind, loving, and unforgiving," she whispered, "but they won't believe he was loving or kind."

28

CERAMIC WHITE RABBITS

Lying in her white hospital gown with her head against the pillow, Jessica didn't need to close her eyes so tightly when nobody could see her. "Did you die for an idea?" she whispered. "I pray not, for ideas are the most stupid reasons to die. Ideas can't justify a life, for they too often die with life. I like to think you died for me."

She owed him the treasure of a life he'd lost for loving her. Bede died for no one's cause, while she had slept.

She should've waited to speak with him or see him Monday morning. She should have left the wine unopened. She should not have bought the tablets. Her errors destroyed a man the world would have done well to follow. They might all have been alive if she had waited.

Jessica remained in bed in wretchedness through Tuesday. If she was not asleep, she lay with her eyes closed so people thought she was, hearing shoes walking and trolley wheels rolling on vinyl floors outside her door. She'd lost her last friend left to lose.

One time she opened her eyes, Jessica saw the edge of a book hanging over the side of the chest of drawers beside her bed. She reached up her hand, until her fingertips held the book by the corner. She pulled it towards her, until it fell onto her bed.

Jessica pulled herself upwards and her head upright. The book was *On the Essence of Truth*.

On the floor stood a small wastepaper basket, in which was a black plastic bag to collect waste. Jessica reached out from her bed and, into the wastepaper basket, dropped the book.

Sometimes that night, Jessica sat upright in her bed, with her pillows behind her back. The small light shone from the wall above her head, while she stared forward into the blanket over her knees and folded legs.

Wednesday morning, the nurse in uniform carefully removed the drip and needle from Jessica's arm, again recording her vital signs. She gave her more mineral and vitamin tablets, Jessica accepted without will. "I know what happened," said the nurse, in calm conversation. The door to the room was closed. "They call you a rebel. We call you a heroine."

"I'm not a rebel, or a heroine, but a little girl with a loving brother, who tried to make money making people beautiful, but who thought when nobody else was willing to think, said what nobody else was willing to say, and wished I never had."

"Please get well," said the nurse. "Where will that thinking of yours go if anything happens to you?"

The nurse reached into the wastepaper basket and removed the book Jessica had dropped there. She read the cover, slipped it under her arm, and left.

The door to her room remained closed, aside from people passing through. Two police officers interviewed her, but neither they nor Jessica had much to say. A counsellor said even less.

More often than not, Jessica laid her cheek against her pillow and stared into the window glass. She didn't recognise the town beyond it. The sheets of graphs at the end of her bed recorded her reluctant recovery.

Introducing his profession to the patient Thursday morning was a new doctor, tall and young. She listened to his words without opinion, before speaking up about her only interest. "I want to go to my brother's funeral," she told him.

"You should rest."

"You can't keep me here."

He studied her eyes, ran his eyes around her face, and nodded. "Someone should take you," he told her. "You come back here afterwards."

After he left, Jessica dressed into the clothes the reverend had brought her. Carrying her handbag, she left behind her nightdress and pink dressing gown, from which no washing could remove the stench.

Outside the hospital, the open air was good to breathe; if only her brother could also breathe it, whether or not he breathed it with her. She looked across King Street, preparing to walk, when a clunking old car, with dints, dents, and scratches, pulled up in front of her. The passenger-side window closest to her was open, and through it came an old man's voice. "Can I give you a lift, my child?"

Jessica bent down to see Reverend Underly driving. "How did you know I was leaving?"

"Sister Avery telephoned me."

"Why haven't you visited me again?" Jessica knew as soon as she spoke, she sounded ungrateful.

"I would have been visiting you for my benefit. You needed time without me."

Several old books lay across the back seat of his car, but not the front passenger seat. Towels covered much of the torn upholstery. Jessica turned the handle to open the door, sat with her handbag on her lap, and closed the door beside her. "What will people say when they see me in your car?" she asked him.

"They might say I need a new car, but they always say that." He drove them away. "How are you feeling today?"

"A little better than yesterday, tomorrow might be worse."

"Your aunt doesn't want you at your brother's funeral."

Jessica shouldn't have been surprised, but still she was. The reverend continued driving.

"I read the *Molong Express* last week," he continued. "No article mentioned Christianity." She didn't understand. "My church is yours. Bede's service commences at two o'clock."

The reverend walked with her from his car to her foreboding little home, opening the gate. The front door was intact, as was the window above it. "You told the police Bede knocked down the door," said Jessica. "Did you repair everything?"

"I had some help."

"How much do I owe you?"

"There are no debts between us."

The lounge room was clean. The coffee table was empty, but for her small glass kitten and onyx tiger. "I'm not returning to the hospital," she told him.

He studied her eyes and face, much as the doctor had studied them that morning. "Call me when you've found a new home, and if you can't find one." The reverend prepared to leave.

"Do you think things will change because of what happened to Bede?"

"Would change make it worthwhile?"

"Change might make it a little less futile."

The reverend closed the gate when he departed. Jessica closed and locked the door.

Shortly before two o'clock, the sleeves and hems of Jessica's darkest dress covered her arms and legs. It reached high onto her neck. Only the most reclusive of subjects wouldn't have recognised her walking along Edward Street and known where she was headed, but she didn't look at anyone she passed to know if they were watching her.

The searing sun shone down on the Uniting Church as perhaps it should not have done, but the sun might've known more than Jessica still knew. Parked outside the church was the long black hearse. The pallbearers in black suits were carrying Bede's coffin into his memorial.

Following them as far as the open church door, Jessica hesitated. On a table were the prayer and hymn books for guests to weddings and mourners to funerals. Jessica left them there.

Stepping from sunlight into shadows, she removed her sunglasses but not her hat. She stepped softly so as not to intrude.

Jessica's eyes adjusted to the darkness. The church hadn't changed since she was young. The large but small sobbing congregation faced the front, away from her, towards Bede's coffin at the far end of the aisle. They were backs of heads, largely unrecognisable, who mourned a man more in death than they'd understood in life.

Jessica sat unobtrusively in the first wooden pew she reached, the last pew in the church, beside the aisle. Ahead of her, her aunt and other older women wore hats. Unaccustomed to wearing a hat indoors and with only the reverend seeing her, Jessica removed her hat and placed it on the pew beside her.

"We will now sing hymn three hundred and seventy-eight," said the reverend. "The head that once was crowned with thorns."

An elderly woman settled in her seat before a page of music, while the one-day congregation and so Jessica stood up. The organ chords were louder than the mournful voices trying to keep pace, while Jessica stood silently, imagining the sounds they made drifting through the town as they didn't normally drift from church.

The hymn concluded. The mourners sat. They responded to the reverend's refrains as congregations should.

Sometimes Jessica listened to something of what the reverend said, but struggled to concentrate on anything. She followed other mourners standing, sitting, and leaning forward to close her eyes in prayer. She placed her face in her hands, before slowly raising it again. The reverend read a passage from his frayed Bible about a valley full of bones.

Her mind wandered into memories. The walls were as Jessica remembered them being, comforting her with familiarity from a better time of life. Somewhere in the pews might be a child's word or letters her brother would've etched. Jessica had been much too good a girl to do so.

"We will now sing hymn three hundred and forty-one," said the reverend. "My song is love unknown."

The reverend stepped into his pulpit. There, he paused, looking over his congregation and even Jessica, before drawing a long breath. "Consider the parable of the seeds," he said, projecting his aged gentle voice more than she'd heard of late. Jessica recognised her influence, if that meant anything. "Whom do we blame for tormenting Jessica Rawlins and murdering Bede? God gave us our minds, but doyens with their dogmas deny us. A thick dark blanket presses down upon the minds across this country, choking anyone trying to breathe."

He spoke as Jessica might once have liked to speak. She sometimes listened.

"An American Supreme Court judge famously said freedom of speech never gave anyone the right to yell 'fire' in a crowded theatre, but our theatre has been burning for a long time now. I smell the fire, but who of you would extinguish it?"

When the service finished, pallbearers carried the coffin back along the aisle. The mourners followed, while Jessica remained seated, looking downwards.

Her aunt Nora's voice interrupted her. "I'm not sure I should feel this way," she said, almost apologetically, "and I'm not able to think about it yet, but I wish you hadn't come today."

Jessica closed her eyes.

"Might you have driven to Orange last Sunday had we let you keep my car?" asked Nora. "Don't answer. I'm too terrified to know."

Jessica's eyes remained closed, until Derek Saxby's voice spoke up. "Bede was an uncommonly good man," said Derek.

She looked up to see him standing in the aisle before her. "Bad things happen to good people," replied Jessica.

"Good things happen to bad ones, but we're too dumb to realise it." His eyes remained upon her. "You were always better than us, but none of us knew." He walked away.

All the other mourners bar one filed from the church, leaving one several rows ahead of her, his head bowed. Eventually, he stood.

Eugene Gallagher stepped along the pew to the aisle, along which he stepped towards her. She considered inviting him to sit beside her, but wouldn't say anything to frighten him away. He stopped beside her.

"Did you know, Bede?" she asked.

"I know you."

She moved along the pew for him to sit. He sat beside her.

"I didn't tell you why I disagree with what you said in the newspaper."

"I'm not interested, Eugene."

"I would've visited you in the hospital, but I don't visit hospitals where I'm not a patient."

"Thank you for coming, today."

"It seemed only fair. You're the only person but Underly to visit me."

"People fear death."

"They fear more than death," said Eugene, as if he had power in his demise. "They fear words. They don't know whether I'm to blame for my death sentence, and I don't know either. They don't know what to believe, so they don't risk seeing me. They talk about sickness but not about sick people."

"I should've been eating lunch with you at the Pickled Pepper Café. I didn't treat you better than did anyone else."

"If you'd said to me what you said to your friends where anyone might've overheard, I might've done what they did. If you're the last white person left on this planet, you're expected to like it, or at least be quiet about it."

She nodded. "I returned to Molong to leave, although London's further away than ever now. Somewhere, far from where I've been, I might learn where I should be."

"What do you want, Jessica?"

"If not a country," she said, "then a town, or street, where I can speak freely of what I feel and believe, where people who disagree about everything still help each other when winds blow roofs from their houses, where we care about each other and might even love somebody." It was all much too unfamiliar.

"They will oppose you," said Eugene. "Few of the people sympathising with you will have the valour to say so."

"I'm trying not to make again mistakes I've made," she told him. "Can you leave Molong with me, tomorrow?"

"Don't be foolish about anything you don't need to be. I'll die here, whenever that will be."

By the time Jessica and Eugene, the last of the congregation, walked from the church, the hearse and reverend had gone to the cemetery. The mourners were at an even more morbid wake.

Standing silently on a small spot a respectful distance across the street, under an aged tree, was Sergeant Vaughan. Dressed in a dark suit and hat, he held his hands together in front of him.

Staring up at the church steeple and Cross, he mightn't have entered the service, but would be the last to leave.

Stopped close to them was a long gold motor car, the door of which opened a little and closed again. "That's my mother," explained Eugene. "She's not coming to any funerals until she comes to mine."

"You better go," said Jessica. "People talking to me lately have been getting into strife."

"She's upset she didn't talk to me about drugs, so thinks people should talk about everything, when so little life remains."

"I look pretty foolish, making stupid choices when you don't have choices."

"My idiot choice put me where I am."

They'd said enough for Jessica to ask him a question she wouldn't ask when first they met. "Did you really contract your virus taking drugs?"

"Is drug taking a socially acceptable means of contracting the virus?"

"What's socially acceptable depends on the society."

"I was at a party with friends," explained Eugene, "one of whom offered me a needle and syringe. He didn't know the virus contaminated his blood, although that doesn't make him any less a murderer. I was too drunk to think I'd ever die, although that doesn't make me any less an imbecile. I injected delusion into my veins for the first time in my life. In the morning, I vowed never to do it again, and didn't, but four months later, I learned I was infected. The virus was a fact about which all of us knew but few of us comprehended. So you see: ruining your life only needs a moment. Worst luck."

Jessica thought of hugging him, but not without gloves. "Some party," she said.

"Some friends." Eugene removed from his pocket a small white ceramic rabbit. "Sometimes I get so lonely, I talk to this. It lets me talk aloud without thinking I'm insane." He held the rabbit with both his hands. "Tilly Peyton gave it to me when I left for Sydney. Loneliness is much easier in a big city, where lonely people are among so many other lonely people.

Loneliness is harder in small towns, where lonely people think no one else is lonely."

The most despondent of sad people were those who sensed happy people near them. The sad people among their brethren accepted their burden more gracefully.

"Here," said Eugene, offering the rabbit to her. "Hold it."

Jessica took the cool rabbit in her hands. She looked most closely at its face.

"I'm not sure if it's a boy or a girl rabbit," said Eugene. "I haven't given it a name, if you were thinking of asking, because I don't address it by name. All I do is talk to it."

If Jessica dropped the rabbit to the ground, it would break. She held it tighter.

"I think I like it because children like rabbits," explained Eugene. "They like to touch them. When the children become adults we call rabbits pests, but the rabbits survive."

"You think a lot," said Jessica.

"Lonely people think too much. Unlike you, I don't say the silly things I think. They don't cause me any problems."

Jessica started to speak, before checking her words. She'd become sensitive to the implications of words.

"You were about to say I could afford problems, weren't you?" said Eugene. "Sometimes nothing left to lose is nothing left to gain."

She dipped her head. She still wasn't very good at knowing what not to say.

"Take the rabbit with you."

Jessica looked up, still holding the rabbit in her hands. "I can't do that."

"If you don't take it, then somebody will destroy it when I die, along with everything else of mine. If you ever stop looking after it, then it's because you don't need it anymore. Thinking of you not needing it anymore will do more for me than talking to it."

"I don't know what to say."

"Haven't you learnt sometimes not to say anything?"

Jessica laughed, held out her arms, and hugged him. He let her touch him, when she didn't know what else to do for him.

29

THE BUS

For too long and short a time, the old Molong Hall had been Jessica's home. Alone, she dumped all her worn clothes into the old washing machine in the laundry. Taking a box from a shelf, she poured and poured detergent onto them, before closing the lid and starting the machine. Her past wouldn't linger on her when she left.

Jessica woke Friday morning not knowing where she would sleep that night. She was heading somewhere she didn't yet understand, but was heading somewhere. The sky was clear, without admitting threat of rain, while Jessica swept the floors.

Dressed in her undergarments, she donned rubber gloves and a scrubbing brush. The water in her red plastic bucket became grey as she washed the wet rooms clean. Her arms became sore, and her knees became tender kneeling against the kitchen floor and then two rooms of bathroom tiles, as she removed every mark she could. She often sat back, collected her breath, and wiped perspiration from her brow with the back of her gloved hand, before cleaning again.

What remained when she finished had been there when Jessica first inspected the premises, so few months earlier. The gloves and brush she left in the bucket in the laundry, below the stainless steel sink. She rinsed the shower recess after she showered, removing any residue.

Jessica ate the last of her food, and packed her last refuse into black plastic bags she left in the garbage bin. All that remained in the kitchen were Derek's last bottles of cider and wine, aside from the small poison baits to kill cockroaches in the darkest corners behind the refrigerator.

Her clothes hanging from the small line in the garden were dry enough for her to iron them more carefully than she usually ironed. She folded them into her two large tan brown suitcases, lying open on her lounge room floor. Their castor wheels and handles would let her drag them along the floor and ground, as they'd done when she returned to Molong, along her way to somewhere else.

Secure within them she stowed her clothes, towels, and toiletries, along with her few glasses, crockery, and cutlery, none of them particularly valuable. Her pictures she removed from the lounge room wall. An album of old photographs and their negatives were more reason to be sad, but they were Jessica's experience. Her diary of names and addresses seemed superfluous, but she packed it anyway. Secure in handkerchiefs and a scarf in a corner of a case, she wrapped her red onyx tiger, glass kitten, and ceramic white rabbit. She might have been none of them.

Her best light frock was almost immodest, with its rich red tones and loosely fitting lines. Her pink wide-brimmed hat would be crushed within a suitcase.

Jessica dialled the telephone number of the electricity company, cancelling the supply to the house. She called the telephone company, disconnecting the telephone service. She sealed her two suitcases with tiny steel padlocks.

A knock came through the front door. Jessica didn't reply.

Another knock came. Still she stood there. A metal key rattled in the lock, the lock turned and the door slipped open, revealing Sophie Fulbright.

"I thought you must have gone," said Sophie. "The whole town knows you bought a ticket for the quarter-to-eleven bus."

"Is the bus company supposed to reveal that information?"

Sophie chuckled. "People who knew told people who didn't. People who didn't asked people who did. They say the mayor's already had his secretary call the bus company to ensure the bus won't be late."

In Sophie's hand was the inspection report signed by Jessica when she commenced her tenancy. It included spaces to compare the condition of the house upon departure.

"Derek told me to go easy with my assessment," said Sophie.

Jessica sat on the sofa watching someone younger than she was inspecting her home and its contents. In another life story, she might've been her.

The furniture listed in the report as being in the house when Jessica arrived was still there. "Are you taking the boxes and books in the smaller bedroom?" asked Sophie.

They were too much for Jessica to carry, and the biology she needed to know she already knew. "I can put them in the bin."

"I can arrange that," smiled Sophie. "There's also a pink box under your bed."

"Nothing there is as important as I once thought it was."

"We have names of removalists for your bed and dressing table."

Jessica shook her head. "The next tenants can have them, without knowing they were mine."

Sophie picked up the telephone handset. It was silent. She flicked the light switch by the door. The lights remained dark.

"That was quick," said Jessica. She signed the inspection report.

"If you want to leave the keys on the kitchen table," said Sophie, "I can collect them later. Where shall we return you your bond?"

The money Jessica had deposited when she commenced her lease would've paid for any repairs to the house or other arrears, but there wouldn't be any. It was thus hers. "Send it to Bede's widowed wife."

Jessica walked with Sophie to the front door, which Sophie prepared to open as if the home was hers. Perhaps it was. "Will you ever come back to Molong?" asked Sophie.

Sophie's words weren't part of her duties. Only they would

know their conversation, safely in the last hour before Jessica departed. People couldn't judge them for what they didn't know. Still, Jessica didn't reply.

"Be careful, Jessica. The mayor has made it known that any friend of yours can expect the same treatment you had. There won't be a soul in the streets when you catch that bus, for fear someone will misunderstand."

"Can he do that? Can he empty the town to isolate me?"

"Mrs Xiedergrain won't be seeing you," Sophie smiled knowingly. "She'll be with the bowling club gardener."

Jessica also smiled; she'd smiled too little of late. After Sophie departed, Jessica closed the door.

An ordinary person would've left the house then and waited leisurely at the bus stop, but an ordinary person wouldn't be leaving. Jessica wouldn't wait where anyone saw her.

When she could no longer risk missing the bus, Jessica hung her handbag over her shoulder and carefully placed her pink wide-brimmed hat on her long blonde hair and head. They made Jessica appear better than she felt, more assured than she was. Her dark glasses were no longer a disguise.

If anyone saw Jessica struggling to carry each suitcase out of the house and down the front step, he or she never spoke up. Through the open gate to the footpath, she stumbled stepping over the edge of one unevenly set stone and almost fell, after which she adjusted her hat and brushed down her frock with her hands. She closed the door and the gate.

Edward Street was without pedestrians or moving cars, vacant but for her and because of her. The breeze that stirred other days was quiet.

Her handbag over her shoulder, Jessica dragged the last of her life in two rattling suitcases towards Bank Street. Hers was the obvious route to walk, but if she surprised them all by walking another street, she might see the rest of the town huddled together.

Bank Street had never before been so deserted at that time on a warm day. The loudest sounds were the measured rhythmic clips of Jessica's heels along the footpath, and the softly squeaking wheels of her suitcases rolling behind her.

Far ahead of her, cars and trucks passed in and out of sight along the Mitchell Highway, driven by people who'd never heard of her, who barely noticed the towns past which they travelled. Beneath the hills outside of town and the broad, spacious sky with nothing to fall down, was the railway station to which trains no longer came. Highway buses stopped there when passengers boarded or alighted. A bus would carry her to Sydney before the day was out.

Jessica dragged her two suitcases along. She passed the town hall, never so quiet of a Friday than it was quiet then. From behind closed doors and covered windows of offices, shops, and homes, evasive people watched her walking: faces she never knew and those she no longer knew. Parents held their children to their sides.

She paused to cross empty Gidley Street, her last street to cross before the highway, from which the highway noise became more pronounced with every step. Instead of continuing along the footpath, she veered into the middle of empty Bank Street. She was obvious, patiently walking with her head high where people couldn't help but see her. Farm people wouldn't enter the town until she'd gone. If a stranger's car turned into the street, then it might need to swerve from her. The stranger might think she was a fool. She would slip out of the way.

Cars were parked facing left outwards from the kerbs, in spaces made wide more than a century earlier for carts and horses. They were like a guard of honour in glass, steel, and aluminium, but not a guard for Jessica. They wouldn't move until the bus had taken her from them.

In one car someone sat watching her, not quite obscured by the outside reflection. When Jessica unfettered had almost passed, the car engine started and pulled out from the kerb. The sudden roar and movement startled her, as the car sped around and past her, emitting a dusty wake of wind that blew her red frock and almost swept her pink hat from her head. Jessica released the handles of her suitcases and turned her face away, before checking that her hat was secure on her head. Again taking the suitcase handles in her hands, she resumed walking.

From the upstairs balcony of the Freemasons Hotel, at the corner of Bank Street and the highway, the mayor in his new mayoral uniform watched Jessica coming; he didn't need to hide. From where he stood, Hector Xiedergrain could also look across the highway to the bus stop.

If Jessica were a bird flying above the town and looking downwards, the only thing she'd see moving in Bank Street would be her solitary figure, slowly dragging her two suitcases. Storekeepers and customers whom she would never again see were watching her, cowering in the shops and offices, doubtlessly dreading that she might veer towards them. They'd tried to make her the same as them and their indifference, but she wasn't and would never be.

The patrons finishing their morning teas and coffees at the Pickled Pepper Café watched her from the corners of their eyes. Lester Cullen waited upon them without looking up. Seventeen days had passed since Jessica sat down with friends for that fateful lunch.

The woman standing at the glass door of the post office wasn't Susan Hodgeson. None of the women standing at the window of the ladies wear shop at which Briony Keyte worked was Briony.

Lynne Delaney stood at the window of her salon. Beside her stood her new young assistant, wearing a white blouse and skirt and with her blonde hair in a bun. Lynne's eyes were trained upon Jessica, and Jessica continued watching her as she walked. Lynne smiled, and raised her right hand in the smallest hint of an innocuous wave. She might've been offering Jessica best wishes, or been bidding her farewell. She might've seen Jessica's clothes sparkle as no other clothes sparkled and thought better of her former charge. Jessica would never hear her thoughts. Her hands were much too full for her to wave.

Jessica felt more disappointed than defeated. Aside from her brother, the life and relationships she'd lost in the past two weeks were never hers. The people watching her were alone, but Jessica had the benefit of having learnt she was alone. They'd defeated but not conquered her, under the mayor's watch.

Derek Saxby's brown bush hat was on his head, ready for him

to leave his offices to meet the Hammonds at their tomato farm after Jessica departed. Sophie Fulbright and their colleagues stood beside him, watching Jessica pass. "We're so weak," he said, his legs not much to hold him up.

"Where will she go?" asked Sophie.

"Somewhere better than I am." She wasn't so far alone as he was. "If we think too much about all possible consequences of our actions and the permutations of them, we would never get out of bed in the morning."

Derek reached his hand onto the handle of the door from the agency offices, pulled it open, and walked across the footpath and kerb onto Bank Street. He couldn't help but sense the mayor from his vantage and all the other people watching him follow Jessica, dragging her two suitcases ahead of him towards the crossing across the highway.

Charlie, without any sense of a story to write, and Agnes watched everything from a front window of the Gatekeepers Cottage. The glass obscured the vision of anyone outside the building looking in without affecting their vision looking out. With a break in the traffic, Jessica crossed the highway. Behind her, Derek was coming into view. "Instability brings change," remarked Charlie.

The mayor had left the upstairs balcony at the Freemason's Hotel. Pushing past people too slow to move aside from the downstairs corner door, he pushed his way onto the footpath. "Go back inside!" he bellowed at Derek, as Derek reached the crossing.

Outside the old railway station, close to where the bus would come soon, Jessica stopped walking. Without releasing the straps to her suitcases from her hands, she turned back towards the mayor's voice.

Approaching her was Derek in his hat, until he stopped several metres in front of her, with the town behind him and his legs at ease because nobody was going to move him. He removed his hat and held it in his hand.

Following him was the mayor. "Mister Saxby," he roared. "Go back to your offices now, or your business is finished!"

His voice reverberated around them while Derek and Jessica

stared at each other. She stood with her suitcases, her face shaded from the sun by her hat. They stood alone, apart. The people who would've damned her already had.

The mayor reached the railway station forecourt. "Go back, Mister Saxby," he continued to thunder, "or you can leave, too!"

A figure in a long dress appeared on Bank Street, walking quickly towards them. Slowly Jessica recognised Susan Hodgeson, where everyone could see her. She crossed the highway where Jessica had crossed, passed the mayor, and finally stopped near where Derek stood.

"Ms Hodgeson," cried the mayor. "You're no longer Volunteer of the Month!"

Following Susan was a third person, a little younger than Susan and Jessica. Lachlan Kincaid stopped as Derek and Susan had, facing Jessica.

"I am your friend," Derek told Jessica.

"I am your friend," said Susan.

"I," Lachlan started to say, "would like to be your friend."

Jessica looked at the two men and woman. They stood spread out and facing her.

"Constable Tarrant," called out the mayor, looking around. "Where's Constable Tarrant?"

The sounds of a bus engine leaving the highway disturbed their little world, as it slowed to stop near Jessica and her suitcases. The bus passenger door opened, while Jessica continued looking at the three people standing before her.

Suddenly, she didn't know what to do, where the best place might be for her. The three were very few, finding courage from the mayhem, but were a group to share the pain they'd suffer being there.

The driver alighted from the bus and opened a door to the low luggage compartment. "Miss Rawlins?" he asked her.

Derek resumed walking towards her, his pace quickening as he neared her. He dropped his hat onto the ground as he reached her, wrapped his arms around her, and kissed her passionately for everyone to see.

Alone within his arms, Jessica's hat fell backwards from her head onto the ground. Her hands held her suitcase handles without embracing him. She let him kiss her without encouraging or discouraging him, although gradually her hands came away from her suitcases. Her eyes closed with him. The town and he were no longer visible to her, as her hands moved cautiously around his waist.

Derek slowly released her. She released him. Their eyes opened as he let their faces slip apart, and they gazed into the dark and light spaces of the other. "I'm sorry, Jess," he said.

The bus driver interrupted them. "We must go, Miss Rawlins."

Jessica stepped back. She turned towards the driver.

ABOUT THE AUTHOR

Simon Lennon has lived, worked, and travelled throughout Europe, America, Australasia, Asia, and the South Pacific. He is married with six children. He is the author of the following books.

Fiction
The King of a Vacant City
Swansong of a Childless People
A Young Man's Tale
The Insubordinate

Non-Fiction
Western Individualism
The End of Natural Selection
The Need for Nations
People's Identity
Of Whom We're Born
Biological Us
A Land to Belong
The Failure of Multiculturalism
Reclaiming Western Cultures
Christendom Lost
Aiding Islam

www.ingramcontent.com/pod-product-compliance
Lightning Source LLC
Chambersburg PA
CBHW030246200626
46816CB00002BA/525